Necromancing
A Tale of Ye Olde Gubbins
By Olly Nuttall

OFFICIAL

Copyright © 2023 Olly Nuttall

All rights reserved. No part of this book may be reproduced or used in any manner without the prior written permission of the copyright owner, except for the use of brief quotations in a book review.

To request permissions, contact the publisher at
ollyjrnuttall@gmail.com

ISBN: 9798860131330
Hardcover: 1
Paperbook: 2
Easy cover: 3
Audiobook: 4
Book a duck 7842

First paperback edition September 2023

Edited by O. J. R. Nuttall (cos no one else would be stupid enough to do it)
Cover art by Ines Funke
Title Graphics: John Matrix
Layout by Oliver Nuttall
Map by Anon (who would admit to that?)
Concept by whoever I could rip off as legally as possible

Printed by monkeys on typewriters

Never mind the B(Ol)logs
Some Dull suburb in Manchester
UK
Europe
Earth
Milky Way
Universe
Giant Toaster
Web Address: https://ollyjrnuttall.wixsite.com/website

2

OFFICIAL

Acknowledgements

Lots of the thanks to the same people as last time. But specifically, my amazing dad for all the support, my mum for always being my mum, Ed and Em. Massive thanks to my beautiful nephews Jess and Sam for ensuring I remain silly and immature (not too much of a stretch admittedly), though please stop the heavy metal first thing in the morning. A big thanks to all Nuttall/Smith/Hickling/Mastracola's past present and future, may the hairline remain strong in one of you.

Special thanks to Ines for once more taking my badly thought-out ideas and descriptions and somehow making an awesome front cover that is a million times more deserving than the novel it represents. Also, for the encouragement and asking how the book is going. I can't thank you enough.

Thanks to Em D for checking a chapter and feedback, its appreciated and needed.

Thanks to The Bens, Ste, John H, Lat, Rek, Sam, Kate, Toms, Jims, Hayles, Ellen, Joyce, Rik, Ems, Jen, Luci, Hazel, Nic, Chiharu, Ri(c)ks, Chris' and all other friends who I've probably forgotten to mention but have definitely helped keep me something approaching only largely insane. I couldn't do any of anything without you.

Also thanks to anyone who bought the first book and more so managed to finish reading it. I owe you a few quid and hours of your life, not that you'll be seeing either from me.

And finally, thanks to Radiohead for the music that reminds me I have a soul, I'm sure they'll be reading this, and if so, I'll be looking for someone to score the film adaptation lads…

For David, who filled a room with his laugh.

Pre-Prologue: Somewhere Ogre The Rainbow

The Late Middle-Aged World was a strange scary place. Danger lurked on every corner, and when danger had a day off, mild peril loitered on every bend in the road.

Geographically It was an odd-looking world, if you saw it on a map, you would think it looked like a blob some idiot with a (underserved) D grade in GCSE art had created whilst having a heart attack attempting to draw a circle with their foot.

The world was inhabited by Humans, Orcs, Elves, Dwarves, Trolls, Halflings, Goblins, Wizards, Dragons, Sports Casual Ogres and weird Bog Monsters that genuinely believed trickle-down economics was an effective means of distributing wealth to the poor that inhabited the land.

These races were in a constant state of war over long held grudges. If they took the time to look at the history books, they would discover a lot of these wars started as a member of race A stepped on Race B's foot at the local barn dance so race B spilt Race A's pint whilst Race C told them to leave it as they weren't worth it. And for hundreds of years pointless enmity and the selling of commemorative plates has ensued.

In this world brave warriors eschew the conventional jobs on offer; Inn Keeper, Bar Tender, Tavern Proprietor,

Alehouse Clerk, Wine Bar Patron, in search of quests and adventures. Scouring the lands, and battling the dangerous creatures that resided in it, for gold, swords, golden swords, shiny things, powerful magic items and Pokemon. Though on their tax return they only ever find, buttons, wooden teeth and boar tusks.

The world was ruled over by a noble King and Queen who when not gorging on large banquets ensured the land was running smoothly. So, for that one day a year, the land ran really smoothly. Still as most of the population was concerned, they were fine rulers. As Gnobrot Splunge the Goblin who lived in a puddle put it "sure, they may spend their time eating gold leaf sprayed lobsters in a huge castle whilst collecting tithes from us, but they really have empathy for the likes of me. And have you seen the quality of the pageantry?" Hard to argue with such sentiments.

In this cruel world for someone to make a name for themselves it took heroic deeds or violent acts or if one was particularly good at multitasking, heroic deeds carried out in a violent manner. And if a warrior was particularly wealthy, they could pay a story teller of the realm to spin the time they saw a dragon in the distance and soiled their armour whilst running off to their mum into a four scroll epic tail of defeating scaly beasties, which bored school children would have to spend whole terms studying. They might even get a day dedicated to their falsely heroic deeds.

The heroes of this story could not afford one of the greatest writers of the land. Or even a semi competent one that lived in a swamp.

OFFICIAL

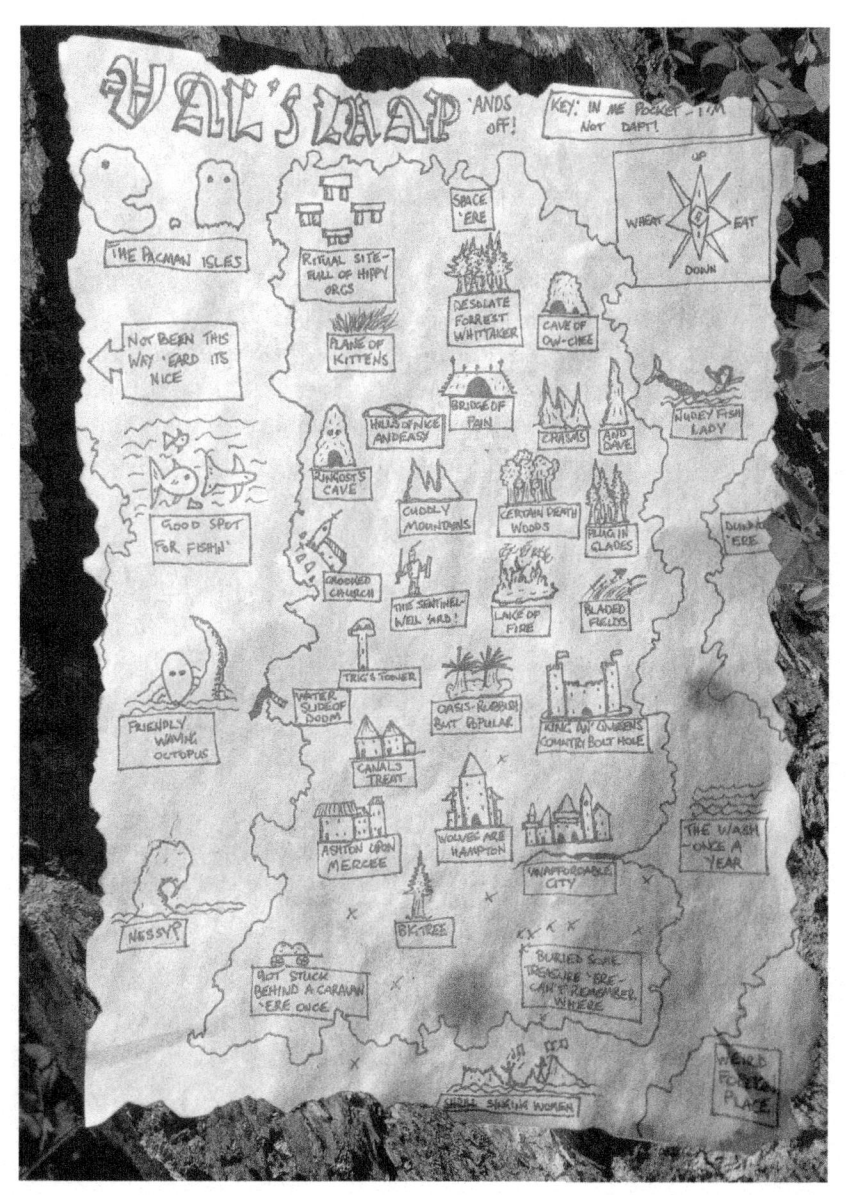

Prologue: I'm Terribly Death?

The last two miles ride to the Crooked Church, also known somewhat dramatically as the Church of Lost Souls, had been a tough journey for Brooker, mainly as he'd had to walk them as his Uber Rider superstitiously had refused to come any nearer to this supposed haunted spot. Brooker couldn't help thinking that if the religious elders had been more careful naming the building, people may not have been so scared of it.

Brooker's expensive boots were caked in mud and much worse and his clothes torn from the perilous route through undergrowth and bracken to reach this spot. Though if he had been more observant, he could have taken the nice dry stone path that led to this place and saved his clothes the damage.

Brooker inelegantly climbed over the broken stone wall and peered all around him, constantly checking behind him as if by a nervous tic, the chill of the lonely night gnawing at his bones. Nothing seemingly moved in the jagged tree line to his right, that had to be a good thing, didn't it? Why did the lack of movement scare him more?

A lone owl hooted in the lost distance, what if that owl was crying out for Brooker and was going to swoop down and steal his soul? Brooker shook his head at the effect of the fear on his own stupid thought pattern, everyone in the land knew it was pigeons and not owls that tried to claim souls.

He was going to have to get better at remembering his lore given what he was about to get himself into. He shuddered and pulled his ermine cowl further around him for warmth, a false comfort.

Once more he questioned why he was here. He wasn't sure he trusted the wooden toothed man who'd brokered this deal. Something about a man who lost an eye and then got a glass eye replacement, but replaced his good eye with it, rang alarm bells with Brooker. Still a deal was a deal, and Brooker was told of a man of such power who could help him become more than the nobody he felt he was.

He'd reached the outer perimeter of the graveyard of the crooked church with the listing spire, seemingly bent at the will of the wind, or a builder who wasn't aware of the concept of a sprit level. From the distance it had looked like some kind of gothic horror stereotype, but up close in the eerily quiet night it became harder to be wryly amused by it.

Brooker climbed the uneven damp stone steps leading to the inner graveyard gate no matter how quiet he tried to keep his tread, the hollow thud of his leather boots rang a discordant note into the distant night and whoever, or whatever may be in it.

Reaching the gate Brooker took one last look around, nothing stirred despite his feeling of not being on his own.

He took a large breath and removed the ornate ring from his finger and placed it in a concealed pocket in his cowl. No turning back now. He pushed slowly on the gate, which made a loud unwelcome creak that called out a song to the night around him, not a particularly melodic song either, the kind of song Hick of the Mucknal would have been proud of.

Brooker moved slowly through the gravestones his feet crunching on the loose stone ground. He cursed that every damn thing in this graveyard seemed insistent on signaling his position to the dark and whatever else was out there. He reached the large sarcophagus to the back of the graveyard; this is where the introduction was to take place. As a reflex he placed his hand on the elaborate short sword he carried, though he wasn't sure it would provide him much protection from who, or was that what, he was meeting.

Nervously he drew his pipe and tinderbox but thought better of it, of the light drawing attention to... to what he wasn't sure. He fumbled the items back into their pouch and his hand returned to resting on his blade hilt. He told himself he was in control and wasn't scared though his shaking hands told of a contradictory tale.

From the other side of the tomb Brooker thought he heard something; he held his breath his heart thudding against his chest. Maybe he was wrong, he couldn't hear anything now... no wait shuffling, uneven footsteps and something else a sort of chinking sound, but it wasn't metal no it was lighter, duller, but what? His breathing quickened, and his eyes darted around. No doubt, a strange tread was approaching, this is what he had agreed to so he knew he must meet it, though why such fear? Perhaps the immediacy of what he was getting into was now hitting home.

He drew himself to as greater height as he felt able to given, he wanted to shrink inside himself and rounded the side of the tomb to confront the source of the sound. He let out an involuntary and entirely unheroic yelp at the shape that approached him from the dark, a skeletal figure in dull rusted armour, its left hand a rusty hook, one leg replaced by a wooden peg and dark socketless eyes that seemed to stare directly into him and find him underserving. Brooker's nerve failed him. He turned and ran.

He stumbled across the graveyard, weaving through gravestones, loose branches from encroaching trees grabbing at his face like cruel claws. Brooker could see the gate ahead of him twenty more paces and he could escape this dread. He was sprinting now, five paces and he was free, his foot caught the edge of a gravestone catapulting him forward onto his hands, his adrenaline too flowing for the pain to bite as yet.

Brooker lay stunned for a split second, before his instincts took over telling him to get up and run, however he became aware of his predicament as a pair of worn brown boots came into his peripheral vision. Brooker turned his head and traced his vision up. He saw a figure in a weather-beaten grey robe, the hood hiding their features bar the slight glint the moon gave to their eyes. The stranger held a crooked staff in his hand, with the skull of some large bird adorning its top.

The skeletal creature from the sarcophagus had somehow caught up with the pair, even though it had one leg, and its top speed was shuffle, it frankly made no rational sense, though rational sense and Brooker hadn't been friends since he got to this dire church. It formed up on his master's flank staring down at Brooker inscrutably.

The robed figure let out a mirthless chuckle before speaking "I heard the rumours but did not think you'd actually come. I can put you to a lot of use. The time is now right for the world to bow to my will, and you will help me achieve that" Silently the man bent down to Brooker and grabbed him with a talon like hand and hauled him roughly up whilst declaring triumphantly "it begins," the words echoing around the graves.

Act 1 Scene 1: It Begins AKA A Rude Message To You

The Herald dug his spurs hard into his steed; Flighty Joanna, before bending to her ears to speak soft words of encouragement. Flighty Joanna wasn't sure there was much need for the kind words given the pain in her sides from the spurs. Though she pushed herself on further to avoid either again.

The Herald could see the unmistakable grey bulk of the royal castle; Frank, on the hill in the distance. The sight of this vast fortress getting ever close filled the Herald with renewed vigor and Flighty Joanna with fears renewed vigor led to renewed spurring.

He was close now and this matter of extreme urgency could be resolved, before any pain was inflicted or bodily fluids were spilled.

Approaching the portcullis, the guards on recognising the Herald's standard dropped the drawbridge and Flighty Joanna carried him over in a couple of easy strides. Inside the cobbled ground of the courtyard the Herald rapidly dismounted and gave the reins to the stable girl whispering something of quiet urgency in her ear. The Herald was a quiet whispered words in ears kind of guy sometimes, it was an extremely irritating habit.

The stable girl pointed to a corner in the yard, the Herald crossed the wet stones of the courtyard in long purposeful steps entering the doorway and pulling the curtain across. He'd needed the toilet for the last four hours of riding and was too prim to go behind a tree. The toilet he was using, even being an outdoor facility, was suitably posh for a royal castle featuring a cover for the hole in the ground and double quilted toads for wiping your backside on.

Business taken care of; the Herald knew it was time to take care of business. He must seek the king and queen Hutter-Schneider to discuss the matter of urgency they requested his personal services for. He strode back across the courtyard reaching the large double doors to the inner keep and once more the guards readily stepped aside on recognition of a person of his importance and renown, or at least that's how the arrogant Herald saw it.

He walked the great entrance hall lined with its showy portraits of kings, queens, princes and princesses past and present. With a wry smile he took in the portrait of Prince Tarquentin The Feckless, the eldest prince, who was known for his love of a party and avoiding anything that could be interpreted as hard work, achievement, or a feck. Though the Herald wondered to himself if that wasn't that the point of all royals.

Next to him was the portrait of Prince Andrestin The Dry, the second eldest, who was keeping a low profile due to some 'unfortunate' incidents with the poor company he kept. His life was now one of punishment, confined to the fourth largest castle in the land, with only the twenty courtiers, left to spend his remaining days holding feasts, sporting events and occasionally opening a local market stall if his mum wasn't looking.

As he made his way further down well illuminated corridor the Herald regarded the portrait of Princess Thandie The Overqualified, who was well liked across the realm, she was intelligent, just, a fierce warrior, kind, caring and unfortunately also a woman and therefore would never be eligible to rule the land under current laws. Due to this she had travelled to the strange worlds over the seas to do missionary work, the concept of work causing much confusion in the royal household, who still hadn't got to grips with the word 'work' as yet, but they had commissioned some courtiers to study the concept for them.

Finally hung the portrait of Prince Brookerston The Who He? The youngest of the current dynasty. A prince no one seemed to really know anything about given he kept himself to himself, didn't like the public eye and who had disappeared from the royal household some time ago, not that anyone had really noticed, but that was the rumour. A strange royal but not a huge miss.

The two guards, in the gold and red armour of the royal guard, on watch at the not quite so great chamber, put their considerable bulk in front of the door crossing halberds as the herald approached but he waved them aside with a relaxed authority and they quickly obeyed. The Herald instinctively removed the ring from his finger, stuffing it in a pocket and pushed the heavy chamber doors open.

OFFICIAL

The king and queen sat on two large elaborate golden thrones that appeared to be made from swords, the Herald wondered why they sat on such uncomfortable, not to mention potentially lethal, looking seats when they had a comfy sofa to the back of the chamber, tradition he guessed, he didn't get it, didn't want to get it.

The Herald hung back at the door as the king and queen were being presented with offerings. Courtiers brought them the usual weekly gifts from the lands, amongst the gifts were an enormous gothic looking mirror (as if they needed another one of those) from creepy Lord Scricketground, some perfumed sweets from Lady Lay of the Eastern realm, elaborate spices to add to the ever growing spice rack (the kokum in the potato and leek soup had rumoured to have been a right royal disaster), a lute player playing songs from the record Hail to T' thief that the weird bearded bloke in the North, who spoke in cod ye olde English had presented them with and finally some socks (admittedly made from gold, ermine and diamonds) from Earl James Jones who clearly couldn't think of a good gift to get the royal pair and applied the 'if in doubt go socks' that was applied by many a parent throughout the land every Christmas. It was one step up from buying flowers from the horse refueling station.

The king and queen's attention had long since waned in this chore, she had picked up The Daily Tapestry crossword and the king was looking at a lewd parchment that he thought he'd cunningly hidden in a scroll about land disputes, though a nude drawing was clearly visible, a bottom being poked poking out from the bottom. The Herald watched this royal dance play out with a smirk.

When the courtiers had taken the last of the forty or so presents out, the Herald stepped forward and gave a bow so mocking it would have been considered heavy handed in an am-dram pantomime "your highnesses."

"Ah... Herald... ?" the king began his tone uncertain "... we have need of your services given what you now do, the realm is under threat of the most dire kind, a necromancer rises in the North West, a being of foreboding power, he doesn't seem to be acting alone some new ally that will help him with his nefarious scheme, our spies lead us to believe he seeks to raise The King of The Undead" that last name made even the cocksure Herald wince, The King of The Undead had once stalked the realm, a terrifying figure of legend, not dead nor alive but a being of great power and even greater blood lust. The history books were full of the heroic deeds of the armies that joined forces to put an end to his destruction of the land. Many lives were lost of all races in ending his bloody reign.

Gathering himself the Herald asked "but how? He was driven away; we were told it was impossible for him to return."

The queen straightened up "It seems this necromancer may have a way of bringing him out of the exile placed on him? Whether it's possible or not this necromancer must be stopped from trying, we need him dealt with."

"And what of your heroic sons and daughter?" he paused and allowed the silence to hang "would they not simply lead the royal armies against such traitors to the land?"

The queen sharply cut across "royalty must not interfere with matters of state." The Herald failed to suppress his smirk 'except when the state threatens your income streams' he thought to himself.

The queen fixed the Herald with a stare "there is one we believe can defeat this evil. You must find Val Kerr the Valkyrie from the Celtic region; we believe she and her rag tag bunch of ruffians can suitably duff up any undead threat."

"Val Kerr?!" the Heralds eyebrows shot up "she and her crew are uncouth savages from what I hear."

The king shifted in his throne, the pointy bit of a sword digging into a place he didn't want a pointy bit of a sword, finally he smiled "and the best at royal sanctioned violence, she can name her price and it will be met. We believe she is drinking in her usual haunts, find her, hire her, stop the necromancer. At all costs." He said firmly.

The Herald went with a slightly less mocking bow and made to leave the chamber "Herald" the queen called after him "Go see Em Queue she has some items that may be of use." The queens voiced dropped slightly "and good luck, these are dark times, stay safe. Please."

****

The Herald made his way back into the chill of the open courtyard and ambled across to Em's 'experimental chamber' i.e., the place furthest from the castle where the inevitable explosions from her work would be least likely to do damage to the expensive royal stuff.

He drifted through the (extremely ineffectual against explosions) beaded curtain into a small square room, lit by the forge in the centre, which smelt of sulfur mixed with curried beetle. "Ah Herald" Em said lifting her head from some liquid in a pan she was inspecting closely, she put her finger in and licked it, before deciding the contents needed more pepper "are you still going by that moniker?" her dark eyes twinkled in the light her forge fire.

The Herald ignored the question and went to the point "what do you have for me Em? It better be good, not like that rocket codpiece you gave me last time, the burns on my… delicate area have only just healed."

Em smiled at the Herald and walked to some heavily stacked shelves at the back of the room, rummaging about with clumsy abandon. After a while she returned with an age worn satchel "ta da!"

"What is it?"

"It's a bag, it helps you carry multiple items at once." Em chuckled to herself whilst the Herald just about managed to suppress his sigh. She tipped the contents of the satchel out onto the work surface, an ornate short sword with elongated runes on it and some kind of medallion. The Herald picked up the medallion and spun it around in his hand, two serpents cast in dull silver encircled a gem of impenetrable black. The Herald cocked an eyebrow at Em.

"Talisman of obsidian, it nullifies all magic cast on the wearer, though be warned, it means the wearer can cast no magic either."

"Nice!" the Herald declared, satisfied he was lessening his chance of getting a magical bolt up his backside, he didn't need that again. He drew the sword from its scabbard and spun it around his hand with casual ease "nicely weighted" he commented as all men do when holding swords, without knowing what it actually means "what is it?"

Em nodded at the blade "Magical sword of true sight." She offered and no more.

"Yeah thanks, care to be more helpful. Tell me it casts fireballs of doom or something." The Herald asked eagerly.

Em chuckled pleased at the back and forth between the two "see that rune under the pommel?" the Herald nodded intrigued "press it." The Heralds fingers clasped the blade and with a sense of anticipation he pressed in the rune; wincing slightly knowing that with Em anything could be about to happen with this blade. The sword lit up in a pleasant bright blue hue.

"And?"

"What more do you want?!"

"It's a light up sword."

"No that's a powerful magical weapon."

"I'm up against unknown forces of darkness and potentially The King of The Undead" the Herald paused to let the name sink in with Em, but she seemed totally unphased "I'm going to need all the help in the realm, and you give me this?"

The Herald could see Em was going to offer no further help. He lowered the sword "it's a glorified torch. Might be useful if I need to take a comfort break in the night and avoid wetting my toes I suppose." He shrugged and stuffed the items into the bag "I'm having this bag too; might be the most useful thing You've ever actually given me!" and with that he saluted Em mockingly and left the chamber.

****

The Herald went back to the keep to see what supplies he could snaffle for his long journey. Passing through the even less great hall (used to entertain the dignitaries the king and queen really had no time for, generally politicians), in the centre of the room was a thirty-foot-long great table, with a delicate silk cloth covering it. The table's considerable weight was groaning under a feast; plates of roast chicken, roast beef, roast lamb, roast duck, roast shrimp, roast parsnips, roast potatoes, roast pheasant, roast eggs, game bird, not so game bird, mashed potato, mashed beetroot, smash potato, curried goat, trifle, broccoli, angel delight, carrots with features drawn on them in coal and decanters of wine. All in all, an average Tuesday's brunch for the king and queen.

The Herald could not suppress his grin at this opportunity, he strolled over to the table and took it all in, stuffing a few spuds in his pocket for later. He reached into his satchel and placed the talisman of obsidian around his neck "nullify magic eh? Let's see" he muttered to himself, he grabbed the tablecloth in two hands took a deep breath and yanked quickly at the cloth. An enormous crashing echoed around the hall as the contents of the table flew onto the floor.

"And the pea is still standing!" the Herald declared delightedly at the single green orb teetering on the edge of the table "let's hope it's better against lesser magicians than me" he muttered to himself.

An attendant, who hadn't been in attendance, came rushing in to see what the ungodly noise was, the Herald caught her gaze "err… one of the courtiers accidently knocked the food off." He stated as a bit of mash dripped from his fringe into his face.

The Herald took this cue as time to leave the castle in his quickest not looking like he was trying to move quickly walk. He did have an urgent mission to save the land to be getting on with and all that after all.

Act 1 Scene 2: In The Beginning There Was An Inn To Begin In

The village of Ashton Upon Mercy is a quiet village. There are a couple of bookies for gullible locals to bet on the virtual finger puppet races. There is a shop selling fried snacks, mainly food stuff closely resembling potatoes, which has been known to have the locals visiting the apothecaries for weeks seeking leaches to cure their gut rot. There was a great excitement in the village once when a particularly crafty fox managed to rummage in some bins, even though they had a stone on the lid, a tale that has passed into folklore handed down from generation to generation.

In the far corner of the village is a tavern, this alehouse sells dangerously off beer, for the cheap alcoholic connoisseur, delightful snacks such as pickled chicken feet or salt and vinegar bats gonads and is populated by the most dangerous cutthroats, cut purses, cost-cutters, bandits, banditos, corsairs, brigands, ruffians, smoothians, brawlers, bawlers and Methodists in the area.

Over the track there is another pub which is much, much worse. This is the pub Val likes to drink in.

The old man with the droopy beard, droopy eyes and droopy other things sat at the out of tune piano playing 'Our Mud hut' by the band Plague Madness to the amusement of no one in the tavern, but that didn't stop his enthusiasm for playing it. Repeatedly.

"Squiz up!" said the extremely tall, muscular lady as she sent the off-duty butcher nearly flying from the bench with her gentle nudge as she sat. "Check out me jugs!" Val declared happily as she opened up her knapsack full of dangerously sharp, badly made pottery "made 'em meself!" she told the table with a misplaced sense of pride.

The merchant with the neatly parted three individual hairs on his head stared intently at the goods but this was mostly the double vision caused by his excessive consumption of the drink Cheeky Vim Toe. His companion in a worse state was only upright due to being wedged next to the wall at the end of the bench.

Val unleashed the bartering skills she had been working on in the toilet mirror to herself "'ow about you buy 'em at a gold piece each or all ten for twelve gold coins? Cheap at 'alf the price, eh?" Val beamed, which given her imposing size sent a shiver of fear down the plump, well-groomed bald merchant. "I'll drink to that!" and so saying she grabbed the merchant's tankard and made the contents disappear before letting out a satisfied belch "not finishin' that?" she asked the comatose companion of the merchant before polishing off his drink too. It was already proving to be an extremely productive day for Val.

On hearing bawdy talk and laughter from another room, Val suddenly jerked her head to one side "'ang on me fine fellows, I'll be back", she rose to her feet and strode purposefully to the chamber at the rear of the inn where the particularly dangerous cutthroats drank round a fire. The merchant Val had been speaking to finally exhaled.

Val stood in the doorway taking up the whole frame "alright then" she gauged the room populated with all the local dangerous types "who said it? I heard ya? One of ya called me pottery a load of thin crap!" the occupants looked at Val open mouthed, saying nothing but giving sideways looks to a particularly brutish sell sword.

He gulped and spoke "Actually what I said was… Waaaarrrgghhh!" Val picked the thug up under one arm and marched out of the chamber, passing the bar she stopped.

"Barkeep, four pints o' Odin's gut punch cider if ya please?" she looked down at the scoundrel under her arm "What can I get ya?"

"I'm OK thanks" the unfortunate wretch managed to squeak out. Val necked one of the pints of cider and carried the man into the vault opposite the bar before pinning him to the dart board with a dagger "You stay there an' consider what constitutes fine art!" she told him before returning to the bar to finish her refreshments.

****

The tavern door dramatically burst open, and a willowy figure swaggered in, a look of disdain at what he saw plastered on his face. The locals all looked at this foppish newcomer in his finery with innate mistrust, anyone who dressed slightly outside the tavern norm was admittedly viewed this way, the grief one of the locals got that time he decided to wear a pair of furry lined boots was the stuff of legend to this day.

The stranger made his way to the bar "barkeep, I seek the renowned warrior Val Kerr…" he glanced down the bar spying the enormous figure with two-pint tankards in each hand at the other end "… never mind".

The Herald sidled up to Val "Ms. Kerr, I need to speak to you as a matter of urgency…"

"Not interested love" Val cut the Herald off before he could finish, giving him a pleasant smile.

"Wh-what?!" the Herald choked slightly sending flecks of spit into the drink of the local on the other side of him at the bar, who either didn't notice or didn't care and carried on drinking. "You don't know what I was going to ask you!" he reasoned.

Val considered this for perhaps a split second "ya were either going to ask me out on a date, or ask me to complete a quest, either way, not interested." Val drained one of her tankards as the Herald sighed "it's the quest innit love?!"

The Herald quickly thought of his options "can I buy you a drink and you at least hear me out?"

"Six flagons of Uncle Buckfast's Psionic Liver Blast an' some porky scratchings and ya have five minutes of me precious time."

Val went and shoved some enormous barbarians off a table and took a seat, the Herald followed over struggling with the weight of the drinks on the tray. "Five minutes" Val stated drawing the stop hourglass from her cloak and placing it on the table, not filling the Herald with any confidence.

"Val you're needed, more than You've ever been needed" Val's expression remained neutral at the Heralds words "there is a necromancer in the North West, he and some strange new accomplice seem to have the power and the will to raise the King of The Undead, if that happens then the land is plunged into darkness; humans, elves, dwarves, halflings, three quarterlings, scallies, village idiots, the lot - all finished. If our spies are right, there will be some kind of ritual at the haunted stone site in the North in eight days' time and if that is successful…" The Herald tailed off before catching himself "… the point is the survival of the realm is currently as precarious as a cat off its whiskers on catnip attempting to traverse a narrow fence."

Val considered the words she was hearing "necromancer this time, is it eh?" she asked plainly. She drained one of the flagons the Herald had brought over "ya have four minutes."

The Herald took out a fancy silk handkerchief and mopped his brow. "Now look, he has the means and the intention to lay waste to this land, and if you hadn't noticed you live in it!" the Herald stated thinking, maybe more hoping, that some actual logic may help.

Val picked up her second tankard and held it to her lips pausing as a thought played across her features "wait a minute..." Val placed the tankard back on the table and stood up, the Herald following her movement with his head transfixed "... I don't think he was criticising me pottery on reflection" and with that she disappeared leaving the Herald stunned. He watched as she entered into another room and unpinned a yokel from the dart board, heavily ruffling his hair and pulling a dart out of his forehead by way of apology. She returned to her seat "now where were we?"

The Herald shook his thoughts free in his head "oh not much, just the small matter of The King of The Undead destroying all life as we know it. Ring any bells?"

"Ah yeah, that. Two minutes." Val supped her drink "been there, done that, last one from memory was the Great Wyvern that was goin' to take over the land, turned out that was some kids who'd stuck some wings on a worm and drawn a picture of it that made it look really big, it was just fake parchment. Before that I think it was Arnold The Great Golden Dragon of the underworld who was gonna set fire to the lands, I soon put pay to that with a little fisty negotiation. Time before that it was some sorceress who had made a really big plank of wood with a nail in it, she was fine just needed a bit of a chat and a couple of cats to calm her down" Val finished her third drink "one minute."

The Herald went to try some other angle "Point is..." Val continued "... there is always somethin' that is goin' to 'end the world'" Val made air quotes "and it's always defeated, else you an' me wouldn't be having this conversation, would we? Humanity an' all the other races always pull their fingers out an' co-operate in the end. Shame it takes such massive threats for them to put their perceived differences to one side an' come together, but people, eh? What are ya gonna do?!" Val drained her fourth drink "So I'm out an' nothing ya can say or do will change me mind."

"So, I'll have to go to Bartok the Balrog Ball Busting Barbarian and see if he'll accept the twenty thousand gold pieces on offer?" The Herald asked taking his chances.

"Now wait a minute" Val hastily came back "I didn't say a hundred per cent I wouldn't do it. A warrior can buy an awful lot of pottery clay for forty thousand gold pieces ya know."

"It was twenty thousand gold pieces."

"So, with that forty thousand agreed You've just hired the V Team!" Val grinned wolfishly at the Herald who sighed and signaled at the innkeeper for more drinks.

Val swilled the new drink around her receptacle and swilled her thoughts around her head "Gonna need to persuade me team back, won't be easy, we didn't exactly part on great terms, but I'll win 'em around with me charm an' me gold, or failing that, I can just put a new team together, there is some real talent in this bar" Val extended her arm at the bar the Herald clocking a mercenary who was making his way around the bar chewing beermats to see if he could get any more alcohol out of them, truly this was a village with its full complement of idiots available, he thought. "We can 'ave an audition, they're all the rage an' so terribly entertaining!"

The Herald went to speak but gave up on that idea, seeing the futility of it. It was days like this he asked himself why he'd given up his last job for this one.

"Yeah, get a team together, get some kind of blade that's good against the undead, I think I know of one of 'em, find the necromancer and the duchess of the dead, or whatever he is called, persuade 'em of the errors of their ways with extreme force, have a celebratory drink, have another fight, get paid, become heroes, 'ave some songs written about our heroic adventures, 'ave a fight with the musicians if the song is bobbins. Easy. So that's the plan agreed!" The Herald wasn't sure he'd understood a word of what Val had just said, but his head was starting to pound from this encounter already, so he didn't have the energy to question any of it. Val stood and walked to the bar giving the Herald a hearty slap on his back as she went.

The Herald composed himself as best he could and picked up his dislodged tooth from the table.

Act 1 Scene 3: A Knave Gave A Grave Rave In A Cave

A light breeze momentarily filled the grim cave with something approaching fresh air, its purity seemingly out of place for the dank evil within. A cowled figure shook off this unusual sensation as he rose from his, comfier than you'd have any right to expect in a cave, chair and crossed to the potion bubbling away in his, again better than you'd expect, nonstick cauldron.

The foul brew bubbled away seeming to move from a light green to a dark mauve, according to ye olde Dulux colouring chart, its stench diffusing in the unusual breeze. The figure had put potpourri in bowls throughout the cave to try and combat the dire smells, but it kept mysteriously disappearing.

The cowled man now crossed to his extensive library, alphabetised by author due to his anal nature. Consulting one of the dusty ancient tomes he took a pinch of dust from a vial and smiled lopsidedly as the fluid angrily bubbled up as he added it, seeming to cloud the room in a putrid mist. Satisfied he put a ladle in the cauldron and took a swig of the liquid, this should blast through his niggling hangover he reckoned.

A second person approached the entrance to this cavern. He went to knock on the door, on seeing no door he rapped on the cold stone where a door could have been, this making no sound. Having achieved zero effect in announcing his presence he coughed quietly, the cowled cavern resident paid him no heed, so finally he tried coughing louder "Cough-I-am-here-cough-cough!"

Without averting his gaze from the cauldron, the grey cloaked character spoke "come over my young apprentice, you've much to learn." The second figure entered the cave rolling his eyes, he'd told the necromancer Ringost Arr many times that he was thirty-two and considered the title young apprentice patronising. He'd agreed to be called just the Apprentice as that made no allusions to his age, young or otherwise and he was learning on the job, so whether he liked it or not the title was appropriate, albeit not the kind of name that would make a Viking go weak at the knees in fear when he heard it.

Ringost reached for a premade potion from a shelf "OK young apprentice, tell me what you see?" he held the yellow sulphuric liquid up to the torch that passed for a light in the dingy environs.

"Plant's Dance Macabre? The potion that summons long legged slow dancing zombies?" the Apprentice declared confidently.

"Good, but it is badly made, what is it missing?" the Apprentice moved closer, though staying downwind, to catch it better in the light. It had a slight green tinge it was lacking something grounding but what?

"Ferrets teeth!" spat the Apprentice frustrated he couldn't get the last ingredient.

Ringost raised an eyebrow "very good!" the Apprentice flashed a disingenuous proud smile.

"I'll go get some right away!" he declared happy at his work, even though he had no right to be.

"No need" said Ringost neutrally, looking beyond the Apprentice. A dread filled the Apprentices bones as he spun to be faced with a creature of bones, a tall figure, what flesh it had left was hanging from its frame, its dead eye sockets appearing to stare through the Apprentice to something interesting it had seen on the wall beyond him, the Apprentice let out a high-pitched scream at the sight.

The skeleton crossed to Ringost and gave him the teeth that it held in its tendrilled fingers.

"Thank you, Kevin," Ringost acknowledged the cadaver. He looked at the Apprentice "he's one of my assistants you know. If you're going to get scared of every undead creature, are you sure the necromancy game is for you?"

The Apprentice bristled at this, "I resurrected that badger, didn't I?" Ringost stuck his head to one side as he considered this. Indeed, the Apprentice had brought a badger back from the beyond, and it had taken them weeks, and cost the un lives of many skeletons to get the aggressive fur ball out of the cave "Kevin just snuck up on me is all."

Ringost ignored this as he moved to a dais in the corner of the chamber, lit by the torchlight burning behind it. He picked up the dented golden goblet resting on it and rolled it around his hand "the time will soon be on us where we bend this world to our will. We will raise the greatest of the undead, those from the grave are a level society, they neither seek nor care about coin or status, they just are and work together, this grasping world could and will learn much from them."

The Apprentice shifted uncomfortably where he stood "and we use this power to try and even the world? No one suffers?"

"Not unless they have to" Ringost spoke quietly to himself "you remember that important lesson I taught you regarding necromancy?"

The Apprentice thought about it for a moment "never use irony with a skeleton, they just don't get it as they're really quite literal?"

"Not that, the other lesson!" Ringost snapped, as he was wont to do.

The Apprentice swallowed "a life for an unlife, a royal life for a royal unlife" he said uneasily.

Ringost attempted to give him a broad smile, but it looked more like he'd burned his bean supper in his cauldron "it's time our cup runeth over with royal blood, my young apprentice."

The Apprentices stomach lurched as he consoled himself by eating some of the dry unusual flavoured thin sliced vegetable snacks that Ringost kindly left in bowls around the cave.

****

The Apprentice had followed Ringost through a maze of corridors to a chamber in the darkest reaches of the cave. Ringost placed the torch in a single brazier which provided little in the way of lighting the large chamber. A large dominating shape in the centre of the room drew the Apprentices eye.

Ringost pulled the sheet from this shape revealing a huge elaborate mirror underneath, its frame a light stone with numerous skulls and grotesque faces carved into it. The glass of the mirror was dark and impenetrable. Ringost held his hand on the cold surface and said an incantation, he paused partway through and turned to the apprentice "remember do not say anything unless spoken to. You do not ask questions." The Apprentice nodded solemnly as the last words came from Ringost.

A face began to appear on the mirrors surface, indistinct at first, but that features slowly built onto it. It was a gaunt, drawn face, it was possibly once something that might have been considered handsome but now was rendered hollow and soulless through the pain it had wrought on the world. "My lord" Ringost spoke reverentially as he bowed, the Apprentice matching him.

The face took a deliberate hesitation safe in the knowledge he had complete control of the room "it is time?" The King of The Undead elongated the words.

"My lord, yes we have all the ingredients for the spell and shortly the royal blood required as the catalyst, then it's just a case of waiting for the night to reach its seventh cycle and you return to remind the world of your total power" Ringost rose as he spoke.

A look passed across the kings features that neither Ringost nor the Apprentice could read. Finally, he decided on the words "Good. I've been in the in this never realm for too long, its time I once more had a physical form to slake my thirsts. People will once more know I am king, ruler, slayer of worlds. Plus, actor."

The Apprentice realised this was his time and with great fear spoke up "About the never world, you're in Lord?" Ringost's head involuntarily fell into his palm and his guts dropped an octave.

A long silence held over the room, unexpectedly, a cruel smile appeared on the face in the mirror "yes, what of it?"

The Apprentice gulped, hesitated and then just went for it "well aren't you sort of better off there? You're not exactly dead, you can command and lead and no one can cause you any physical damage whilst you're in that realm?"

A loud cracked sound which may have been a laugh answered the Apprentice. "True I can communicate? But what else? This between realm of being not dead or alive hold no interest for me. I am invincible up to a point, there are ways though no one has the skills or wit to attempt or achieve it, though I wouldn't want to risk perishing in here that would truly be the end and an ignoble one at that. Besides, have you ever felt the look of your foe as they realise they've drawn their last breath on your blade? As their life leaves their eyes…?" He didn't wait for the Apprentice to reply for he knew the answer "… this realm enables me to escape the death fate had planned for me" he sighed "but too long have I been denied my rightful place ruling all worlds. There are so many things that I miss."

"The violent things?" the Apprentice asked.

"Oh yes!" said the King of The Undead in a tone that suggested it was the obvious answer.

"We will make that happen quickly sire" Ringost quickly cut in, still unsure of the term of address he was meant to use with The King of The Undead.

"You will not fail me" The King of The Undead stated in a way that left no doubt "now go make my will happen Ringost." Ringost bowed once more and made to leave, the Apprentice following as quickly as he was able "Apprentice?" the Apprentices blood ran cold as he turned to face the mirror "if you're interested in the between world, I can teach you some of its ways. Its important someone knows its decrees so that they may better know my fate and its workings, it's always good to have a contingency." The King of the Undead allowed himself a mirthless laugh as the Herald gulped hard in fear of the world, he had just talked himself into entering.

Act 2 Scene 1: Badminton Norse Trials

Val got her considerable bulk comfy behind the picnic table they had liberated (i.e., brazenly stolen) from the tavern and set up in the multistorey horse park outside the pub. This was where they intended to audition potential new recruits. There were rumours of some strong potential, apparently there was one guy who if he ate enough spicey sprouts could knock out anyone within a ten-foot vicinity, truly a power from the gods not to be played with lightly.

She looked through the numbered score cards she'd had the Herald create, though Val wasn't as strong on numeracy as she was on clobbering things around the headeracy. She picked up a number ten card and dropped it on the floor "doubt I'll need that 'un!" she said playfully elbowing the Herald in the ribs possibly cracking a couple in the process "We ready d'ya think Herr?"

"I wish you wouldn't call me Herr" the Herald responded wearily "no man in any part of the world goes by the name Herr."

Val totally ignored the Herald taking a swig of her super strong sour strawberry and sole scrumpy "Next!" she bellowed causing mild to severe hearing damage in the Herald next to her.

The first try out emerged from the tavern's smoky doorway, Val having paid a wizard for a smoke spell to make their emergence more 'dramatic', though this effect had been slightly spoiled when a lost drunken local staggered out first and had to be shooed back in as they weren't auditioning. In front of them coughing from the inhalation stood a lanky slight man, in decidedly manky furs. His hair had been greased back in a failed attempt to hide an obvious bald spot. "Name?" Val asked politely.

"Cough Beastmaster cough" came the reply.

"Abilities?"

"Beastmaster"

Val cocked an eyebrow and grinned "'Ere, are you saying ya can control all the beasts an' animals?"

Beastmaster nodded enthusiastically and produced a jar from within his rough furs "behold!", he unscrewed the lid, and a wasp flew out at a gesture of his hand. The wasp produced a few loop de loops before resting on Beastmaster's upturned palm.

Val clapped delightedly "Imagine what this 'un could do with a Cockatrice?" she asked the Herald excitedly.

"Ah no" Beastmaster cut in "it's just this wasp I've mastered. Though I am hoping to move up to hornets soon."

"Wh… What?!" the Herald sputtered "We're up against pure undead evil and all you can do is make a wasp fly around in circles? What impact can a wasp have?!" the

Herald shook his head despairingly, one try out in, and he was already seeing the futility of this recruitment.

Beastmaster allowed himself a sly smile "You've clearly never been to a picnic, have you?!" and with another signal the wasp flew out of his palm straight at the Herald's head forcing him off his seat running for whatever cover was available whilst wildly flailing his arms.

Val was doubled up with laughter but managed to reach down to the ten card on the floor and wave it enthusiastically. "You good sir are definitely in!"

Beastmaster drew himself up happy at this news and called his wasp back with a cheerful "come on Bernard" to its jar-based housing, he was going to the tavern for a celebratory drink, he'd allow the wasp a cheeky half for his performance too.

A flustered Herald gingerly took his seat back next to Val. "Next!" called Val, the volume nearly sending the Herald flailing off his seat again.

"Ahoy there!" answered a jovial voice from the tavern door. Val looked but could see no person, she did a double take looking at her drink to make sure she hadn't drunk herself blind again. "No, it's not you, it's me." The voice clarified "I'm the invisible man but you may call me Ash."

Val relaxed a little happy she wasn't going to have to get another restore drunken vision spell. "Oh, 'ello love, you're starting to show" she responded cheerily on seeing half of Ash's body.

"Huh?" Ash answered confused looking himself up and down "oh no that's normal, I can only make half of myself invisible, be that my top or bottom half or my left or right side" he clarified.

"Ash the half invisible man? Genius!" the Herald muttered to himself "and what, pray tell, is the use of half invisibility?" he spoke louder.

Ash stood and pondered "well imagine this, if the three of us are in a room and wish to hide from the enemy and said room only has a curtain big enough for two and a half people to hide behind, well with me on your team we're all safely out of view!" he half smiled pleased at this idea.

Val nodded at the notion even though Val was as likely to hide from an enemy as she was ride an arthritic hamster backwards into battle, though now she thought of it, there was that one time she'd got drunk and did something a bit like that for a bet. "You're in pet!" she declared waving away the Heralds attempts at intervention. The half invisible man disappeared.

"I mean come on that's just a pathetic power" the Herald attempted to reason to Val.

"Oi!" came Ash's reply from behind a tree right next to the Herald. Val howled with laughter as the Herald flushed.

"Ooh I am enjoying this!" Val stated happily whilst taking a hefty swig of the Herald's drink. "Next!" Val bellowed, the Herald being ready for it this time by with two breadsticks he'd rammed in his ears.

There was a flash and smoke in front of the table then a pause before finally a man dropped down on some kind of rope. "Cool!" said Val instinctively. The powerfully built man wore a green cloak with what may have been a stag shaped clasp, though it might have easily been a mouse bagpipe hybrid creature shaped clasp given it was clearly made by someone who wasn't especially into art. He wore a face mask with a pair of antlers precariously roped to his head. He had a belt that seemed to feature a number of stag themed implements, one of which was definitely a spork. "Name?" Val enquired.

"I'm Stagman" he growled in a register that sounded like it was hurting his voice box.

"Oh, hullo Stagman" Val responded cheerily "That voice sounds sore, I think I've got a lozenge in one of my belt pouches somewhere…" Val began to pat down pockets on her belt "no sorry just pointy and sharp things actually, not sure they'll help much but you're welcome to try. Anyway, if ya don't mind me asking, what do ya do?"

"I'm Stagman" he rumbled back in a tone that seemed to suggest he felt he had covered everything before he took out a disc from his belt, probably meant to be stag shaped but it was hard to tell, it may just have been left to near a fire and melted a bit. He took quick aim and threw it at one of the village drunks, Val had persuaded to stand by a tree as a practice target, felling the yokel.

Val nodded her approval, "OK Stagman love, like the theme, you've got a good aim, you're in." Stagman threw a smoke bomb to the floor and attempted to disappear.

Val could see him struggling to heave himself back up his rope but chose not to shatter his illusion out of politeness.

"How many more of these… whatever these are do we have left to see?" the Herald groaned.

Val didn't pick up on the implied criticism "as many as we need to make up our super squad. Now go get me a couple of drinks Herr, I'm parched. I can see the rest meself." The Herald got up; it was probably a merciful release to head back into that grim tavern.

Val looked at the parchment in front of her "'ere lemme see, ah looks like one more eh? Next!" a dog howled in the distance confused and startled by the loudness of Val's shout.

A blur backflipped out of the doorway landed in a splits pose before bouncing back up to her feet and starting to clap out a rhythm "She's looking to form a super squad, she's got a totally amazing bod, she's gonna stick evil with her sword, then form a semi peaceful accord. Gimme a V!"

"V!" Val responded almost involuntarily.

"Gimme an A!"

"A!"

"Gimme an L!"

"L!"

"What's that spell?"

"Err… V plus an A and then an L…" Val began to count on her fingers and then her toes "… Val?!"

"Goooo Val!" and with that she performed a forward tumble and threw her armoured pom pom at the remaining standing drunk, who seeing the projectile heading for his face accepted his fate willingly, as it smacked him square in the chops, knocking him off his feet. Val stood and applauded unsure if the athleticism or the song had impressed her the most.

"Nice work love. What's your name?"

"She-ra-ra. I lead, I do good deeds, I make the enemy blead and afterwards I rustle up some mead" she curtseyed.

Val beamed "you are definitely in! This calls for a celebratory drink when that useless bloody Herald shows back up. Honestly he had one job."

****

Val left the tavern with her heavy adventure bags under her arm and a couple of 'borrowed' adventure flagons of ale in her hand. She made a strange clinking noise as she walked, and the Herald hearing this in the distance had a sneaking suspicion she was bringing her pottery with her on the quest. She rounded the corner to find him holding the reins of his elegant horse and her enormous steed; Power and no one else there.

Val looked bemused "what happened to the new supergroup?"

The Herald looked at the ground and cleared his throat a couple of times "Well I mentioned we were going after a powerful necromancer and maybe The King of The

Undead and that seemed to change the atmosphere somewhat. The half invisible man said he had to disappear, though I could still see half of him. Beastmaster said he'd forgotten he'd promised to take Beastmrs out for a romantic all you can eat greasy spoon and that he'd catch up with us. She-ra-ra said she has an allergy to skeletons and needed to get some antihistamines for them. I say she said this, it was more in song format really, I was kind of impressed she found a rhyme for antihistamines. Finally, Stagman growled something and all I caught was something about Stagman but also some vague thing about shining a stag signal in the sky, not sure what the cripes he was talking about. So, I guess we're back to square one, whatever that means."

Val put her hands on her hips and then let out a hearty laugh "not a problem Herr love. I'll just have to put the original gang back together!"

"Didn't you say it ended in bitter recriminations with you all vowing You'd rather die by the claws of a Pain Beast from the Ouch Realm rather than see each other again?"

Val put her bags on Power and stroked his nose affectionately "what that? Oh, that was nothing, we didn't mean any of that."

She finally attached a large jar with a fairy like creature inside it to her horse. The Herald's eyebrow shot up "what on late middle-aged earth is that?"

"Theme music love, every good hero needs it" Val stated as if this answered the Herald's question. The Herald shook his head, the day had been long enough, and he wasn't going to get any further into this.

She mounted her horse with a surprisingly easy grace "Let's go see that dwarf Bumli first, he'll be a miserable sod as per usual, but he loves an adventure. An' gold. An' an adventure that pays in gold!" Val made to start off.

"Wait a moment" the Herald caught her "Bumli? That's his name? Bumli? Seriously!?"

Val didn't seem to understand the Herald's angle "Bumli is a very noble name in Dwarven tongue, it means rulers of those that dwell at the bottom, he's very proud of it."

The Herald shook his head "Whoever gave him that name is moronic. What's his surname pray tell? Fartypants?"

Val still seemed bemused by the Herald's line of questioning "don't be ridiculous Herr love" she chided "Its Air Quaker, one of the great Dwarven lineages that."

The Herald buried his fist into his face and mutter "moronic" again. Val didn't hear this as she had kicked Power on. "I didn't sign up as a counsellor" the Herald muttered as he mounted his ride and started on after Val "Mind you not sure what I did sign up to here, a right load of nonsense as far as I can tell."

Act 1 Scene 4: I Want To Market With You

The Herald and Val had been riding hard for some time since meeting in the tavern, the lack of feeling in the Herald's backside told him it had been many hours, The Herald being very good at time keeping based on feelings in his bottom. They were heading ever further North as the grey dank sky seemed to be telling them. The path they rode through nondescript fields tricked the mind into thinking the landscape stretched on forever.

And yet seemingly from nowhere, into view appeared a range of bright lights which highlighted tents and stalls, the drift of the smell of strange foods, some of which may have been actually edible, being cooked, artisan breads being sold for extortionate prices and all kinds of people and creatures slowly milling around spending time staring at items they had no intention of buying.

"Market day yay!" Val whooped noisily very much to the Herald's irritation. "Come on Herr love, let's see what they got going on!" she called excitedly over the noise of the trade.

The Herald's face was set in disgust "was I not clear earlier Val, we're against a clock and when that clock runs out we're dealing with the small matter of the total end of the wor... wow look at those shirts!" the Herald became distracted by the stores 'Shirt Hot' and 'The Right Cuff' one of which was selling a gaudy gold lame shirt with cuffs so large is looked like the sleeves were blowing out smoke "five minutes, not a second longer" he stated begrudgingly, steering his horse down the side of the track and towards the activity.

The Herald and Val allowed themselves to get lost in the throng of characters who'd appeared from nowhere who seemed quite happy to put aside eons worth of enmity to trade a sword for a mystic goblet (goblets only claim to mysticism appeared to be some much later badly added 'ruins' in pink paint, still some warriors were a sucker for a novelty goblet).

The Late Middle-Aged Earth was truly an odd place where people bought things they probably didn't want, absolutely didn't need and that wouldn't afford them any real happiness five minutes after purchase, but by gad they had to have the item and have it now.

At the store 'Pants a Picture' some young dwarf was looking apprehensive at the trousers his parents had just bought him from the friendly troll vendor. Given the four-foot height discrepancy between him and the troll, the dwarf was not convinced these were the pants for him. Still, his parents assuring the juvenile dwarf that he would 'grow into them' and in the meantime they would just take the trousers up a little bit, about three and a half feet up the young dwarf guessed.

Val was busying herself at the weapon store 'If You Have To Axe, You'll Never Know' looking at sharp and pointy, blunt and heavy or blunt but heavily sharp pointy items on the weapons stalls. She was particularly interested in the latest mace, a long-handled weapon with a spiked ball at the end that when you pressed a button on the shaft the weapon fired an incapacitating liquid in the face of a would-be foe. Val decided against buying this weapon as it went against her instincts of how a fight should be delivered with knuckly justice.

She drifted over to a pottery store 'Kiss My Vase' where she decided to buy some bright coloured Blarrice Bliff vases that the dwarf, with a tan so strong and hair so grey he looked like a photo negative of himself, behind the stall had assured her were 'cheap as chips'. Val had no idea what that meant, she didn't like the pottery, but she was a sucker for a cheeky nonsensical catchphrase and figured it could give her creations a new lease of life if she 'borrowed' its designs, so she put them in the bag she carried around her neck.

Happy with her purchases, she hunted down the Herald, who was at the clothes store 'Blouse of Glory' trying on a particularly ostentatious set of emu feathered pantaloons and chimera skinned shirt. "Whit woo! Check ya out, proper noble looking aint ya? Fit to be a king!" she teased him.

The Herald blanched and began to remove the clothes "Kings Pah! What do they do? Sit on their fat backsides ignoring all the complicated things they don't understand and instead concentrate on the unearned fealty and trappings of a luxury life. Who wants to live that life?!" He handed the clothes back to the store holder, who looked keen to still haggle over the price of the zero items the Herald had just bought.

"Nah, I'll keep my Herald's wear, it's a purer more honest, earthy existence." Val regarded the Herald's finest gold leather breaches with foie gras silk shirt and otter fur lined cloak and contemplated commenting on this, but pointed barbs weren't really Val's thing.

The Herald changed tact "what about you then Val? You from some ancient royal or noble lineage?"

Val smirked "you're kidding right love? Us Valkyries don't go in for any of that pomp an' ceremony nonsense, an' we don't have a one person who we're told is our ruler without us havin' a say in it" she stated with pride.

The Herald didn't seem to comprehend "so how do you have order? And leadership?" he asked.

Val laughed "I dunno, we just kind of get on with each other an' make sure we do the important things, seems to work. If you're a decent person an' handy in a scrap when some smackin's have to be handed out, then you're alright with us Valkyries" She smiled at the Herald "let's go. Necromancer busting time. He doesn't know what's in store!"

The Herald let this pun go but part of his soul killed itself as an act of mercy.

Act 1 Scene 5: A King (And Queen's) Ransom

"Ghastly lot" the queen stated chucking her hot water vole out of the bed and onto the floor. She then began plumping her pillow, annoyed the courtiers hadn't got it to within the millimeter of the exact height she wanted it.

"Pardon?" said the king from the other side of the bed.

"I said gha…"

"… No, it's no use, let me get a bit nearer" the king cut in shifting ten or twelve feet across the bed to be next to his partner. "What was it you said my radiant one?"

The queen clicked her tongue "I said, I hate those ghastly industrialists, wealthy businesspeople, and lickspittle politicians we have to entertain. All in it for themselves and constantly staring at the serving ladies, who they treat with arrogance and disdain. Appalling people."

The king sighed "true, true, but alas we need these people to keep us in royal coin. Those gold dusting rags for staff do not come cheap; you wouldn't want them using cloth rags now, would you?" The king had to admit he agreed with his wife, but he hated hangers on slightly less than he liked royal coin. And he liked royal coin rather a lot. "Though the royal coffers are nearly full enough for us to look at the programs you have in mind to help the disadvantaged people and races of the land, we may even be able to afford that school for training stray marmosets, with wild mood swings. Truly you have the largest heart in the land my dear."

The conversation was broken by a large metallic crashing sound from outside the door and a muttered "arse!" that followed it.

"What was that?!" the queen asked sitting bolt upright "its slightly too late for Timothy to be dusting the royal pictures and ornaments, we let him have an hour off at this time of night."

The queen's question was answered as the heavy chamber door bursting open and into the candelabra lit room entered two hooded characters accompanied by a couple of, actually the king and queen couldn't tell what the other two things were, they were definitely not of the royal world.

The shorter of the hooded figures spoke an incantation under his breath and pointed at the king and queen who had remained frozen in bed "Who-are-you-and-how-did-you-get-in-so-easily?" the queen said in an extremely fast high-pitched voice.

"Blast!" the hooded man replied hitting his hand on his head in admonishment "wrong voice spell" he rapidly said another incantation and again pointed at the royal pair, who now found no words would come out at all.

"Good. Now I have your full intention. You will be coming with me; I need you for a spell." The figure laughed for a full thirty seconds, immensely pleased with himself and his weak pun. "For once you will be actually serving a purpose to this land" he said gleefully. He nodded and swords raised the, what turned out to be undead troops, moved to the bed to *encourage* the king and queen out. The second hooded character with the mask of a beaked bird preferred to stay at the back watching intently, not getting involved in the interaction.

The first man puffed out his chest proudly "Oh and your highness asked a question" he spoke as the king and queen were brought in front of him by his undead servants "Who am I? I'm the future ruler of this overstuffed, complacent realm, but you may call me Ringost Arr the Great". The Apprentice's eyebrows shot up under his mask, he wasn't sure at which point Ringost had decided on 'the Great' as a moniker. 'The passable on a good day, but a real grumpy short arse git' would have been more accurate as far as the Apprentice could tell, but he figured now was definitely not the point to get into it with him.

Ringost gave the royal couple a mock bow which had enough theatricality to get an eight-month run in a small room off Ye Olde West End. "As for how I got in here so easily, a little knowledge and a pinch of magic can open a lot of doors to a person."

Ringost was feeling inordinately pleased with himself. He made a sign with his hands and a portal appeared on the wall opposite the bed. Ringost stared at it, something was not right, it quickly came to him, and he made another sign to create a doorknob to get into the portal. Ringost should have known this, knobs were one of his specialties.

"In time you will see how your royal birth through royal death will finally be of use to the land" and with that the corpses pushed the king and queen through the portal.

Act 2 Scene 2: I Did It Mine Way

The Herald encouraged Flighty Joanna into moving up the grey slate path that wound between the mountains looking to him like some great stone serpent, a real snake mountain. The Herald stared at it wishing he was better at similes and metaphors. "This, am I really going to have to call him this, Bumli? Where is he now? How do we find him?" he called to the hefty shape of Val just ahead of him on the path.

Val turned in her saddle, smiled and pointed, at the side of the path was a wonkily erected brown sign that read "The North Dwarf Wharf and Mines – Guided tours available. Beards optional all days except Tuesdays."

"And you know him to be here?" the Herald asked not sure that a tourist sign could be trusted at the most accurate means of finding a former adventurer.

"Oh yes Herr, I've got me Valkyrie instincts for these things. Plus, he mentioned it was where he was workin' in the card he sent me last Christmas" Val filled the Herald in.

The Herald carried out a near perfect double take, which caused a couple of passing pigeons to pause and contemplate applause such was its mastery. "Wait? What?! You send each other Christmas cards?"

"Every year love."

"But... but I thought you all had a massive fall out and said you never wanted to see or speak to each other ever again. In fact, didn't we have nearly this exact same conversation as we left the tavern?" The Herald asked flustered, worried like most entertainment, this quest was full of repeats.

"Oh yeah we did have that fall out an' said those things. But its Christmas innit? You've gotta send each other cards, its tradition, like cooking sprouts no matter 'ow much ya don't like the disgusting little things," Val spurred on Power down the slate aisle her large strides quickly taking her away from the Herald as she wound down the path towards the bottom of the crags.

"Bloody adventurers!" was all the Herald could manage as he shook his head in disbelief, kicking his horse on the match Val's stride.

The Herald followed Val down this path, albeit more cautiously, wary that a badly placed step and his horse could slide on the loose shale to one of the many lethal looking drops available.

A calling sound from the sky caught the two adventurers" attention as a black winged bird came descending down to land on The Heralds arm. The Herald looked at Val a mask of worry etched on his face on seeing this corvid. "Reverse charge raven. This one has come from the royal house looking at the seal" he stated. He pulled the note from its leg and paid it the required gold coin before it flew off.

As the Herald unfurled and read the attached note colour drained from his face. He turned to Val "the king and queen have disappeared, foul play is suspected, details are scarce, the royal armies are searching the lands for them, but so far not a single sign or clue. It's got to be the necromancer and his vile magic, hasn't it?" Val nodded slowly knowing this to be the truth of the matter.

She rested her hand on the Herald's arm "don't change anything love, we round up the gang, get rid o' this necromancer and save the king an' queen" she paused "though of course, this may raise my fee somewhat" this got the Herald to smile and the two kicked on their horses with renewed vigor.

The Herald attempted to start a conversation to distract himself and the thoughts in his racing mind "yeah those ravens for communication are all well and good, but they'll never be any substitute for the speed, skill and eloquence of a herald" he stated sounding more like he was trying to convince himself.

Val half smiled "Oh yeah Herr love, you're totally safe in what you do, it's the personal touch o' the messenger who takes days crossing the lands to deliver a message that a bird could have done in hours that the public want. People will always pay for the personal touch" she replied whilst trying to stuff the mobile dove she carried further down into her saddlebag lest the Herald saw it. She didn't have the heart to tell him everyone she knew had a communications bird these days, the Herald wasn't having the best of days as it was.

****

As the path evened and opened out the Herald could hear horn and bagpipe music and the outside of the mines became apparent. There were large tents, stalls selling artisan slate and slate-based snacks and some of what looked like highly unsafe slate themed rides. The 'bone chipper' looked the least appealing as it appeared that you sat on a large piece of slate as you were pushed down a steep slate filled slope, how you stopped appeared to be in the hands of whichever god you prayed to or any passing gods that took sympathy on your plight. "So, they've taken the eons of Dwarven back breaking labour and heritage and turned it into… a theme park?" he asked himself as much as anyone.

Val was hooking Power to a wooden fence post and looking in her purse for the correct change to pay to leave her there. "Get used to it love. Seems the old ways always get replaced by some kind o' expensive leisure activity." Val scanned around the grounds "wonder where the little hairy ball bag is?" she mused to herself.

The Herald as a reflex began scanning around though was not clear who, or what exactly he was looking for "this Bumli, what exactly does he look like?"

"Short, stocky, bearded" Val responded. As far as the Herald could tell, that description appeared to match all the dwarven men, women, and for that matter children, plus one particularly unusual looking sheep going about their business in the area.

Val started wandering around the fairground, the Herald watched in wry amusement as Val got in a heated discussion with a dwarf manning (dwarfing?!) the 'hook a dwarven duck' (even harder than its non-dwarf counterpart, those bearded ducks were really rather small) stall. She stomped back to the Herald "I told that guy he was Bumli, but he wasn't having it!" she fumed.

She stopped for a moment, hands on hips, unsure what to do "Aha!" Val's tone brightened as she saw the tourist information sign. She weaved her way through the velvet ropes which would have given the illusion of a shorter queue had there actually been anyone queuing. She returned looking much happier this time "Turns out he is chief tour guide for the great mine, I've got us a couple of tickets, which is definitely going on expenses for this quest. We've a little bit of time to kill before it starts." She stated as she made her way into the fairground attractions.

After much of the aforementioned time killing, Val stuffed the last of her large cuddly dwarven toys, that she had easily won, on the "test your strength" and "the coconut not so shy" stalls into her saddlebag. The Herald had to settle for a goldfish, which he'd given to a young dwarven girl as he wasn't sure a quest was the best place for aquatic themed pets.

"Tour fifty-four!" bellowed a grey-haired dwarf using his false leg as a loud hailer.

"That's us!" Val grinned getting behind the queue of elves, sprites, fantas, treemen and gnomes. The Herald shrugged and followed, a role he had seemingly been playing a lot of late.

The queue formed under the large imposing arch entering into the mine. Val could hear a familiar, albeit more well-spoken than normal, sounding voice echoing off the cavern walls, as they descended down the narrow dimly lit paths. Val and the Herald could hear Bumli spinning some kind of yarn about the Dwarf Lords allowing the dwarf people the joys of smashing the rocks in the seams of the cave, searching for precious metals, which they gave to the Lords in return for their below minimum wage job and a damp cave to live in.

The party descended down narrow winding tunnels with low ceilings (especially if you were a Val, not so much if you were a Bumli), the grey green sides damp with running water, the walls reaching above higher than the torches could illuminate. Finally, they stopped descending and their boots crunched on loose stones as they made their way between a narrow gap in two rocks into a clearing cave, the unmistakable sound of running water echoing around it.

"And here is the cleansing chamber of the Dwarven people" Bumli's voice almost sang the words "where the past was washed off for new beginnings and foreshadowing was extremely welcome" he pointed at the gushing water cascading from the rocks above into a clear pool, the depths of which was unguessable. "This is a good place for you to get some memento sketches" Bumli declared to the tour leaning on a rock to take the weight off his feet. The tourists drew out their parchment and began drawing pictures of themselves in front of the prominent features.

Val crossed the chamber, the Herald in tow, to where Bumli was looking at a small magazine on real ale he'd hidden in his beard. "I wondered when You'd come over" he stated flatly not looking up from his tract. "You're not really the right size for stealth Val, nor just dropping in on old acquaintances" again he did not look up.

The Herald thought maybe now was the time for his superior diplomacy skills "Mr. Wind Quacker" not sure if he'd correctly remembered Bumli's surname "if we could just have a moment of your precious time…"

Bumli quickly glanced up to look the Herald up and down in a disconcerting manner "and who is this floppy fringed wet hemp sack?" his voice dripped with contempt, plus some ale fumes from the night before.

Val stepped closer into Bumli's vision "He's with me, gave me a quest, he's sort of OK once you get past all the other stuff." The Herald wasn't sure where to look or if he should disappear behind a rock to spare him this conversation. He was particulary perturbed by what "the other stuff" was.

Bumli laughed without humour "quest, eh? And you thought old bygones would be bygones, all the things that happened the last time we adventured are done and we'd just pick up from where we used to be?" he looked back at the waterfall "a lot of water has run on from then", being a Dwarf, he was somewhat heavy handed with his metaphors.

"Maybe, maybe not but a split o' thirty thousand gold pieces can maybe build a pretty decent bridge" the Herald was unsure if Val's memory of the agreed fee was really bad, or actually really good and she wasn't giving her companions the best deal "an' the chance to defeat a pretty lethal necromancer says it's worth a try." Bumli swallowed hard, he did his best to keep his eyes on the waterfall. The Herald stood motionless still trying to work out Val's math's on the reward, none of the formulas he used added up well.

"Meet me in the picnic area after. I've a tour to conclude" he said gruffly and wandered off without looking back, to round up the tourists.

"You know he's not wearing any trousers?" the Herald spoke quietly to Val after he'd gone. Val shrugged and moved to join up with the tour.

****

Val and the Herald sat on the splinter encouraging picnic bench outside the great mine. "… And another thing…" the Herald began, Val sighed "… he's what? Five foot six, five foot five? Does that count as small enough to call yourself a dwarf?"

A fly landed on Val's shoulder; she absentmindedly flicked it sending it thirty feet into a crag. "You want to take that up with him love?" she turned and gave the Herald a thin smile. The Herald swallowed and then pretended to take great interest in a rollercoaster based around the lung damage sustained from long term work in a mine called 'Simply The Chest'.

Presently a stocky figure huffed over to the bench, sat down drawing a stone flagon and unwrapping a paper package that contained some bread that looked suspiciously like it was made of stone. He tucked his beard into his tunic and began eating.

A silence passed that seemed to go on for an eternity, or for at least as long as a bard comedy. Val finally went for it "Bumli?"

"Aye?" the dwarf grunted.

"Fancy a quest? Lots o' gold in it."

"Aye."

Val smiled and took a swig of the "water" from the flagon in front of Bumli, the liquid felt like a punch in the gut and made Val's eyes water stinging wet tears, and she had superhuman constitution.

Bumli let out a bitter laugh. "This tour guiding isn't for me, though it's a steady wage. Prior to this I did try and form a new gang 'the hells rejects', but everyone said we were too nice, to be fair, the name was open to misinterpretation. I mean you carry your gear in one goat's bladder for life and everyone sneers at you for being soft. So yeah, that didn't last long" Val and the Herald exchanged quick puzzled glances. Bumli declined to go into any further details "I'll get my armour on."

****

Val and the Herald held their horses by a slate deposit to the side of the great mine. A distant chinking sound grew louder as over the ridge a stern helmed face appeared, next his heavily plated body came into view and finally his short legs which were not wearing plate and still seemed to be sans trousers. This vexed the Herald, but he was definitely not broaching the subject.

Bumli nodded at Val and put his fingers in his mouth and attempted a whistle that actually sounded more like a wet fart. The Herald hoped it was the dwarf's mouth that had made the noise but wasn't brave enough to look down at Bumli's trouserless legs to make sure. And yet on cue a heavily laden donkey rounded the corner and pulled up next to the heroes' horses. "Ah nice ass, it's good to see ya" Val said patting the donkey on its head.

The Herald couldn't help finally looking Bumli up and down trying to avoid looking at the down for too long "Bumli?"

"Aye?"

"Err… you're not actually that shor… I mean where are your trous… what I'm trying to say is… nice armour." The dwarf did not reply and mounted his steed.

"Let's go, I've our next stop slated in!" Val said cheerily. The Herald preyed that the quest was going to be easier to deal with than the level of Val's puns.

Act 2 Scene 3: In Rude Elf

The three companions kicked their steeds along the tree lined dust track, midges on a constant suicide mission heading at their faces, seeming to take great pleasure flying to a saliva-based doom in the riders" mouths. This didn't seem to bother Bumli one jot who seemed to enjoy the taste.

"So…" Bumli began "… how do we find… the elf?" he struggled to spit out the last two words.

Val smirked at Bumli "I heard she an' her band were looking to break the Western realm. Some kind o' large stadium tour, according to the last correspondence I had with 'er. Dead successful sounding she was."

The Herald drew level with Val flicking midges away from his face before speaking "We are recruiting a musician?"

"Depends on what yer definition o' music is love" Val answered "there is no doubting she is lethal with a bow though, an' I don't mean the one used to hit an instrument" Val took a swig of her water, or at least the Herald's working assumption was it was water.

"We can be in the Western realm in a few hours. Just got to cross the Planes o' Peril first." Val read the startled look on the Herald's features "so called as it's that plain an' boring, people often fall asleep when crossing an' fall out of their saddles. The outer region councils have to deal with all kinds of litigation cases for it. Hence the warning signs" Val pointed at a sign that read 'long rides are tiring. Especially across the Planes of Peril. Take regular breaks. Oh, and look where you're going, don't read this sign'.

With that, the track reached its apex and in front of the Herald lay an expanse of featureless land in the least exciting green/brown and improbably, somehow grey hue possible "Crikey, I'm feeling tired already" Val said stifling a yawn as she slunk down into her saddle.

****

After hours of riding, which felt like it may have been geological ages the gang reached the tavern 'The Beige Squirrel' which was situated just as you exited the planes. After a quick enquiry within (and a much-needed toilet stop and wizard crafted energy drink) they had gathered that Ansafety's band 'Don't Leaf Me This Way' had a big gig to the river south of the tavern, a thirty-minute ride through the woods beyond. Wearily the trio kicked on.

Exiting a clearing in the woods they were confronted with a shallow pebble bottomed river which they crossed to head South to where they were told the band were playing "'Ere, what's that noise?!" Val asked cupping her hands to her ears.

"Sounds like the death scream of an enraged Kraken" Bumli answered in hushed tones looking around alert, his enormous axe drawn.

"No, sounds much worse. Could be a Scarebeast from the Terrorsville realm" Val rested her hand on the pommel of her great sword.

The Herald shook his head and laughed "I've bad news for you, it's worse even that all that" he kicked his horse on ahead of Bumli and Val. "That. That is a pan pipe solo. Prepare yourself for what awaits fine folks" he turned his steed in the direction of the scattering of trees to his right and the source of the unholy noise.

A short ride (and a lot of sonic suffering) later the trees totally thinned out revealing a clearing, in the distance appeared to be a hastily erected stage with four elaborately dressed bodies playing music they, if no one else was, were enjoying. The no one else in this equation appeared to be five bored looking elven youths sat in a circle smoking leaf. Two further elves whose mechanism had clearly gone from too much leaf and wine were dancing in front of the stage in a style that could only be described as 'mechanism clearly gone'.

"Big gig, eh?" Bumli stated with what was as near as the Herald had seen him smile in the small time, he'd known him. And as near to a smile as Val had seen in the long time, she'd known him.

The three dismounted and made the decision to stick twigs in their ears to minimise the musical damage. They stood as far away from the stage as they could manage as an extra precaution until the music finished.

"We'll be taking a break now, don't go anywhere" the lead singer, come clam shell player shouted to the audience, who met the news with a degree of pleasure. The band paused waiting for applause that never came so sheepishly they made their way off stage.

"Now's our chance" Val motioned to the other two striding to the back of the stage, daring the Roadie (Trackie?!) with a glare to challenge her progress. The other two followed through the breach Val had punctured in the flimsy looking security arrangements.

"Ansafety!" Val shouted warmly, ignoring the cold looks of the other elves in the equally hastily erected 'VIP' dressing room, which looked like a couple of stumps to sit on and a mirror someone had put in between them with a few candles around it to look glamorous "we liked your… err… sound… didn't we lads?"

Ansafety looked nonplussed, though it was hard to tell with an elf. The Herald saw his cue, nodding vigorously "Yes amazing… err… vibes… people say you can have too many flutes playing a solo, not I!" He dug Bumli in the ribs whilst glaring at his ears, Bumli twigged and removed the twigs from his ears.

"Aye… very..." He stopped even trying to think of words and gave up at that.

Ansafety slowly drew a notebook from her pocket and looking dissatisfied made a couple of notes before retuning it. She took a sip of her expensive elven wine. "Pleasantries done. What do you want?" Her voice melodic, unlike her music.

The Herald shifted awkwardly unsure how to play it, but Val had no such concerns and went at the problem head on as was her modus operandi. "We've got a quest. Stop the big necromancer an' some potential undead king thingy, probably 'ave a few other unplanned fights along the way for a laugh, get paid. Big. Need your big bow skills." The elf looked disdainful but again that may have been her resting face. "Don't ya miss the adrenalin hit of questing Ansafety?"

The Herald tried to press home the point "Think of all the tales of heroism and daring a do you'll have to fuel the accordion solo on your next album?"

To the Herald, Ansafety's features changed little, if anything she looked more disgusted, but Val recognised the tell and as was her wont, exploited it immediately "thirty thousand gold pieces buys a lot o' effects pedals, whatever they are, for your lutes. You could also get a promotor, whatever they are. I'll be honest I know little about the music business love, but I'm sure 'avin' wealth in it takes ya a long way over skint people with talent."

The face of the elf looked less and less impressed with each word "Aha! Gotcha!!" Val declared triumphantly.

The elf took another deliberate sip of her wine. "OK. But you stay to hear our next song. It's a sure fire hit in the making."

****

Eight hours, fifteen minutes and forty-five seconds later the now four were ready to set off.

"I will lay a bloody vengeance on anyone" Val spoke solemnly "to get that bleedin' pan pipe solo out of me head." She gripped Power's reins tightly.

The Herald found himself humming the tune, which was no easy feat "I actually quite liked it."

Act 2 Scene 4: They Say Necromancing Is Dead

The Apprentice followed Ringost down the uneven echoing winding steps to the lower parts of the cave where the makeshift dungeon had been set up. Ringost wanted it to be called an oubliette but realised he didn't know how to spell it, or pronounce it. He wasn't entirely sure what the word meant either, so dungeon it was.

Somehow the lanterns they carried managed to highlight the gloom more than lift it if anything, a lingering suppressive gloaming. Finally, the two reached the bottom their feet pattering on the shallow pools of slimy water, the noise of the constant dripping off the walls their third companion. Their breath clouded in front of them as they made their way deeper into the cavern.

Rounding a corner that seemed to go on forever, where the bend teased it was at its last before curving further on, they finally saw the bars that had been mounted against one of the caves in the chamber. Within its bars sat the king and queen using a crate as a makeshift means of being as comfortable as they were able. A torn blanket, the Apprentice insisted they were provided with, wrapped around their torsos offered their only real means of heat. It was a real comedown from sitting on a giant swan whilst wrapped in the fur of the famed toggle otter.

Ringost noticed a shoddy sign had been hung on the wall saying "no cage like home". Clearly one of the skeletons had developed something approaching a sense of humour. Ringost made a mental note to check out which skeleton had done this, as if the raising the King of The Undead plan went wrong, he could tour the Northern comedy circuit with that skeleton as a backup plan.

Ringost approached the bars whilst the Apprentice hung back in the dark of the chamber keeping his head down.

"Comfortable?" Ringost asked with wry amusement and more than a hint of a sneer. The king stood and approached the bars, Ringost did not flinch from his position.

"Whatever you want" the king spoke with the confidence of a man used to getting just this "name your price, all the riches you want for our freedom" the king maintained his eye contact with Ringost, though this did involve him having to stoop somewhat to take into account the height differences, even with Ringost in his built up boots. Which he wore in a failed attempted to convey not being a short arse, like the famous irritating hobbit singer Probono.

Ringost allowed himself a smirk "and that's how your mind works isn't it? Riches for me is all I, and indeed anyone needs in this life? No what I have in mind is something a little grander than your spoilt mind could imagine." Ringost began pacing along the bars "with your sacrifice, I will raise new royalty, one who will help deliver a slightly grander vision, The King of The Undead will return to level things a little and with that I will rule the land and see if I can't make it a more interesting, better place for all. And I mean all." Ringost said, essentially revealing his whole plan even though it was entirely unnecessary to do so.

The queen barked out a laugh, without any humour from the back of the cave, it echoing around like a taunt. "The King of The Undead, really? That? That is your plan?! You would seek to do business with that vile monster? Does your memory run as short as your legs, on what he did to this land before he was finally, and with the blood of many people and races spilt, banished? Do you think he has any need, much less want of a pathetic mortal like you once you have him back in this world? It'll be a more even realm for all races alright, as they'll all be dead." She snorted with contempt "and I thought Necromancers were supposed to be smart."

Ringost inwardly flinched and then allowed himself a slight outwardly flinch before getting his internal/external flinch ratios about right. He placed his face near the bars sneering "You'd do well not to underestimate me your highness. I've had enough people do that in my lifetime and you and they will both learn the error of their ways. You will all learn! Ringost Arr is not a man to be dismissed!" He spat the last word dripping in venom.

"Besides" he continued in a lighter tone "I've NVQs in raising the dead, summoning ghouls, communing with the beyond, zombie obedience, skeleton herding and home economics. How's that for not being smart?" he folded his arms with pride, he really was proud of that sausage plait he'd made to get his pass mark for cooking, though coming to think of it, he'd never bothered to make it again since.

The queen was unmoved by his speech, even less so his list of qualifications "I do not even know where to start with all that. And anyway, what of your silent friend over there? What does he get?" She nodded at the Apprentice, who was steadfastly staying out of this, though fully noting the logic of the arguments.

Before Ringost could speak, the Apprentice cut in "the chance of some power on my own terms, as myself. More than that though a society of fairness and merit" he muttered in a quiet neutral tone as he paced the back of the cave, his enigmatic response somewhat undermined by him clearly stubbing his toe on a loose rock no matter how much he tried to hide his pain and refused to wail in agony out loud.

The King stepped into Ringost's eyeline and addressed him as sternly, as the unusual situation he found himself in, enabled him to do "your idiot plan will never meet fruition. We are the prominent rulers of this realm and are known to be missing. Enjoy this moment whilst you can little man, we have the greatest and smartest heroes of the world coming for you!"

Act 2 Scene 5: Busting A Nut

Bumli dismounted Nice Ass to approach the gold chain hanging from a branch in the small woodland clearance. The party watched this charade from the saddles of their rides from the tree line just behind the dwarf.

Ansafety curled her lip "he does know that it is most patently a trap, right?" she said disdainfully, flexing her body to warm up for the trouble that was waiting for the first idiot to come along, seeing that they had now provided said idiot.

"Clearly!" Val declared eagerly, spotting long ago it was an obvious trap, but having withdrawal symptoms of not being in a scrap for a couple of days, she was happy to see how this one played out. "Them dwarves love their gold. What are you gonna do?!" The Herald moved his hand to the pommel of his sword with great speed as Bumli closed in on the pendant.

Bumli eyed the gold pendant dangling in front of him, his tongue slightly lolling to one side. He took a long look around, weighed up the options and then finally went with plan 'yank the sod' "Got it!" he yelled triumphantly at the trophy in his hand a large grin on his large beardy features. At this point there was a snapping noise and a twang as a rope snaked around his leg hauling him upside down, and leaving him hanging in the air, gravity taking over his skirt giving anyone looking a view they could do well without. "Come on then, I'll take you all on!" Bumli yelled arms windmilling aggressively as he dangled upside down.

"Didn't see that one coming" Ansafety said in an almost bored tone as she drew her bow and notched an elegant arrow. The Herald sighed and drew his ornate sword and dismounted to see about cutting his companion down. Val giddily leapt off her ride, a massive grin on her face.

Most of the bushes around the clearing began twitching as figures with their faces hidden behind the foliage began to emerge, their swords, axes and clubs (one appeared to have forgotten his weapon so was wielding a garden trowel as menacingly as he could manage) drawn and pointed at the interlopers.

The largest of the masked intruders moved closer to the party who had formed as best protective ring around Bumli as they could manage with three people, it was perhaps the pioneering outing of 'the protective equilateral triangle, though it may have been an isosceles triangle, this point didn't feel like the time for geometry. "Now then my fine friends" he orated in a rich well-spoken voice "hand over all your valuables and you're free to go unharmed."

Val's laugh echoed around the clearing startling a couple of squirrels who had come close to the gathering to see if any of the humans would drop any nuts on the off chance. "Ladies an' lads, you've really misjudged this 'un. Yer only running at about five of you to one o' us, including me upside down matey." She gave the nearest raider a pantomime wink "but I'll humour ya. Say we hand over our goods, what will yer do with 'em?"

The lead raider cleared his throat "Well, since you ask, we'll take them to the oasis, in the dessert, five days ride from here and then we stash them beyond the wit of any mortal" he said firmly and sounding a little pleased with himself.

"Err… mister raider…" the Herald jumped in "… not to tell you the best way to do your job, but Wolves-Are-Hampton city is but a day's wander from here. You could take our objects there and exchange it for gold, wine, women, amateur dramatics. Whatever your heart desired. Not to give you incentive to steal our gear though."

There was approving murmurs throughout the gathered posse. "No, no" the lead raider spoke again "We stash them at the oasis, this is the way."

"This is the way? What kind of codswallop is that?!" a raider to the back muttered quietly.

"What then boss?" the raider nearest to the front asked their leader.

The leader was momentarily dumbfounded "What…?! Well, we just stash it there don't we?! That's the noble art of what we do, it's a tradition handed down from our forefathers and foremothers and forestepparents and tradition is important in raiding" the leader regained his composure "So my fine friends what choose you?

Handing over all that lovely gear I can see, or lots of pain?"

"Neither!" Val declared with positive relish. The lead raider looked confused, or as possible as it was to look confused wearing a mask and shrugged before closing in on the party, his posse following in, closing from all sides. Ansafety drew back on her bow, the Herald spun his sword ostentatiously and Val cracked her knuckles loud enough for a distant woodpecker to think they had a new rival in the area, and they best brush up on their aggressive pecking.

The fight that was about to ensue took a quick breath in as the parties weighed each other up. This was finally broken by Val's battle cry "Lets 'ave it!" she charged the nearest raider and before he could react, she picked him up and swung him into the raider next to him, sending both back into the bush they emerged from. She looked around for her next raider target, quickly identifying them, pointing her finger at them and closing the gap menacingly in their direction.

Ansafety let off two arrows at ferocious speed, quicker than her assailants could see dropping two opponents before firing a third arrow which ricocheted off the helm of the raider it hit. "Ha you missed!" this raider declared triumphantly not seeing the intentional rebound had sent the arrow at the correct angle to cut the rope holding Bumli up sending him crashing down heavily on the overconfident bandit.

The Herald was engaged with three raiders using a series of elaborate feints, elegant parries and spins to dispatch his opponents with a graceful ease. With a grin on his face, he thrust at the last of his opposition who stepped to the side and kicked the Herald's legs away sending him sprawling to the ground, landing hard, his sword spiraling out of reach.

The Herald looked up aghast as his foe raised his sword and began to charge where the Herald lay. At this point, Val casually stepped into the raiders path, who had too much momentum to avoid her, she swung her iron toe capped boot into the raiders never regions lifting him a full six inches off the ground, he landed and crumpled to the ground howling in a tone only audible to particularly vigilant dogs. "Count 'em don't rub 'em" Val counselled her beaten enemy.

Val helped the Herald up "Impressive. You've clearly 'ad some fancy an' expensive training with a blade" she dusted him down "but don't be afraid to go route one, love" she affectionately ruffled his hair and wandered off to check on the rest of her gang.

The Herald drew a mirror and ensured each hair was back exactly as it should be. He then turned his attention over to the sobbing heap in front of him trying to think of something that may help with the pain, or some words of comfort. Seeing the impossibility of this, he offered an apologetic shrug and made his way to his colleagues.

The two squirrels returned figuring they may have judged this one right after all.

Act 2 Scene 6: Barbaric Queue Sauce

The woodland foliage became less and less dense and a dim dusk light greeted them as they came out into the open. Down the slope of the hill, they came to, the torches were being lit in Canals Treat, also known as Ye Olde Gaye Village, truly the liveliest, funnest social epicenter of the realm. The pleasant smell of oak wood being burned in chimneys wafted into the nostrils of our heroes filling with them some form of comfort.

Val encouraged Power down the decline and the party reached the large wooden village gate. The crew pulled up as an enormous ogre in a black jacket with a luminous armband barred their way.

"Purpose?" he said chewing gum aggressively and staring over the heads of the crew, in a way that managed to somehow sound both bored and threatening.

Val responded for all "We're meetin' an old mate, usually 'angs around this way. He'll be well chuffed to see us!" she said cheerily.

The Ogre's face remained the same unreadable setting, as if a sprite had just farted up his nostril. "You're all a bit casual" he decided. The Herald shifted in his seat about to point out three things; firstly, what the hell did 'too casual' even mean, were they atop their horses in a maverick free form way or something? Secondly, that when you were questing to defeat the forces of pure evil that are intending to end the world, you didn't wear your best dinner jacket and deerskin pantaloons (although it had taken the Herald much agonising deliberating not to start out the quest in these clothes) and thirdly, despite points one and two he still looked utterly fabulous, and how dare this brute suggest otherwise. However, before he could speak Val put her arm across his chest in a gesture that said she had this.

"Aye, but we've a load o' gold to spend in your fancy overpriced bars and posh street food stalls." The granite expression of the ogre remained neutral, and he said nothing, but he pushed the heaving weight of the gate to one side with zero effort. He grunted at the party which was his way of saying "come on in my dear fellows, we are well met, and I wish you the fortunes of the stars in your endeavors in this world and the next."

The four trotted down the main thoroughfare, past a lot of huts and shacks. At the end of this row was a tall, tower made of light blue stone, which seemed to almost glow in the evening light, giving the tower the impression of beaming into the stars. It had a large balcony at the top and 'wait here' painted many feet down from this with an arrow pointing up to the balcony.

The Herald looked up at this impressive spire "what is that?" he asked anyone who would answer.

Ansafety would answer "The Enchantresses' tower" she stated.

The Herald nodded though he was not sure what that actually meant. Bumli took pity and decided to fill the Herald in some more. "She is a powerful magician; warriors visit her, and she grants them boons for their quest. However, her mood can be a little, err, variable and one in six visitors, on average, she turns into a toad for a little while for reasons no one has been able to fathom, she's certainly not one for revealing her motives. Once a quester is a toad, fellow warriors generally steal all their quality gear, being it's not easy to carry around a fancy sword with short, webbed feet. So, seeing her is a risk but many take it. It's all a bit random if you think about it, but that's questing for you."

The Herald did think about it, this was indeed a strange phenomenon, which made little sense to him. "Any of you ever seen her? If so, what happened?"

Bumli smirked "now that would be telling. Let's just say I have a newfound appreciation of a good Lilypad, and the nutrition value of flies." The Herald smirked at this as he wondered if a toad version of Bumli retained the beard.

The party reached the tavern 'The Frog and Musket', they had as their destination and tethered their horses to the post outside. The noise of bawdy music, animated conversation and plain shouting carried to the outside.

"And you're sure the big lad is in here?" Bumli asked Val.

Val nodded "yep this one looks and sounds the most lively!" and by lively Val meant that everyone is there was either drunk, fighting or drunkenly fighting "an' let's face it he's either gonna be in the most full-on bar that's available to him, or the library." The Herald seemed confused at Val's words, but he had come to accept this as a regular occurrence as he followed her through the rotten wooden door that just about clung to its hinges.

The inside that greeted them was a picture, and not a particularly competently drawn picture at that, more the kind of drawing You'd get if you attached a paint brush to the tail of a disinterested (is there any other kind?!) cat and asked it to draw the creation of the universe on the garden fence.

Immediately in front of the party was a cut-purse in a bareknuckle punch up with a girl guide, to their left a poker game was on the cusp of breaking into a fight over who was cheating (all of them were), a mercenary was joyfully sliding down the banister from the mezzanine too drunk to notice the splinters in his bum turning him into some kind of arse porcupine, three nuns were practicing their knife throwing in an alcove and to the right a ranger was casually urinating (mostly) in a plant pot. In fairness to the ranger this was a safer bet than using the actual toilet and the plant in the pot looked like it needed no further help in dying.

"We were nearly too casual… for *this*?!" the Herald asked rhetorically, his eyes on stalks as a naked whooping figure ran joyfully past them.

Bumli gave the Herald a sideways glance "they only let you in cos you were with a couple of lasses."

In the far corner a sinewy man in a wax jacket drank his pint slowly as the chaos unfurled around him, everyone being careful not to bump into him or spill his drink.

Ansafety noticed the Heralds gaze and decided to be more helpful filling him in this time "The farmer. People have often got into fights with him, again tends to happen about every one in six times for some reason, but it seldom ends well for them if they do take him on. He's not to be trifled with." The Herald nodded slowly along with Ansafety's words.

The group weaved their way through the disorder in front of them and just about made it to the bar dry and unruffled. Ansafety was looking particularly disgusted at what was playing on around her and her default facial expression was pretty much disgust.

A stout barman with a walrus moustache and matching walrus boots sidled over to Val and nodded "Aye?"

"Edin in?"

"Aye."

"Back room?"

"Aye."

"Scrumpy please."

"Aye."

"Thank you."

"Aye."

"It's the fascinating in depth discourse, exchange of ideas and thought-provoking discussion that really marks these places as a special location for the meeting of minds isn't it?" the Herald muttered to himself.

Val necked her tankard and turned to her companions, she went to speak, paused, belched then tried again "He's in the rough bit o' the bar" she pointed over her shoulder. She turned to walk off throwing her tankard over her shoulder as she did, it landing in the middle of the just settled from fighting poker players who immediately began fighting again at this intrusion and who was to blame for it.

Val casually rounded the bar and entered the snug, so called for the large number of people packed into such a small space to cheer on the brawls that took place within its walls.

The Herald used his sharp elbows to get through the throng, his eyebrows shot up at the sight of probably the biggest human he'd ever seen, every considerable muscle looking like it was trying to inflate away from his body, crude tattoos – some clearly self-penned, the upside down one on the leg saying 'hello you!' a dead giveaway – adorned any blank body space available to them and a look on his face that could curdle whisky from fifty paces.

This giant was being held aloft by an even bigger, cruder tattooed being who was casually pressing him above his head as a gentle workout.

Val smirked and shook her head "Same old Edin, always lookin' to get a pump on, even in the middle of a fight." She put her fingers in her mouth and let out a wolf whistle so loud a couple of the cage fighters began to cry. "Oi Edin, put 'im down, there is gold to be 'ad an' zombies to be chinned!"

The Barbarian gave Val a toothy, well more like mostly toothless, grin, and as if it were no effort to him threw his opponent into the nearest poker game which immediately broke out into a fight.

After picking up his vanquished foe and giving him a slightly too long a lasting hug, Edin powered through the assembled crowd. Parting spectators and clasped hands with Val. At some point an unwritten rule at this gesture kicked in and it became a battle of strength to see who could win this mid-air arm wrestle, though in reality it was no contest at all as Val forced Edin's arm down with minimum fuss. Edin laughed at his loss "Ye really oughta take up the bar brawling Val lass, you'd clean up!". He regarded the rest of the party, grinning at Bumli and giving Ansafety a nod, for all the reaction he got from her "who's the stiff?" he asked fixing his eyes on the Herald.

"He's the paymaster" Val clarified "He's sort of alright once you get used to 'im" the Herald wasn't sure what to make of this description but remained quiet. She put her arm around Edin's shoulder "somewhere we can talk love?"

Edin nodded "Aye my star dressing room should do the trick." Edin led them to a door under the stairs and the five of them squeezed into what appeared to have once been, and judging by the smell may still have been, a toilet. The space would have been cramped for a party of five quarterlings, but when two of the party were giants like Val and Edin it was more of a squeeze than a python stuck in a beer bottle with the beer also still remaining in it.

"We good?" Val asked, those two words seeming to convey a lot more than appeared.

Edin nodded "it wasn't me who you fell out with."

Satisfied at this Val kept the background to the quest brief to save breath, particularly as it was hard to breathe in the quarters. Besides, Val had Edin at 'lots of gold' so any other words were unnecessary.

The five agreeing on terms made their way to leave the bar, just as they reached the door Edin spoke over his shoulder "Barkeep!"

"Aye?"

"My tab."

"Aye."

Edin flung a bag of gold onto the nearest table, where people happened to be playing poker and thus a brawl ensued.

Act 2 Scene 7: A Moon With A View

Ringost led the Apprentice by torchlight further into a chamber he hadn't been in before, something of a regular occurrence of late, though in his defence, Ringost was very precious about who he let enter his dark tunnels.

The flicker of the lantern revealed on the walls what the Apprentice assumed were wards, but on closer inspection some looked like amateur attempts at still life drawings, though he didn't comment on this lest he risked hurting Ringost's feelings. Ringost could be extremely prickly about his work especially if it was the more creative side of what he did. Actually, Ringost was just prickly about everything.

Finally, they reached the back of the chamber and Ringost lit the torch attached to the wall. The room was full of charts, scrolls and books, a couple immediately caught the eye of the Apprentice as of extreme interest. Whatever could be levelled at Ringost, he certainly had books covering all the elements of the dark arts from Aardvark Resurrection to Zombie Zumba Classes, the Apprentice made a mental note of the books that looked like they could be of much use to him and his learning.

Ringost purposefully went to a stack of scrolls and pulled one out before preceding to unfurl it on the stone alter in the middle of the room. The scroll had a large drawing of the moon on it. "That is the moon" Ringost said pointing at it.

"Thanks Ringost."

"This full moon is what will power our spell to raise the King of The Undead" Ringost impressed upon the Apprentice.

"It's always the moon isn't it?" the Apprentice muttered, Ringost totally ignoring him at this point.

"In seven days, the full moon is upon us, and we sacrifice the king and queen to raise a far greater and more useful power. This scroll" Ringost picked up and unfurled another parchment "shows the ritual. The steps we must take and the factors that must be in place for us to be successful. It won't be easy but I'm fully confident we can pull this off."

The Apprentice rubbed his chin, he wasn't sure why only now Ringost was revealing his full plan, but Ringost moved in mysterious ways, or sometimes just plainly in the wrong direction. "Speaking hypothetically, as this is just a threat right? We're not actually going to go through with it, but couldn't we just sacrifice them now? You know then its mission accomplished and less chance or time for things to go wrong." The Apprentice quickly corrected himself "not that there is any chance of our plans not working obviously."

Ringost let out a weary sigh "you respect nothing of ritual. It has to be with that moon and in seven days' time, nothing else." He regarded the Apprentice "Did I ever tell you the story of Richard of the Cliff?"

The Apprentice shook his head "you did not."

"Well, this Richard of the Cliff was an extremely powerful necromancer, he featured regularly in Wisden's Necromancer of the year. Through his learning he discovered the secret of how to raise an unbeatable undead army that would surely lead to him ruling the world. Problem was, there was no deadline for him to perform this spell, it was open ended and spells can be a load of hassle and admin. He kept putting it off thinking he could do it another day, he always had something to occupy his attention on the day he was thinking of performing it, you know how it is when you've a wash load to do and you need to get some food in as the cupboard is bare, and there is that picture of a ghoul that needs rehanging. Anyways. So, he delayed and procrastinated about performing the spell and one day he passed away in his sleep having never gotten around to having immortality and the power to rule the world." He fixed The Apprentice in the eyes "So you understand now why we have a deadline?"

The Apprentice nodded. "Seven days it is" Ringost affirmed.

The Apprentice smiled at the news of the number of days before the spell would be cast. The game was afoot, possible even achariot, it seemed the plan had yet to pick its preferred mode of transport.

Act 2 Scene 8: Having a Super Wizard Time

The now five rode up a thin strip of a path that wound round a dull grey mountain, every step cautious lest they plummet down the sheer face to the beckoning jagged rocks below. Reaching the top of the mountain the ground levelled to a small bare plateau but for tall dark purple tower in the middle of the outcrop, a bruised finger pointing into the unknown above. Val pulled up and handed Power's reigns to the Herald. Ansafety made to dismount but Val shook her head at the elf, who reluctantly stayed in the seat.

The Herald craned his neck up looking to the top of the tower, which seemed to pierce the skyline. He then turned to Val "Err, what are we doing here? This doesn't seem on the way?"

"Picking up some firepower. An' some random explodin' animal attack power" Val stated as if that covered everything.

The Herald took a swig of water from his flask "Val, not to tell you how to do your job, but for the how manyeth time we're up against the clock a little here. Can you make these diversions as minimal as possible please?"

Val considered this statement for as long as it takes a goblin to consider picking his nose if he thinks a juicy bogey lies within. She smiled at the Herald "I said we 'ad to get the gang back together an' that's what I'm doing. Still, plenty o' time to pick up the sword an' kick that necromancer in the pants until he gives up. You've loads to learn about adventuring Herald, it's not all about slavishly sticking to the clock, sometimes it's about feelin' your way through an' enjoyin' the ride!"

The Herald coughed out some of the water in his mouth "What?! No, it is very much about the clock on this one, we have an end of the world deadline that won't... wait sword? What sword? You didn't mention anything about a sword?" he spluttered.

Val's expression remained bright "I very much did right at the start. You need to pay more attention love, it's all there."

The Herald went to argue his case but once more decided it was about picking his battles, plus there are times on this adventure where his brain had switched itself off for its own protection at the idiocy attempting to assault it. "Humour me. What sword?"

"Oh, you know, some drunk orc in a tavern I was once drinking in in told me about a cave in Old-Early that holds a sword that gets rid of all kinds of undead, half living or generally a bit grave-y types, you know like those kids who dress all in black an' mope about outside the corner stall. Sounds like jus' the blade for us!"

The Herald stressfully ran his hand through his hair "but Old-Early is three days ride from here! It's not on the way to where the necromancer is said to be, by our intelligence reports. It's at least another two to three days ride from there to reach his destination. If we do all of this, the time is going to be so much against us!" he implored Val.

Val simply laughed "You've never ridden with me before!" she replied as if that answered everything again. She made her way to the narrow doorway in the tower and just about got her bulk through, her words "bugger me that's a squeeze!" echoing out to the rest of the party.

"And you still haven't properly told me why we're here!" the Herald bellowed hopelessly after her, he was painfully aware of the other three riders sniggering at him and his constant naivety.

"When you're up against magic, you bring a little magic to the mix yourself, an' we have the best magic maker and mixologist!" Val's voice echoed down the stairs from within the tower in reply to the flustered Herald followed shortly after by "bloomin' 'eck this is a lot of stairs!".

The Lesser Great Medium Wizard Trigonometry The Maroon, Trig to his friends, placed the frog on the metal dish and took a step back. He then quickly took another five steps back. He checked the parchment in his hand a couple of time, it making less sense each time he looked. He was as ready as he'd ever be "Teleportation a Hoppit!" He incanted. There was a loud bang, a flash and then a splat sound and where the frog had been was a large pile of green goo. "Ser Hoppalot? Ser Hoppalot?" the wizard called confused.

His concentration was broken by a round of applause from behind him "Nice exploding amphibian spell Trig, I bet that's dead useful!" Val said happily.

"Explosion spell…?" The wizards' features set in a confused frown "… yes that was it, wasn't it?!" the wizard concluded.

"Come here you!" Val said crossing the chamber in a few giant strides pulling the magician into a huge embrace.

The wizard looked at Val "Hello… err… you… err it's nice to see you too" he said distractedly. Val was a little put out by the exchange "Ah yes hello to you!" Trig smiled and spoke with greater clarity as he looked over Val's shoulder at Ansafety who had defied Val's orders and entered the room. She came over to Trig and enveloped him into a long hug.

Ansafety put her arm around Trig and she and Val escorted him to his small table by the window in the room, which had impressive views of the mountains that stretched out below. Ansafety helped Trig into a chair and stood next to him, her arm resting comfortably on his shoulder and seeming to ease the wizard's agitation. Val took the seat opposite him failing to get her legs under the table without the table rising slightly.

"I've got a job and I need your expertise in the magic arts for it. Lots o' gold in it for you." The wizard smiled politely at Val but looked slightly vacant "an' it's a noble quest that will save the realm!" these words seemed to lift the clouds in Trigs eyes, and he sprang to his feet with surprising speed, sending Ansafety's arm flailing backwards.

"Quest, yes good!" he crossed the chamber to some cluttered shelves and began eagerly rooting through "We'll need supplies, let me see…" he picked up a satchel next to the shelves and began throwing things in "spell book, spelling book, colouring book, magic wand, magic eye, dispel magic scroll, fireball scroll, multiply rabbits scroll, fake bat, concentric rings, fish of fate, ginger biscuits, hot pepper sauce… yes I think I'm ready… Val?" Val smiled and gently took the satchel from him, Ansafety helped the elderly magic user to the stairs.

Outside the Herald was staring into the middle distance trying and failing to work out the timescales and in what ways it was actually possible to do all the things Val had in mind before the world ended, these sums were causing him considerable stress.

Edin had got off his horse to lift some enormous boulders as he hadn't done any weights for a couple of hours, and he was worried about muscle wastage. Bumli was keeping himself entertained by drinking something that smelt distinctly like alcoholic pondwater with a tadpole chaser.

Val and Ansafety emerged from the tower doorway with their arms around Trig both towering over the smaller frailer man.

Edin casually threw his boulder over the mountain range and grinned. The boulder possibly also grinned as it caused a near landslide on its rapid descent to the bottom. Bumli cackled "Trig you old band stand!" he called cheerfully. Trig smiled and gave everyone a shy wave. Val lifted the wizard up as if he were a trinket onto the back of Ansafety's elegant steed, Easy Raider.

"Let's go get us a sword!" Val whooped kicking her horse into a speed which was surely too quick for the path they had to traverse back down the mountain though Val seemed not to care. The Herald, not for the first time sighed and attempted to keep pace with this enthusiastic ball of chaos, figuring if he died riding at this speed at least his death was in honour of trying to stick to a schedule.

Act 3 Scene 1: Go Quest, Life Isn't Peaceful There

The six adventurers stood around the tree stump looking intently at a tatty parchment which was marked 'Val's Map – 'ands off!' that Val had produced from a saddlebag and rolled out in front of them. It definitely appeared to be some kind of map, being that it had something vaguely land shaped in the middle of it, with some crude drawings, some very crude drawings, some scrawled words and some "Xs" marking spots, although they may have been kisses, it wasn't immediately obvious on first viewing. The map seemed to be missing a lot of villages, towns, cities, seas, mountains, bays land mass and accuracy. Essentially the map looked like it had been drawn by a sleep deprived four-year-old child with a bag over their head using their wrong hand, but not quite as professional as that. The Herald was convinced Val had dipped it in tea to give it an 'aged' look.

"Right, I've got our route mapped out for us" she intoned. She began pointing at some of the drawings on the map "We travel through The Planes to The Devil's Forest, cut through there 'avin' had a good scrap with any an' every beastie that gets in our way an' maybe even a few that obligingly get out of our way. Nice little journey over The Lake of Fire, quick right through The Certain Death Woods, cross The Screaming Chasms an' Dave which brings us right to where that orc, swore on 'is big green god, an' some of 'is smaller but still green gods, the cave where the sword lies!" to emphasise her point she brought her finger down hard on the map, but missed her mark and landed her digit on the stump next to the parchment, seeing where it had landed she quickly moved it across to one of the Xs on the map. There were approving nods from Elf, Dwarf, Barbarian and Wizard the Herald looked puzzled at them.

"Then we hightail it over the bladed fields, through the doom pass, over the bridge of pain an' work our way up North to the old ritual site where we expect that Necromancer to carry out 'is dumb ritual, we smack 'im round the chops and get 'im to apologise for his stupid raising the dead lifestyle choices an' then all over to Uncle Tom's Chophouse for extra strong ale an' guess the fried animal skin you're eating!" The murmurs of approval grew louder from the group, though Ansafety's lip curled at the choice of refreshments and snacks, whether this was a criticism at the choice or her look of approval, it was impossible to tell.

The Herald studied the map intently, it didn't make much sense to him, he wasn't entirely convinced it was the right way up, come to mention it he wasn't sure it was even a map of the realm for that matter, or any realm, if he didn't know better, he suspected it was a made up map that certain chains of restaurants gave to children to colour in in a (failed) attempt to pacify them whilst their parents tried to eat a nice meal for once in their lives. "You know, looking at the map this looks a much quicker route" he traced his fingers across a line going straight up.

Val looked at the route he was picking out "What, you wanna go via the Cuddly Mountains, the Fluffy Forest, the Planes of Kittens an' The Hills of Nice and Easy? An' miss out on the scenic, action-packed route I've got planned? No chance! Besides, knowing you're a bit soft like, I've spared us taking the route past the Sentinel, to make life a bit easier."

The Herald was getting more rather than less confused "sorry, the Sentinel?" he asked.

Trig decided to fill the gap in his knowledge "Ah yes my young friend, the Sentinel he guards the passageway between the regions, an incredibly powerful warrior, no one knows why he has taken to this guarding job, doesn't seem like he was asked to, he doesn't seem to be getting thanked, let alone paid for his efforts. I guess everyone has to have a hobby?"

Edin took up the story "Aye, my mate said Grotti Ting the ogre pit fighter once necked a load of potions of strength and sparked the Sentinel right out. Well proud of himself he was. Next day he comes back, and The Sentinel is back where he was in perfect nick guarding the route again challenging anyone who wants to pass to a barny. Didn't seem to hold a grudge against ol' Grotti but he wasn't for letting him past unless he beat him in combat again, which Grotti decided better of all things considered. Weird guy, but pretty organised and persevering, not to mention well hard. Gotta admire those traits in a weirdo."

The Herald decided to disregard this story and appeal to Val's logic, accepting it wasn't exactly her strong suit "but we've six days until the full moon reaches the sky, your route doesn't look like that timescale is achievable?"

Ansafety gave the Herald a look which may even have passed for pity "Have you never been at one with the wind?"

"I have after some extra hot curried penguin!" Bumli roared nudging Edin who burst into a deep rumbling bass of a laugh, Val and Trig were chuckling away. Ansafety tried to look disdainful, but her face was already set to maximum default position, and she had nothing left to give.

Val stood up to her considerable full height "So are we doing this then?" she held out her arm, her four old companions exchanged looks, smiled and placed their hands on top of Val's. They all turned to look at the Herald "yer one of us now, love" Val said encouragingly. The Herald tentatively added his hand on top.

"Let's do this!" Five of the party said in unison.

"… do this!" The Herald came in a fraction after them completely missing his cue, though in his defence the party had given him zero training in the team shake.

Bumli cleared his throat and looked awkwardly at the ground "I have to use ye olde bog."

"Tree there mate!" Edin said merrily.

"Err, no it's a bit more than that…"

"In the thick bushes over yonder then love." Val gave instruction.

One hour and fifty-four minutes later the party set off onto their quest late, much to the Heralds chagrin, next quest he was going to remember to factor in dwarven bowel movements to his planning, as it seemed they were a significant factor.

Act 3 Scene 2: Recruitment Drive Dive

Deep in the Necromancer's cave, a variety of mages, sorceresses, mercenaries, sell swords, orcs, trolls, goblins, ne'er do wells, and some bored teens who'd been tempted in with the offer of complimentary drinks and ginger biscuits mulled around the chamber exchanging tales and rumours.

Ringost bustled into this hive of activity, pleased at the turnout he had got, and made his way to the front of the crowd "My friends, my friends..." he attempted to speak like an orator, however the party were enjoying their free drinks and snacks and cracking jokes with each other too much to pay the small, strange man much attention. This was often a feature of Ringost's life.

Ringost fired off an extremely loud thunderbolt spell from his fingertip that knocked a nearby goblin clean of its feet "My friends" Ringost began again to a room that now had his full attention, just how he would like things to be "thanks for the attention, it means a lot to me."

"Bugger me that was loud!" a random voice bounced around the cavernous walls of the chamber.

Ringost let this comment go and addressed the warriors in front of him. "We hold captive the king and queen of the realm" he paused to let that sink into the crowd knowing the power of the statement, satisfied with the murmurs it created "and in six days' time, in front of the full moon, we sacrifice them to the dark powers and raise the King of The Undead."

Now there was frantic chatter beginning amongst the army in front of him, Ringost smiled as he'd been expecting this "and what then? He will destroy all life in the land in front of him, I've no wish for my people to have to witness him returning to the land" said an Amazonian warrior dressed in elegant curved white chainmail armour, an enormous golden axe by her side.

Ringost took a couple of paces to his left to be able to address the woman face to face, or as near as face to face as he could manage given she was many, many inches taller than him "I am a necromancer of great power, with my abilities, when I raise him he is supplicant. I'll let him destroy the enemies of my choosing and no more, he will obey me. What remains in the land is ours. We will be the new power in the world and shape how it looks! No longer will any of you be the marginalized, outsiders looking in on a world that expects everything and offers you nothing." An excited murmur lapped round the cave like a wave.

"We raise the king of the undies?!" an extremely loud voice boomed through the cave. This was the voice of Ant Gi who had seen the advert for fighters of all shapes and sizes, figured he most definitely met one of those criteria and decided to sign up. Being a giant, he couldn't fit in the cave so was attempting to listen to the plan from outside, with mixed results. Ringost knew he should have given the speech outside, but his weather parchment had said rain was likely and he'd done his hair specially to look good in front of his would-be army, his hair got very voluminous when wet and he didn't think the bouffant look was the right image to persuade a ferocious army to fight for him.

"No Ant. I said we raise the King of The Undead!" Ringost bellowed at the cave entrance. He turned back to the room "So my friends, what to do is we…"

"… What?!" Ant's voice boomed back in, louder again, cutting across Ringost's speech.

Ringost just about kept his anger in check. "Look, I'll come out and explain it to you after Ant" he yelled even louder, his face turning red, his throat sore from the effort. Again, he turned to the room, clearing his throat to try and sound less hoarse after all the shouting "so what say you all to the proposition I am…"

"… OK!" Ant's voice rumbled back.

Ringost flattened his robes and took a breath, this part wasn't going as he'd imagined it when he was practicing in front of the mirror the night before, he'd looked a lot more heroic and composed in the image in his head. "If you sign up to help me then…"

"… Something about king size underpants, I dunno. He says he'll come out and tell us!" Ant's voice once more filled the room.

Rigost's face moved to enraged puce on the anger colour chart "Ant… what the… I said… I'm making a big speech here!"

"It's not very rousing" a brigand muttered to his companion. Ringost heard this but made the decision to ignore the slight, whilst making a mental note to be particularly passive aggressive to the warrior at a later date.

"Sorry! An orc just turned up late and I'm trying to fill her in on the plan." The voice once more shook the cave.

Ringost clenched and unclenched his fists multiple times. "OK Ant that's fine, but from now on until I come out there you just say nothing!" he yelled, his attempts at looking unflustered long gone. Once more he addressed the crowd "so what say you…" Ringost paused to make sure there was going to be no interruption this time, satisfied not he continued "… to this plan, for your services I offer you…"

"… Gotcha!" Ant confirmed.

Ringost kicked a nearby goblin in his frustration sending it flying into the buffet and spoiling the plate of egg and cress sandwiches, a pirate had earmarked for a later snack. "So how do you fancy helping me rule the land in return for your fighting prowess?" he spoke quickly lest any further interruptions.

The Apprentice, who Ringost had planted in the crowd, remembered his role after a few seconds of the silence that had ensued, he kicked himself realising he'd missed his cue by a fraction but decided to make up with enthusiasm what he had given away with tardiness. He began cheering and clapping Ringost, this response began to be taken up by the other cave inhabitants, growing into a deafening din, Ringost turned his face to hide his enormous grin, his spirits and other parts raised.

He let the cheer die down and composed himself "So here is how it works, Dark Sorcerer" he said to the large gentleman to his right who was so called because of his all black robes which he wore as he was a fan of the group of minstrels Ye Cure and also as he thought it was slimming "anyone tries to get near the ritual I will perform, you're our magical defence" the Dark Sorcerer attempted to give an enigmatic nod, but it looked more like he couldn't remember if he'd left the cauldron on at home or not.

"Lady Heyve-Ho" A lady in jade armour, with a lion helm and with finely made dual short swords at her waist looked up at the necromancer "Your warriors and half the mercenaries in here are to patrol the west of the ritual site, when the time comes for us to move to that place. In the meantime, you are to guard the cave to make sure no unwanted visitors. Deal with any with extreme prejudice, freeform violence is wholeheartedly sanctioned". A smile crept over her fine features at these instructions, she turned and nodded her approval at her troops.

Ringost moved over to a group of exceptionally powerfully built orcs. He addressed the largest of them "Allt, you will protect the cave and its entrance with Ant… you can fill him in on all the details…"

The orcs face didn't move, he crossed his musclebound arms firmly across his chest and fixed Ringost with a hard stare "and where does all this destruction get us? what of the arts?" his rich voice asked. This question stopped Ringost in his tracks, it wasn't one he'd prepared for, truth be told, he was going to try and fashion an answer, but the erudite orc continued "this chaos and violence has its place if it can create a utopian society but beyond that, what of the yang to the ying of destruction? What about creation? The things that stir the soul and give us glimpses to the meaning to be truly alive? I want a good share of the profits from this endeavor to go towards art exhibitions, music, dance. And I want a guaranteed sum to go on the playwright Launchjaveline's shows I'm putting on; 'Two Gentle Orc's of Verona', 'As You Pike It', 'The Flaming of The Shrew'. Without the enrichment of spirit and soul, what land is worth ruling?" he took a step toward Ringost using his bulk to emphasise his point.

Ringost considered the Orc's argument, he'd never been too into the arts, but he wasn't going to lose some muscle over a shonky play. "OK, we smite all or foes, putting on a jolly good show and then we put on a jolly good show."

This time violence was going to take the unusual step of preceding a bad play.

Act 3 Scene 3: High Pains Drifter

Ansafety expertly steered her elegant horse over the uneven ground and caught up with Val. "These planes feel like no short cut to my Elven instincts Val".

Val scanned the horizon, "Them Elven instincts are no match for a Valkyrie hunch me dear!" She smiled at the Elf "I'm telling ya up over that ridge yonder we'll find a river which we cross, and that will bring us nicely to the Devil's Forest an' bang on time too I may add!"

Ansafety rolled her eyes, she knew it was impossible to talk Val out of her plans so she dropped her ride back so she could keep an eye out for any danger from the rear of the pack.

Through a combination of planning, route plotting and most likely pure luck, the group did indeed find a river, though Ansafety tried to argue it was more of a stream or brook, but Val wasn't for getting into a volume of water-based argument. They crossed the as yet to be agreed on body of water and they came into trees just about dense enough (about as dense as Bumli) to be counted as some kind of forest, and as no one from the local borough had thought to put up a helpful sign they have to assume it was Devil's wood.

The horse's hooves crunched through the golden brown of the fallen leaves that carpeted the ground. "Wits about you" Bumli muttered to his beard, though the party were way ahead knowing when you go to a place called Devil's woods you didn't generally take a picnic, although Edin was getting peckish and was wishing he'd brought a picnic, just a few legs of lambs to fill a hole until it was tea time proper.

A glint from a break in the trees shone a bright emerald light which caught the parties' eyes, a high ethereal voice seemed to call to the party on the gentle breeze "I'm going to take a look" the Herald stated. An unexpected bravery taking over him, gripping his sword and steering his horse through the gap in the foliage.

"Here we go again" Ansafety said with a groan "I mean we could just have carried on and got on with the quest, but no." Trig who had been absent mindedly taking in the beauty of the trees and really not paying attention to what was going on smiled behind her in the saddle and patted her back "nice day in here isn't it? He decided on.

The Herald dismounted and crouched, on the floor was a tall dark green misshapen bottle covered in an intricately etched pattern with a pyramid shaped top encased in sliver which gave a twin glint with the green when the light caught it right. The Herald slowly bent down and gently picked up the object "it's just a bottle" he said carefully turning it in front of his face.

"Best not to take the stopper off my friend" Trig cautioned seeming to gain focus presented with this unusual, possibly mystic object.

"Not the slightest intention of going near the stop... ah..." the Herald tilted the bottle barely through forty-five degrees and the cap against the best advice of bottle design, physics and even the intervention of gravity, dropped off hitting the leafed floor with a muffled thud. The Herald froze holding his breath whilst his companions reached for their weapons. Nothing happened. "Huh?" the Herald exhaled relieved, though his heart still thudded against his chest like an over enthusiastic six-armed chimp drummer.

A beat later there followed a loud whipping noise and then again nothing, the Herald spun around hyper alert but still saw nothing untoward. "Got away with one there. What was that all about?" he asked confused.

"That was me!" came a response in a high reedy voice that could cut through glass and probably plate armour too.

The Herald spun around again, starting to get dizzy by this point, failing to where the voice had come from but seeing nothing. The rest of the party dismounted and closed in on him with weapons drawn "What? What?!" the Herald asked perplexed by the events of the last few moments and his companions" stance.

"You're mine now posh boy!" came the cackled a response he wasn't expecting.

"Who is saying that? What's going on? And hang on, how can you tell I'm posh?!" The Herald asked, flustered for multiple reasons.

"Oh, you can definitely tell" Edin answered his third question.

Trig considered the situation that the Herald had got himself into and thought back on all his years studying lore "It's one of those... erm..." he began counting on his fingers and then seemed to get inspiration from his thumbnail "Poultry geese! Yes that's what it is!"

"Poltergeist?" Ansafety ventured.

"Better name!" Trig confirmed.

"I am" the harsh voice confirmed "but you can call me Polly."

Edin shook his head "Polly the Poltergeist, what were your parents thinking? Wait do poltergeists have parents?"

Polly ignored the rhetoric, feeling now was not the time to get into her genealogy. "By freeing me from the bottle, this chinless wonder must now carry me on his back for eternity!"

"Or until he crosses running water" Trig clarified having found the P section in his "Bumper Wizard's book of beasties, ghoulies and miscellany weird stuff that life throws at you."

The spook stopped cackling "Wh... what? Who told you that? That's not true!" she wailed loudly.

Val took her turn to laugh, throwing in a cackle to rub salt into Polly's wounds. "Right-ho young fellow me lass, that's you found out innit. Bumli ya always need the toilet, a quick Jimmy Riddle, our friend Herr here crosses the stream an' we're a polka guise lighter!"

Bumli began to hitch up the part of his tunic that covered the modesty of his trouserless lower half "No wait! That's never going to work!" Polly said with more than a trace of fear in her voice, which made it even more grating that if at normal timbre.

"Never mind that!" the Herald cut in "I'm not walking through Bumli's golden stream. No offence" Bumli seemed not offended in the slightest. Edin was struggling to contain his mirth at all this.

"OK. Exorcism it is!" Val state cheerily drawing her enormous broadsword, which she spun dexterously in her hand before bringing it crashing down butt first on the Herald's back. "That do it?" she asked.

"Nnnnnooooo…" groaned the Herald and Polly in unison.

"OK I'll have to use the reverse Protty Stance version for the exorcism. Hold him lads an' lasses, this is gonna hurt him a lot more than it is me." The other four grabbed the Herald. Val could just about trace the shape of the otherwise invisible poltergeist on the Herald's back.

"No wait, we can negotiate!" Polly wailed the Herald nodding his ascent, but it fell on deaf ears as Val brought her sword down in a series of rapid blows on the Heralds back in the area she guessed the Poltergeist should still be.

"OK, OK I'm leaving" Polly said in a resigned tone, unaccustomed to dealing with Valkyrie sword-based spiritualism. Val gave it another whack just to be on the safe side. There was another loud cracking sound, and a voice came forth from the bottle "OK I'm gone, happy now?"

"Not really" the Herald just about managed to groan in pained tones.

"Who ya gonna call?" Val yelled in triumph.

****

Edin piled the last of the far too large to get a fire going logs onto the pile and reached into his loincloth, searching for his tinderbox. "Leave this to me my good chap!" Said Trig kindly, and before anyone could question the wisdom of this he pointed at the fire and recited the magic words "Flamosaurus wrecks!" there was a blinding flash and a great wave of heat as suddenly the fire was blazing away.

Everyone around the fire had a look of shock on their face as their eyebrows were singed, well every part of them was singed. "Bloody hell!" exclaimed Polly the poltergeist from the glade many leagues back, startled at the sudden explosion.

Bumli finished pitching the tents which he'd volunteered for on grounds of being a Dwarf and good at engineering. What he had erected looked suspiciously like some material badly traipsed over a log which was listing terribly as it wasn't large enough to be load bearing even for some lightweight cloth.

Val ended taking some items from her side saddle and returned to where the party were starting to make themselves as comfortable around the, what would surely count as a conflagration, as they were able to. Val placed her flask next to her and six surprisingly ornate tumblers. She poured a dark viscous liquid into each and passed them around the fire.

Bumli held his up to the light the liquid was impenetrable "Is that Belcher Bobbit's Bowel Busting Brew?" he asked excitedly.

Val tilted her head in appreciation of Bumli's recognition of a strong drink "Aye, that it is" she confirmed happily. The Herald took a swig of a liquid that tasted exactly of pickled herring mixed with seasoned tar with just a hint of nutmeg, the Herald wasn't sure how he knew that's what it tasted of, he just knew. The power of the drink blasted the Herald's throat like a fiery javelin all the way down, he could feel the days it had taken from his life leaving his body.

The rest of the party actually seemed to enjoy it, except Ansafety who the Herald couldn't read what she thought of it, but if he had to guess, he would have gone for disdain.

"So, what make you of our chances of completing this Val?" Bumli asked. The Herald was struggling to work out if this was the groups chances of completing the quest or chances of surviving the drink they had just imbibed. The Herald could already feel the pain of an elephant in plate armour jumping up and down on a particularly sensitive part of his brain.

Val pondered the question for as long as it took her to let out a glorious belch. "This? Piece of fried goblin cake!" she decided, pouring more drinks for everyone passing them around "Remember the Quest for The Crown of Command? Now that, that, were a quest me loves."

An approving murmur spread around the campfire. "Was that the one where Ansafety got her pants burnt off when she was struck by lightning?" Edin roared with laughter "Again!" The rest of the party bursting into laughter, except Ansafety who's facial expression you can guess.

"Every time you're going to bring that up?" Ansafety muttered moodily.

"Every quest we go on, old haughty knickers here gets her trousers blasted off by lightning!" Bumli struggled to get the words out from his laughter, clarifying for the Herald's sake.

Trig shook his head "I think it's time to re-evaluate that standard she carries, it's a veritable lightning conductor" he mused.

"That is a sacred Elven battle artefact!" Ansafety protested with what might have been a trace of mirth in her voice "it must be mounted on a twenty-foot pole by law and lore, nothing less."

"Still, helluva quest" Bumli said finally getting the better of his laughter. "Though the one after, not so much. Pity for

Will the Unwise" he said quietly his face dropping. A silence befell the party and Val stared glumly into the fire.

Edin broke the fug "to absent friends!" he said draining his shot, the Herald reluctantly accepted his fate and knocked his drink back.

After a pause, the Herald decided to break the less upbeat mood that seemed to be hanging around the camp. "This necromancer is no match for us and will perish on the end of my magic sword!" he declared the strong hooch giving him a sense of confidence, or foolish bravado. More worryingly the drink was giving him the urge to show off what a tremendous dancer he thought he was too.

"What magic sword?" Bumli asked amused.

"This one" The Herald said pulling his sword from his scabbard and turning it in the fire light.

Edin tried to stifle his laugh and gave up "What magic powers it have oh wet one?"

The Herald welcomed the question "watch this!" he said gleefully and pressed in on the pommel as the sword offered a greater light to the campfire, the blue mixing in with the flickering orange.

"That should help me find the toilet later Herr love!" Val rocked with laughter as did the rest around the campfire.

"So, it lights up? Anything else?" Ansafety asked, but she read the Heralds face before he could answer "that's no magic sword!"

The Herald looked a little taken back "I said the same thing, but I'm assured its magical. You guys won't be laughing when I have the necromancer impaled on it!". He placed the blade back in its holding, its glow fading from his features.

"Well, we'll be able to see it at least" Trig said drily sending the camp into hysterics.

Not long after this conversation party decided to go to bed, the Herald just about drunkenly rolling into his sleeping space, as he held onto the ground to stop the floor moving away from him.

Act 3 Scene 4: Toll Trolls Take Their Toll

The Herald awoke cold. A light breeze had inevitably done for Bumli's 'indestructible all weather' tent construction. His head was pounding from the drink he has consumed the night before, but the Herald found he was OK as long as he didn't move fast, move slowly, move at all, think, blink, breathe or exist.

"Morning!" Val called breezily as she boiled a kettle by the fire, looking clear eyed and chipper. She was in full armour and weaponry and appeared ready to take on the world, which she was easily capable of and may have to do before the quest was out.

After a little time getting ready, mostly due to the Herald being confused and scared by everything in his current state, the party were mounted and ready to go. The warriors edged out of the trees onto an even expanse of long dry grass which a river, deep and fast, wound its way through. A large stone bridge presenting the safest, perhaps only way to cross the torrents of the water.

In single file Val led the team cautiously to the bridge. Within feet of using it to cross a deep gurgly voice rang out "Not so fast!" From under the bridge a towering green figure, easily a head taller than Val or Edin, emerged to bar their way.

Bumli sighed "Great, an intern ate troll". The hulking creature took a couple of long strides nearer to the group. The Herald had his vinaigrette working overtime to try and counter the putrid smell of dead fish emanating from it.

The creature cast its gaze slowly over everyone "You all look magnificent" it stated matter of factly, the party stayed silent but muscles taut betrayed their feelings "No really, you look like a wonderful group of warriors, you look ready to take on the world. Its lovely to see such an eclectic group of races, sexes, creeds, ages and beardedness working together. What a wonderful example of our modern old world, this is a thing to be celebrated."

Val relaxed a little and moved her hand away from her sword "thanking ya very much me green skinned lovely" she smiled at the troll.

The intern ate troll bowed "You're very welcome me lass!" the creature smiled, but with the amount, shape and formation of teeth it had, it was difficult to tell the expression from a snarl, or a creature suffering irritable bowels. "Now that will be five gold pieces, each, to cross my brilliant bridge and you're on your way."

"Oi Herr, pay the man, beast, green guy his dues" Val ordered happy to do business with someone with such a positive outlook. The Herald inwardly cursed but thought better of taking Umbridge with either Val or the fishy smelling wall of muscle that barred his way.

""Ere Mr. Troll?" Val changed tact "do you like pottery?" she opened up the satchel from around her chest and showed the troll the wide variety of thing shaped wares that she had made.

The troll's eyebrow shot up or would have done had he actually been in legal possession of one "ooh I like that vase" he said pointing at something shaped like an explosion "me water daffodils would look grand in that" he nodded his head at a yellow mass of what once were flowers but now resembled some kind of chicken vomit from water saturation.

Val smiled appreciatively "ya have fine taste me lad. That will be five gold pieces". She looked at the Herald, who tired of this whole escapade handed the five gold coins to the troll who handed them straight over to Val. "Pleasure doing business with ya!" Val said before crossing the bridge and onto whatever ridiculous and time-consuming encounter came next.

****

The heroes rode hard over the plains, leaping hedgerows and splashing through streams, they could have stuck to the track to avoid all that but decided it wasn't 'impactful' enough as a gesture. The Herald was still a little bitter at the increasing expenses Val was accruing, though his prime concern was still the irregular pounding in his delicate head and whether it was possible to actually die of the ennui brought on by a hangover, he was thinking it may just be possible.

After a long hard ride, a small cloud of smoke from a scrub area caught their eye. "We're making extremely good time, let's go have a look" Val decided.

Ansafety, not for the first, or last time, rolled her eyes "haven't we had enough of these stupid, pointless encounters to last us a quest-time?" she whispered behind her to Trig who smiled pleasantly but seemed to be thinking of something else somewhere else.

Due to her superior hearing Val had overheard these hushed words "Gotta have encounters!" She called and moved Power towards the smoke "it's often how ya get the good stuff!"

They pulled up and dismounted. The grassy enclave had some logs and rocks moved to work as surfaces for potions and books. A large pot bubbled away over a fire. A striking woman in a celestial blue robe, corkscrews of dark hair spilling out of her hood in every direction, tended to the contents of the pan.

Without looking up she spoke in a calm whispered voice "Greetings Val and your band of questing warriors."

Val was temporarily stunned but then regained her composure ""Ere, 'ow do you know me name?"

Trig moved up next to Val to politely whisper "Nice day isn't it?" Val looked at Trig confused, Trig read the look and seemed to remember why he had come over to Val "that is The Prophetess, a legendary figure in magic circles and the magic circle, she is extremely powerful, and it is said can see and interpret the frayed strands of the future."

"That I am and more. But you may call me Antonia should you wish. Thank you for your kind introduction Trigonometry you do better than you have any right to" she clarified mysteriously, having somehow overheard Trig, or maybe foreseeing his words, it was hard to tell when figures have the slippery ability to see into the future.

Val made her way over and stood on the other side of the fire. The Prophetess was clearly making a strong potion or potato and leek soup if Val wasn't mistaken. "Future eh?" she smiled deferentially at the lady "Well young lady, Miss Profit hiss, I mean Antonia, can you tell us if we are successful in our quest to defeat… ya already know what our quest is don't ya, I don't need to tell ya that bit?" she caught herself "please?"

A thin smile broke across the strong features of Antonia "alas not" the gang exchanged looks "there are so many factors at play even I am struggling to weave the pattern of the future, so much is yet to come into pay and the paths of what is to be, twist and turn like a twisty turny thing" she finished stirring the pot "besides if I told you how it plays out, you might not make the choices you have to make. And there are always choices to make, and the right path often isn't the easiest path."

"Useful aint she?" Edin muttered to Bumli.

"But I will tell you this" she looked across each of the party "successful or not you will lose and gain from this quest. Whether you feel you end in credit or deficit depends entirely on you." The party remained silent trying to fathom what her words meant.

"Always got to speak in riddles these people, haven't they? I swear it's in their contract." Bumli whispered back to Edin who nodded his agreement.

She lifted a small globe from her robe and moved it around her hands like the renowned be-mulleted wizard Jareth had shown her how to. "I will give you one glimpse of the future", she stared into the orb which whilst remaining transparent to the warriors seemed to be showing her complex patterns. "In the future, I see one of you practicing their kissing on a dog?" The gang exchanged puzzled looks once more at this bizarre revelation. They had hoped for something a little more illuminating for their perilous adventure.

"Who would do such a despicable thing?!" Bumli asked aloud.

Antonio pondered "I cannot see who the person in the vision is, they are obscured by a large beard."

The gang all turned to face Bumli "That could be anyone of us!" he protested looking at their not especially bristly features. "OK I did it once as a teenager to practice, she must have that orb on the looking back to the past setting!"

Antonio smiled "the orb only sees the future."

"Harumph!" harumphed Bumli.

Antonio regarded the group and smiled "I wish you all luck on your quest, truly you are a noble crew" she turned back to her cauldron "oh and Herald?" Antonia continued.

The Herald stepped forward eagerly "Yes?"

"Sorry about your boots" she stated with a trace of sympathy in her voice.

"Huh?" the Herald was confused by this.

The party bade farewell to Antonia who wished them luck as they left her den. They were just making their way to their steeds when the Herald cursed loudly "By the prickly horns of goatman!"

"What's with him?" Bumli asked.

Edin responded "Just stepped in some animal mess".

"Oh."

"Yeah."

"Dog?"

"Bigger."

"Bear?"

"Bigger."

"Oh."

"Yeah."

****

After a long day of hard riding the party decided to camp on the outskirts of Certain Death Woods. Finding a suitable clearing they began to look at unpacking their saddle bags.

A rustling caught them unawares as they reached for their blades a pair of couples emerged from the bushes.

"Oh... err... hello!" called the man cheerily with a note of uncertainty in his voice, as he pulled his poncho a little further down. "Are you her for the... you know..." he stumbled his words out.

"... Questing?" Val asked eagerly though unsure of the whole charade.

"Ha ha ha questing, yes that's it!" said the lady at the back of the group with seeming forced levity.

The Herald took in the surroundings and the people and decided to make a decision for the group. "You know what, it's OK, you have this spot, and we'll camp further into the woods".

And with that, the unusual couples blended back into the woods whence they came, as our heroes quickly packed up, avoiding an encounter perhaps too dangerous by far for them.

Act 3 Scene 5: Teleport, Teleport, Did You Get Very Far?

Once more the Herald slept under stars, this wasn't some romantic notion of sleeping outside, more a reflection on the effectiveness of Bumli's shelters at staying over the heads of our heroes.

The Herald rose sorely and made his way to his steed and began jamming his camping equipment into the satchels having long given up on getting the items to fit neatly as when he had first packed.

A quick breakfast ensued. Val swore this was the most important meal of the day, but the Herald wondered if this really was the case, and if so why the king and queen never threw a lavish banquet breakfast for dignitaries. He decided against taking up this point with Val.

Saddled up, Ansafety had taken point as they broke from the woods, a low early sun covering them in a warm golden light, and the gang enjoyed the momentary deception that all was calm and well in the world.

The terrain became rockier and the trees more dispersed and the party travelled in silence lost to their own thoughts. They travelled on further through a canyon of rusted orange rock, loose boulders scattered across the path, the now high sun basking down on them filling the trench with a dusty light.

They wove their way through these rocks for several hours when from nowhere a small man in a green suit with bright red hair and matching beard materialised on a large rock next to where they rode.

The party all saw this man but decided to politely, or not so politely totally ignore him, having had enough of these tedious encounters with the various oddballs that populated the realm. The creature made a point of loud coughing to gain attention, having to reach the point of sounding like they were having an episode given the heroes were still doing all they could to ignore him. Finally, Val gave in "oh hullo there love" she said with a resigned politeness.

"Hello, my fine companions" the stranger returned the greeting, bowing his head a little revealing the considerable work he had put into the brushover with his hair, the unforgiving sun pointing out the numerous gaps to his scalp. "I'm Shame-Us a free-lance teleporter, I'll take anyone anywhere, anytime for nearly any fee. Anyone fancy a ride?" he asked cheerfully.

The party shook their heads in near unison, knowing better than to get into a teleportation with a complete stranger, working of the principle of if that person couldn't manage their own baldness how could they be expected to manage the vagaries of instantaneous movement across time and space.

However, the Herald's curiosity was piqued, this may just have been a consequence of his decision-making being impaired through a lack of sleep and still feeling the effects of over strong booze. Still, if he could teleport anywhere, he could complete his mission before the king of the dead was even close to being raised, saving the day before it even got close to being too late, that would sound good in the songs dedicated to him by the greatest minstrels in the land. Plus, this allowed more time for celebratory wine drinking and grape eating. Most importantly of all it meant no further nights under one of Bumli's shelters, or out in the open as it might be more accurately described.

"OK, I'm game. How does it work?" he declared. He dismounted Flighty Joanna and handed the reigns to Ansafety whose facial expression was as predictable as this encounter was ridiculous.

Shame-Us smiled "it's as simple as having your atoms instantly pulled apart and reassembled by the fates" he stated, using an opening gambit that probably wasn't the most reassuring. He clicked his fingers and a five foot in diameter purple vortex of possibility opened hovering next to where he stood. "Pay me ten gold pieces and step through to your destination."

The Herald paid Shame-Us and made to step through, he paused, "wait, how do I get to my destination?"

"Just imagine where you need to be" Shame-Us stated hoping the Herald didn't pick apart the fact that didn't make a jot of sense. The Herald took this on board, reminding himself not to get distracted imagining himself in a posh wine bar surrounded by serving ladies. Having got this out of his system, he took a breath and stepped into a purple glow, there was a blinding flash and some kind of exotic, and difficult to describe particularly well, whizzing sound.

The Herald's vision cleared, and he was facing an empty rocky outcrop, there was a smell of burnt hair that he was doing his best to ignore. So, this was where the fiendish Necromancer hid, he thought to himself. Well, the Herald would see to that, he would find the entrance to his lair, flush this evil out and force him to concede on the end of his blade and return home to a hero's welcome and all the fair maidens wanting to run their hands through his luscious hair, but not so much that they messed up the neat styling he'd done with it.

The Herald was broken from his daydream by a sniggering noise behind him, he turned to face Val and the party pointing and laughing at him, as the teleportation had done nothing but spat him back into the canyon albeit facing the other way.

The Herald spun to face Shame-Us anger coursing through his body "why you little…"

"Time to disappear!" Shame-Us yelped opening and diving into a portal but proving equally effective with magic gates for himself as he was with strangers, reappearing a yard closer to the Herald. After refunding the Herald his ten gold pieces, plus two gold pieces compensation and two gold pieces for emotional damage done to his hair the parties went their own separate ways, very much by foot. A journey of a thousand miles begins with the first step and a small teleportation, followed by another thousand steps.

Act 3 Scene 6: A Bone To Pick Up

Moving swiftly around the chamber making mental notes, Ringost handed the Apprentice a large knapsack, which still had a rotten apple at the bottom from when Ringost had taken it to the Necromancer's of the West picnic and performing arts festival, there were some acts to chill the bones that day, nothing to do with necromancy just a standard performing arts festival entertainment.

He went over to the shelves in his 'most magical storeroom' as the sign next to the shelves helpfully said. To the Apprentice it just looked like another section of the cave but with a candelabra unsafely suspended from the ceiling by some fraying hessian cord.

Ringost had moved over to a large chest and was rummaging in an agitated manner. Muttering to himself he began handing items to the Apprentice "vial of sparrows blood, special magic dust, black candles, skull of vole, I'll definitely be needing that… what else… cat's whiskers, the last straw, hells teeth, bumper book of gnome jokes, set square, snacks for later…"

The sack was getting heavy, and the Apprentices arms were aching "wow there is a lot to this ritual" he said more to himself than anyone else, as Ringost wasn't seeming to listen to him, which was a fairly common occurrence.

However, this time he was paying attention, Ringost heard this and chuckled "good grief no. We don't particularly need any of this for the ritual, but, you know, people expect a bit of spectacle, some razzle dazzle, so we give it to them, it goes a long way."

The Apprentice wondered who the actual people watching this ritual would be, a few skeletons, who as far as he was aware weren't especially into their big shows, zombies that were mostly interested in brains to feed on and the king and queen who were set to be killed halfway through it, so probably not that in the mood for a performance. All in all, he wasn't sure the ritual actually had much of a market for some glitz.

The Apprentice shrugged and pushed down on the contents of the sack to free up some space. He heard a small cracking sound and figured he'd probably just broken the vole's skull. He hoped Ringost hadn't heard so he could blame it on the Barry the skeleton later.

As if they had read his thoughts, Barry and his skeleton companion Eva arrived. The Apprentice had just about learned to control his involuntary scream whenever they showed up, but for an apprentice necromancer he still wasn't great with the dead, a mild flaw that he could work on, he figured. The skeletons were encouraging the king and queen (and by encouraging they were prodding them with their swords whenever either stopped or slowed down) into the chamber cramping up the supposedly magical place.

The queen sneered at Ringost, "still think this half-baked idea, though even calling it an idea seems a stretch, of yours will work?"

"Friends, orcs, goblins, lend me your spears!" echoed into the chamber.

Ringost momentarily stopped what he was doing and regarded the royal couple "think? No" He picked up what the Apprentice thought was a bag of magic dust, though it may have been paprika "I am certain it will work. In four days', time we'll be welcoming a royal who actually gets off their backside and achieves things in this world."

The queen snorted her derision "if you call mass murder of all in his path an achievement, then sure, what a wonderful utopia he will create for the realm."

The king attempted to wrestle some control from the situation "why don't you just do it now you pathetic wretch?" he turned to the Apprentice who was trying to stay out of it in one of the chamber corners "you and your spineless masked lacky show us how tough you are."

"Is this a dagger I see before me? And a sword? And a cleaver? And a club? And a trident? Oh good!" rang as a response through the cave from somewhere.

Ringost turned back to the shelves and made as if he was seeking something out "all in good time, we will be finishing you off but we want to make sure we put on a good show doing it," he smirked to himself "in the meantime, Barry and Eva will take you to the new transportable cage I've had made up for you, should make getting you about a bit quicker." He turned and nodded at the cadavers, who got the king and queen moving again.

"To be or not to be, that is the question. For my foes its always not to be. With extreme prejudice!" these words roared down the cave.

"What is that?" the Apprentice asked agitated at these bellowed random phrases that kept interrupting.

Ringost let out a long breath "its them bloody orcs practicing their tedious plays" he then lowered his voice conspiratorially "it's a good job they're useful in a fight, as they're bloomin" terrible at acting. Though some of the skeletons seem weirdly really into it."

Act 3 Scene 7: Lake A Like

The horses and mule made their way down the long shingle path that wove between dunes of shale. A strong smell of eggy sulfur assaulted the Herald's nostrils as he wondered if Bumli had brapped his pants again, it remained a permanent distinct possibility.

As they neared the dune that Val assured would bring them to The Lake of Fire, the Herald could hear some ungodly sound, it was the sound of high-pitched cackling crossed with some terrible dirge music about some ancient queen who could dance and have the time of her life. As they climbed up and crossed the dune a flat expanse met them with a grey green water glistening in the distance, the noise continued seeming to get louder from the water but with no source revealing itself.

The party made their way down the bank, the stones getting smaller and smoother as they reached the shoreline, the steeds hooves sinking in the softer ground. The party dismounted.

The Herald looked out to the murky water "Call me old fashioned, and I don't mean to be a pedant, but when you said we were crossing the lake of fire, I kind of expected more fire on the lake?"

Trig pulled up alongside him and smiled "no?" he clicked is finger which created a spark which he blew, and it gently made its way out towards the lake like a luminous snowflake caught on a breeze. As the spark floated close to the water there was a great 'whoof' sound as the lake before them became a raging conflagration.

The Herald took a few paces back from the raging heat that now endangered his haircut "I was going to say I was totally OK with the lack of fire" he muttered.

Trig looked at the incendiary wall in front of him "I probably shouldn't have done that" he said a mite sheepishly. The two backed further away from the inferno hoping no one would put the sudden increase in temperature on them.

Ansafety seemed distracted as she furiously sketched on her pad by the shoreline seeming none too troubled by the fire or the ever-increasing volume in the strange sound.

The Herald decided to stand next to Val "err, what now?"

Val scanned the horizon "we wait for t' boatman an' pay him to get us across" she answered, as if that was the most natural thing in the world to do.

The Herald followed Val's gaze over the fiery expanse and sucked his teeth 'surely not across there?' he thought to himself.

The horrific noise continued to get closer, the Herald's hand fidgeted nervously by his sword hilt. Edin crossed to him and rested an enormous hand on his shoulder to hold his draw and pointed out to the fiery expanse.

Through the flaming waves the prow of a ship was becoming visible, fashioned in a dark wood, the prow carried the shape of a ram's head held in some primal scream. More and more the body of the ship became visible. The boat was populated with a lot of women, no fairies for their backs bore wings, swaying around the boat, drinking brightly coloured liquids from bottles and laughing wildly. At the back of the boat was a party of elven musicians playing music for them, some song about some warrior who was simply the best and better than all the rest. The fairies sang along in a variety of different volumes, tempos, keys, melodies and lyrics.

"Fairies? No Sirens? Here to lure us to a watery or fiery or watery fiery death?" the Herald found himself asking Bumli who shook his head slowly.

"Nah. Worse. Hen do." With that, the boat reached the shores and the fairy women dismounted seeming untroubled by the flames, stumbling up the shore making a number of lewd suggestions to the Herald before trudging up the bank of dunes. The musicians shrugged disembarked and followed their paymasters.

The Herald watched them depart wondering how on this earth they were going to get home. He dismissed the thought and wondered back over to Val who was admiring the drawing Ansafety had sketched of herself stood in front of the flaming lake looking out of the page.

"What's that?" the Herald asked.

"It's an Elfie" Val responded.

"You did not just say that" the Herald groaned disgusted. He turned to the boat and nearly jumped out of his skin confronted as he was by a character at the front of the boat. It was tall and dressed entirely in a black robe with a hood that concealed all of its features. The creature moved silently to the prow and reached out a skeletal clawed hand to the party.

"Well Herr love" Val declared "pay the good gentle-skeleton creature thingamy bob 'is coin."

The Herald inwardly groaned as he placed a gold coin in the taloned hand. The hand remained outstretched, the Herald placed another coin in its hand. The hand began to curl its fingers inwards in a repeated motion. Exasperated, the Herald just dropped the bag of coins into its hand.

This seemed to satisfy the creature who transferred the coins into a bumbag it had hidden under its robes. It moved to the stern of the boat allowing the party and steeds to embark.

Somehow, despite being surrounded by fire, the boat was taking no damage from the flames and the heat on board was minimal. The Herald took a seat next to Ansafety on a creaky bench to the side of the boat near where the boatman stood. The boatman turned the boat and pushed out into the fiery expanse.

After travelling a short while, the boatman spoke in an accent the Herald couldn't place "Sorry I took so long to turn up, some bleedin' numpty set the lake on fire!" The

Herald and Trig exchanged nervous glances "We turned the bladdy thing off to save on the ol' heatin' bills. Gonna cost us a bladdy fortune that!"

The Herald felt himself sinking further into himself the boatman seemed to change tact "D'ya know what's wrong with this land?" No one responded to his question, figuring ignoring him was the best option, but this seemed to not deter him one bit "I'll tell ya what's wrong with this land, all them bladdy Orcs, coming over here stealing our jobs, none of them learning how to speak the language too good. An' another thing, bladdy Goblins undercutting an honest boatman with their cheap raft services..." The Herald considered the vast sum he had just paid the boatman and wondered if the goblins weren't maybe offering a better value service, probably with less of a whiff of xenophobia too. Though again, the Herald thought better than taking this up with their strange pilot.

"... And the bladdy elves, don't get me on those bladdy haughty pointy eared little tree huggers..." the boatman started to slate the entire Elven nation for some perceived slights, oblivious, or uncaring of the elf sat right next to him giving him disgusted daggers with her eyes.

The boatman continued telling the party about the ills of the world, most of his sentences seeming to start with "I've got nothing against a certain race..." before he went on to detail exactly what he had against that certain race. The Herald switched off his brains and ears and stared into the now inviting fiery expanse.

Act 3 Scene 8: Failing To Avoid Stepping On The Crags

Bumli smiled looking back at the jagged walls of black rock, with enormous steep drops between that stretched behind him "well those crags were easily traversed; I don't see what all the fuss is about. That and The Lake of Fire all crossed no trouble at all, with no interesting stories to tell" he spoke with more than a hint of self-satisfaction "I hear some people spinning pages and pages of yarns, bloomin' songs included. about how they crossed them."

Trig had caught his breath now and agreed "Ah yes, very bracing, reminds me of where I grew up in Woodfleet, I'll tell you about it some time. Anyway, where does the map say we need to go next?"

Val nodded "lemme see" she stated reaching into a number of pockets but seemingly dissatisfied in what she found in each of them. "Give me the map Herr!"

The Herald spun from where he was checking the saddle on his steed (how they got their horses across the crags is quite the tale, though again not told here) "me?! Why would I have it?"

Val puffed out her cheeks "we were looking at it together on that rock way back there" she pointed her thumb in some random direction, the Herald wasn't sure that was the direction they had actually come from "an' when we were done it was implicit that you were to pick it up" she explained, what she thought was reasonably.

"No, no" the Herald countered "You explicitly said I wasn't to so much as look at the map, let alone touch it, as that was your special map with all your hidden stuff on it, and that if I went near it, you'd batter me."

"Well, we both have␣our versions of events" Val concluded.

Ansafety, who had been standing back in case the idiocy was contagious approached "So, what we're saying is the map is back at the start of the crags are we?" she asked with a touch of apprehension, knowing what the answer was going to be.

Val smiled at her, ignoring the look on her face out of habit "seems so love, not a problem, we'll just nip back across an' get it, shouldn't take a jiffy" she stated breezily, as if the task were as simple as making bad harp music. "We got across 'em once, it'll be even easier now we know the route."

At this point there was a low rumble as the ground shook beneath their feet, then a loud splitting crack as the sound of debris and large stones crumbling echoed around the area. Once the dust settled the party could see an enormous fissure in the rocks they had crossed, and the landscape had changed to become even more pointy and sharp and generally more dangerous looking than it had resembled before.

Val contemplated this for about the time it takes for a fly to work out it doesn't want to be splatted by a fist "doesn't change a thing!" she decided "now come on ya lazy bones let's do this, we can be there an' back in the time it takes for Bumli to have a tinkle!"

The Herald went to put up a counter argument, but Edin gave him a look that said, "if you are preparing to argue with Val at this juncture, prepare to receive a boot to a part of the body which prefers to remain a boot free zone." The Herald didn't need telling twice where boots to painful parts was concerned.

After giving this helpful and extremely descriptive look, Edin made his way to the rides and began unpacking the rope from his saddle bag and getting out the crampons. Even this fearless warrior wore the look of a fearful worrier.

****

After many hours of hauling themselves over jagged vertical rocks, narrow ledges and sheer faces, with a few narrow falling escapes and some undergarment near soiling the warriors had completed their journey so fraught as to barely be able to be described. Again.

Still, they had found the map, pinned as it was between two rocks as they had left it, before making the even more perilous crossing to be back where they were at the start of the day.

The group lay around trying to catch their breath, take on water, or alcohol and generally trying to blot out the journey they had just taken whilst thanking their lucky stars they weren't a splat at the bottom of the canyon.

Trig, a wonky grin across his face, sidled up to where the Herald was sat on a rock, his head resting in his hands staring blankly into space "well that was a blast wasn't it? though we could have just used my magic bridge to cross!"

The Herald nodded in agreement and then did a very natural and very large double take "sorry, your what now?"

Trig traced the route they had just taken with his eyes "oh yes, I could have summoned a magic bridge very easily. Big enough for all of us and to span all the canyons. We could have crossed there and back in a matter of minutes. Though I guess if I'd done that, we wouldn't have had the same sense of accomplishment and team building. Still, I am surprised no one considered the offer."

The Herald went to count to ten in his head but got about as far as one and a quarter seconds "you didn't mention it!" he growled through gritted teeth.

Trig looked taken aback "did I not? I'm sure I did. Oh well. We had some larks though didn't we?"

The Herald just about got himself calm enough to speak again "maybe don't mention that to the others eh?" he spoke quietly "they may be holding slightly different definitions of what constitutes 'a lark', I know I am."

Trig smiled at the Herald and tapped his nose. He then patted part of his colourful robe "plus I have a spare copy of the map in here, in the pocket where I keep my magic gerbils" the Herald just stared at him dumfounded "never know when we might need that!"

"I know when we might have needed a copy of that map. Just now, when we nearly died on some rocks trying to find that exact map, we might have needed it in that exact moment!" he spluttered, he could see Trig wasn't really following him "maybe don't mention the map to the others just now as well" was all he could manage, setting his vision back to staring into space, it seemed safer there.

After some gentle corralling, followed by some not so gentle corralling from Val, the party started off again heading away from the rocky outcrops, down a slope that wound out of the stone mountains.

It was not long into this new journey when as if from nowhere a group of hooded figures jumped out of parts of the new larger bouldered terrain. The Herald recognised these interlopers as the fearsome warriors from the 'swords of many angles' tribe, on account of them having four sword wielding arms. That and the banner they had with the tribe name helpfully written on it.

Their leader, a particularly sinewy and tough looking swordsman cleared his throat from within the oversized helm which didn't fit him so well. Before he could go to make any statements or demands, Val shot him a look which said "look mate, it's been a very long day and we've had to do a load of climbing over some particularly jagged rocks, cos some burk, probably the Herald, left the map behind, so although you're very intimidating, with your four arms and four swords and all that jazz, I will individually pull off your aforementioned forearms from your four arms if you even think about messing with me." It was a day for communicating in strong looks.

The leader took a moment to think and then spoke "sorry to get in your way, we jumped out by accident, have a lovely day, here is a bag of gold. Safe journey". With that he threw a bag of coins, that Ansafety caught, before they all quickly hightailed it.

"Some people are quick learners" Val said approvingly.

Act 4 Scene 1: Nick (From The) Cave

The party followed Val very carefully, ensuring their steeds used the same tread as her as they wound down the dust slope into the sparse valley below.

Val pulled up at a ridge and her crew formed up alongside her. She pointed at the semicircular clearing below some rocky outcrops as a crescent at the back of it. There was a large gaping mouth in this rock formation, like a skull screaming from the stone as if it had been forced to listen to another song by the (unfathomably) popular bard Shed Earen.

"That there" Val said in hushed tones, or as hushed as she could do, which was about as hushed as goose that had been goosed "is the entrance to the dungeon that holds the sword of Ow-Chee, the undead bane, skeleton skewerer, zombie zapper, ghoul gorger, vampire vapouriser, Wight Walloper it goes by many names, probably too many to list. However, to get to it, we're gonna have to fight through caverns full of creatures, beasties, bloodthirsty warriors, an' spooky things. Not to mention all the various part traps, pit traps, tip traps, pit prats, prat traps, mouse traps an' the like. Should be a blast I reckon."

"If anything, you're underselling it friend" A voice boomed from behind causing them all to jump at least the height of a decent sized halfling in the air and reach for weapons and for the Herald to check his underwear. They turned to find themselves confronted by an ogre the size of a large outdoor toilet facility, with flat features in his granite face and a mohawk that reached for the sky. He was covered in rusted, but sharp armour and carried a club with 'this bit does the hurty stuff' etched into the thick end. He grinned at the party "I'm Plotpointe, I work at the cave" he introduced himself with a half bow.

The party weren't sure of their place in this encounter and hands instinctively stayed near weapons, though the ogre seemed quite relaxed "it's not a great job, the pay is terrible, and the working conditions are atrocious. The foregoblin is constantly tracking our movements, to make sure we're in the right place looking fierce. Even when there are no raiders in the dungeon, he insists we 'look busy', he's getting more doubloons than us, how about he imagines us looking busy? I can't believe I studied hard for three years on that philosophy degree to end up doing this" the ogre sighed as he went off on a tangent.

Plotpointe seemed to stare into the middle distance for an eternity, the heroes just looked bemused. "Anyway, I'm running late, I best get in there and clock on." He started to shuffle his enormous shape down the slope, his armour clanking with every step. "Oh, if you're planning on raiding that cave for any of the treasures within, and we have a cracking assortment of riches and weapons in there, there is a tradesorc's entrance just twenty metres to the right of the main cave entrance. It cuts out all the hazards and defenders and leads you straight to the good stuff. Right, I think I've done the bit I was put here to do, best be cracking on. Cheerio!" and with that he carried on his journey.

The Herald smiled at this fortuitous but extremely detailed information that had just fallen in his lap. The four days left to get to the necromancer seemed like it might just be achievable, despite Val's 'best' efforts.

Act 4 Scene 2: Dead Flock Holiday

"I'm not sure this is a good idea" the Apprentice tempered Ringost as he followed him through the winding passages of the cave. "Shouldn't we actually wait until, you know, we've succeeded in our mission… not that I'm saying we won't succeed, but you know there is a traditional order to these things" he caught himself quickly.

Ringost waved an arm at the Apprentice behind him as if try to cast some particularly elaborate spell or waft away some unpleasant wind breaking, or maybe a little of both. "Nonsense! We can't fail!" he stated as close to cheerily as he seemed capable of achieving, rapidly ascended the uneven steps to the main chamber "and it will be good for everyone's morale, some of the zombies have been proper mopey of late." The Apprentice was confused about Ringost showing any interest in morale but the 'Being a Charismatic Successful Boss For Dummies' scroll he thought he saw on the bookshelf made more sense now.

Ringost entered the chamber, which was awash with buzz from his various troops, who'd heard via officer gossip that there was news. He spread his arms wide open by way of greeting, the chamber ignored him and carried on with their conversation. Ringost decided a statesman like bellow was the way forward "Oi! You lot!"

a minute or two later, when everyone had finished their conversation they started to give Ringost their attention. Ringost toyed with not making his announcement now out of spite.

"My wonderful friends" he decided he'd give them the benefit of the doubt.

"We're only your friends as you pay us" an Orc muttered though alas the cave once more amplified the volume, the inhabitants really should have mastered this by now all told.

Despite how much this stung, Ringost regained his composure "Ahem, my fellow… hang on, can one of you Mauve Elves go outside and tell Ant we'll give him a write up of this conversation, not that I think he can read…" once more the cave carried the sound loudly to Ant.

"Hey! I've an Open University degree, joint honours in English and stomping people underfoot!" he yelled in, hurt at the slight on his intelligence and his qualifications.

Ringost buried his hands into his head, figuring his head into his hands wouldn't be effective enough, and shook his head as he did so, to try and shake the stupidity out. He once more regained his composure "My… colleagues, we've worked extremely hard, and the assured moment of triumph is but four short days away" he paused for cheers of which a halfhearted smattering eventually came. "And to reward you for your efforts, we're going to have a celebration tonight, a pre-celebration if you will" this gained more of a cheer, but Ringost couldn't help feeling the atmosphere still fell a little flat "there will be drink, the finest feast, song, dance…"

"… Wine from the Border Dough region?" a rough voice cut in impatiently.

"Yes!" Ringost said, not entirely sure where that area was but he was going to leave the Apprentice to do all the organising and shopping, so he wasn't overly fussed with the details of such things, besides he was just happy to seemingly get a bit of audience participation at last.

"Pork scratchings?" Asked one of Ringost's particularly verbose skeletons, Ringost couldn't remember his name, it may have been Terence. He wasn't aware how his boney minions had picked up a taste for unhealthy, fried skin snack-based products, it really not being an area of expertise for them, but he wasn't going to let that get in the way right now, those unhealthy snacks might help the skeletons put on a little weight.

"Yes, sure!"

"Pin the tail on the cockatrice?" a sell sword piped up.

"Yeah why not?!" Ringost shot back.

"A game of begorge my neighbour?"

"Err... yeah…"

"Elf tossing?" asked a particularly eager looking satyr.

"No, no we won't be doing that" Ringost decided, feeling that was as good a place as any to draw a line. The satyr looked miserable, but the rest of the room was buzzing with excitement. Some skeletons were chatting about the cocktails they were going to make; Long Island Sliced Tea, El Diablo, Bloody Mary and of course a Corpse Reviver. They weren't so keen on drinking a Zombie though, knowing where they'd been.

Even the king and queen, from their cage in the corner, seemed strangely invested in the party idea, though this may have been withdrawal symptoms from fine drink and gout inducing food.

The mort the merrier.

Act 4 Scene 3: Dungeon Quest Ion Time

The Herald had a sprint on now, drainpipe legs pumping like pistons, he'd tethered his steed, was past the main cave entrance and almost at the secondary door the strange ogre had told them about, he shouted over his shoulder "Come on fellas we'll have this sword and defeat the villains in lickety…" he turned around to see his companions going in through the skull mouth of the main cave entrance "… spit!" he spat, turning to find out what the hell they were doing.

The Herald ducked down into the darkness of the entrance his companions had vanished into "Err hello?" his voice rattled around in the dark, he couldn't see anything, but he was pretty sure he heard a noise that was Bumli falling over something and cursing. "Why are we going through here? We can cut out all the hassle and peril if we use that other entrance. Were none of you listening to that enormous ogre that explicitly told us that literally five minutes ago?" he asked exasperated.

"Look Herr love" Val started patiently from somewhere fairly close by "you're very new to all this questing lark, else you'd know it's all about the peril. The peril an' the bounty. An' the drunken songs. An' fighting whilst singing drunken songs." The Herald could hear the happiness in her voice and none of the others in the party were dissenting, not even Ansafety and Trig, who seemed to have a chunk, well perhaps a slice, no maybe a slither of sense between them.

"But we're really against the clock? End of the world in a matter of three days and all that? I really shouldn't need to keep saying that it should feel like a pretty significant milestone that is in people's thoughts at all time, without me ramping up the tension" the Herald thought he'd try a different, albeit thus far unsuccessful tact.

"Pft!" A voice from slightly further ahead in the dark expanse answered him, he thought it could have been Edin.

The Herald realised he wasn't going to win this battle, so he puts his hands where he thought his hips were "in which case, bullocks to this dark!", he drew his sword and pressed the pommel which immediately flooded the chamber with an eerie blue light. His companions were all close to him, Bumli prone on the floor, struggling to get off his back like some bearded, trouserless turtle.

The chamber was large and yet surprisingly neat. The walls had been hewn flat and someone had actually hung a few pictures of orcs in fine robes eating grapes to brighten the place up. There was a few sparse furnishings to make the chamber airy. The Herald saw the party all staring at him in the newfound light, he looked at his blade "who isn't carrying a magic sword eh?" he grinned.

The party weren't particularly impressed and walked off to explore the cavern further "just a light up sword" Edin muttered.

After picking their way through the labyrinthine tunnels off the main chamber they reached the end of a corridor with a large arched doorway and a great imposing thick oak door filling the frame. The huge door had some runes that despite being painted in black seemed to have a dull glow, around the side of it in a language none of the party recognized, the party really only specializing in language to make a brigand blush.

Val and Edin put all their might into pushing the frame but not even their considerable strength could budge the barrier a fraction. They turned to look at Trig who could possibly offer a different approach "where I grew up in Woodfleet was quite the place…" The party stared at him, but he seemed to have nothing else and was lost thinking about something else.

"Err, Trig? Any ideas on getting past the ruddy great door blocking our way?" Edin gently prompted him.

"Oh… yes that… well in Woodfleet… I mean, I think the runes must be the key" spoke Trig. "Let me consult my runes book" He produced a tome for his robes and began reading, the party were not convinced Trig was going to provide the solution when they noticed the book he was reading was 'bird throwing for beginners.'

Bumli who had been staring at the door, with his hand rested on where his chin began in his expanse of beard, trying to look intelligent, suddenly stood bolt upright "ah its well-engineered I grant you, but no thing is engineered beyond the knowledge of a dwarf" so saying he placed his hands on the door and began to feel around "Aha! As

I thought!" he declared excitedly as he'd found a hidden lever carefully concealed in the pattern of the frame. He gave a yank, after a moment there was a clanking sound then the noise of metal grinding against metal. Bumli stood on the spot eagerly waiting for resolution, at this point a latch dropped down and a flame sprayed out where Bumli was stood and if he'd been of human height he would be suffering a very singed beard, luckily it went over his head, like so many things in life seemed to.

Ansafety put away the journal she had been writing poetry in and unfurled herself from the rock she had been sitting on "alternatively…" she walked up to the door and pulled open a smaller door cut into the body of the main door.

The party squeezed themselves through this new opening "of course I was getting to that" Bumli protested at the backs of the crew as they went through as he walked through he lent on the frame pressing another lever which released a hobnailed boot on a pulley which fair booted Bumli up the backside and into the corridor on the other side. The Herald was very impressed with how specific that lever had been to their current situation, the timing and height of the boot had been strangely prescient.

A short corridor took them into a new chamber. This room was torchlit with mounted flames across the walls, the floor was a marble check, it had dark grey pillars carved from the granite walls reaching high into the ceiling, the centre had a gleaming white stone fountain with a green hued water trickling into the pool below it.

The Herald made his way to the fountain with a look of awe in his eyes. He dropped to his knees and whispered, "this must be the fabled pool of life, immortality awaits!" before cupping his hands and drinking from the basin, he winced "tangier than I was expecting."

Trig surveyed this scene and spoke quietly to Val "I think that's actually where they do their washing at best, at worst it's the toilet for this lair" Val valiantly attempted and failed to suppress her snigger which echoed around the room strangely ornate room.

"Feeling invincible Herring?" Edin asked the Herald tauntingly.

The Herald gulped "err not really, feeling a little nauseas truth be told, why?"

Edin drew his enormous square bladed broadsword and gave it a hefty practice swing "no particular reason, just looks like we're about to be attacked by rat people who seem to have got somewhat attached to this fountain."

Out of the walls and concealed gaps in the floor were crawling legions of dark furred humanoid rats, their red eyes glowing in the room and their whiskers twitching as they scented these intruders. A couple looked like they may have been mice people who had been drinking a lot of protein mixes and that the rat people had got too scared of to stop them joining their gang. Either way they were all well-armed rodents with a variety of crude clubs and spears.

Multiple arrows flew over the head of Edin and the Herald, felling furry creatures where they landed, Ansafety as alert as ever had decided the battle had started and she wasn't waiting for permission to do her thing.

"Does anyone have any really big pieces of cheese?" Trig asked, as Val and Bumli roared past him swinging their blades to help Edin and the Herald at the front of the fight. "Nothing to do with the rats, I'm just a bit peckish and would like some cheese." And with that he drew a pouch from his robe and casually chucked it where a couple of rat people were lurking near him, the pouch flashing on impact and immediately making the rodents disappear in a smell of singed fur, singed flesh and a hint of nutmeg.

Everyone was now engaging in fighting, their battle cries bellowed in defiance, the Heralds being the least bloodthirsty of these shouts and possibly containing the word 'please'. He was still very much a work in progress.

Despite their considerably greater numbers, the rat people were being cut through by the superior strength, weapon craft and swearing of the raiding party. It was at the point where Val picked up five rat people on her sword and flung them at another four, that their will broke, and they disappeared into the holes as quickly as they'd appeared. Probably quicker, given their wish to avoid further beatings. The Herald swore he heard one squeak "sod this!" as it disappeared into the ground and pulled the rubble covering over its head.

The Herald dusted his hands "Well rats the end of rat!" he declared, much to the disgust of his companions.

Act 4 Scene 4: Duvet Day of The Dead

The Apprentice had been summoned to Ringost's private chamber by a slurring even more than normal but jovial zombie. The Apprentice pushed past the drapes over the cave entrance and called "Master, what is thy bidding?" his voice echoing off the sparse walls, except for the wall that carried the portrait of Ringost that a ghoul with supposedly artistic ability had painted on commission from Ringost, Ghouls and art are generally not to be mixed, though the ghoul had certainly captured Ringost's ear lobe.

Ringost recoiled at this noise. He was lay flat on his bed, eating what looked like melted cheese slices and drinking a black fizzy potion. He had a blanket pulled tightly over him and was hanging on for dear life.

"I am here Apprentice" he called, each word painfully ricocheting off his brain. The Apprentice moved to the chamber where the noise came from and was more than a little taken aback by the sight of Ringost, he was noticeably even more pale looking than normal, the Apprentice was struck by how gaunt and beaten he looked, and the Apprentice spent most of his days hanging around with the undead.

Ringost caught the look and though it pained him spoke again "when using undead magic, sometimes one must lay down, meditate and pull the sacred blanket of power around them." He reached down to a bowl by the side of the bed and emptied the crunchy snacks from within into his mouth chewing greedily.

He went to sit a little more upright, winced and slowly lowered himself back down again. "You show promised my young apprentice. Its time you showed how far you have come with a… err… development opportunity." These words struck the Apprentice as odd as only last night Ringost had been saying how useless he found the Apprentice and his work, before later in the evening slurring about how much he loved him and how he was his best mate.

The Apprentice thought better of bringing this up, unaccustomed as he was to Ringost dishing out praise and happy that his brilliance was finally being recognised, he'd personally been very happy with the zombie frog he had recently created until it drowned in one of the shallow cave's puddles. "What bidding would you have me do master? I have learned much in the ways of controlling the undead and not brapping my pants when in the presence of a reanimated cadaver."

"Yes, yes" Ringost said entirely unengaged, he painfully shifted the weight on his aching buttocks "you know that celebratory party we had last night…"

"... the one where you and two of your skeletons were loudly singing 'I can't get you out of my dead' and then you started trying to breakdance?"

"Anyway" Ringost cut him off hurriedly, as the memory came back and painfully dug him in the ribs. "If we are to be successful in sacrificing the king and queen, thus raising The King of The Undead and taking control of all the realms, then I really need you and some of the skeletons to clean up the main chamber where we had the party. You know what they say, 'clean chamber, effective undead army to lay waste to the lands and destroy all your enemies.'" He pondered a little "maybe check the other chambers for detritus too." With that Ringost fell silent as he chased the stringy part of the cheese with his tongue unsuccessfully.

The Apprentice shrugged and left the chamber beginning the journey up the winding steps hoping to locate some skeletons to help him with this vital mission. His focus was broken when a skeleton stepped out from a side chamber into his path on the corridor. The skeleton spoke embarrassedly "I'd... err... give that a minute or two if I were you..." pointing at the room behind him before ambling off.

"But that's a magic store cupboard" the Apprentice spluttered.

Act 4 Scene 5: Fixing A Whole Lotta Hole

The Herald led the party cautiously (or as cautiously as he could get Val to behave) through the twisting corridors, tendrils that dug further into the land, his sword torch just revealing a few steps into the gloom, of the serpent of corridors hewn into the ground by who? Or what? And were they unionised and getting plenty of tea breaks for this backbreaking work?

For some time now the party had explored these gloomy tunnels picking the route at junctions based on what Bumli insisted was his innate Dwarven ability to know which route to take underground, though the Herald was certain they were lost. Still, they ploughed on Val seeming happy with the plan, though nothing seemed to make Val unhappy for long.

The Herald followed the passage round to the right when he heard a "Waaaarrrgghhh!" followed by a heavy crashing sound coming from somewhere at the back of the team. He spun round quickly and walked straight into Val which knocked him onto his backside. Gingerly he rose again.

"What was that?" he asked.

"Bumli fell down a hole" Ansafety's amused voice came from further behind them in the dark.

"Not true!" A voice echoed from deep below, it sounded a long way down. The Herald moved his way through the pack and shone his torch at a large hole that was in the ground, he couldn't see the bottom with the light. "I thought the corridor exploration was having mixed results, so I thought I would participate in an independent subterranean search. Us Dwarves being blessed with steel tough backsides I took the judgement that I'd take the quick route down to do this" Bumli attempted by way of an explanation.

Val looked down the hole and smirked "genius work Bumli, my little Dwarven friend. We'll come join you down there in the search." Val bent her knees as she prepared to happily leap into the dangerous unknown.

"Wait!" Bumli bellowed out, several minor key notes of panic in his voice at the prospect of being trapped in a very deep hole and secondly having a fourteen stone Valkyrie jump on his head whilst you're trapped in a very deep hole. "Err… no need… I've… err… done a quick pre-emptive search and my cast iron deductions tell me what we seek isn't this way, but it hasn't been a wasted journey for by being down here I've gained further insight on where we must go. It's up there somewhere."

The five none pit based heroes turned to begin the search once more with a voice saying "… would one of you mind throwing me down the rope…?" ringing around the passageway behind them.

****

Many, many hours later, the party had taken a break at a junction which had a large skull of some enormous unidentified beast, carelessly left lying around, which made a useful seat for some to take on some water and food before renewing their search further.

"'Ere Herr, when we got split up earlier, did you say you had an encounter with a monster?" Val engaged trying to piece together part of the adventure she had missed when The Herald had taken a turn the others hadn't and had come back looking more flustered than usual.

The Herald slugged back his water at the memory "that I did Val, strange creature I think it was some kind of woman snake cross breed thing."

"Sounds like a Gorgon dear boy" Trig answered utilising his study of creatures of the land.

"Did she have snakes for hair?" Ansafety asked curios.

The Herald pondered this "Err… yeah I think so, I can't remember all the details of what she looked like fully."

"Definitely a Gorgon" Edin grunted utilising his knowledge of punching the creatures of the land.

Trig tried another angle "Did she have a stare that petrified anything she looked at, that means anything she stared at turns to stone?" he asked.

"Yeah, you know what, I think she might have" The Herald replied.

Val took her turn "did you look into her eyes Herr love?"

"Yeah I might have done that for a moment too" came the answer. Ansafety looked the Herald up and down to see if any stone-based features and shook her head in disgust, he was the same stiff as always albeit not now hewn from rock.

"How did you defeat her then Herr love?" Val asked always keen to hear about a good old fight.

"I... err... well... you see... she looked pretty scary, and I wasn't sure of the best angle to take her down so... I... err... I chucked a rock at her head and then ran off. Turns out real legs are quicker than having the lower half of a serpent."

Bumli necked his hip flask and winced "Great so we may have an angry Gorgon on our tail somewhere in these murky depths." He spoke grimly not noticing the pun. The whole party privately concluded the Herald was useless and made themselves ready to explore the maze of corridors further, with more than a whiff of the possibility of a grudge bearing gorgon pursuing them. The dungeon quest was proving to be as successful as the time Bumli bet them he could leap a cyclops in a single bound.

****

After what seemed like endless further exploration the Herald saw a small doorway to the side of the corridor and cautiously entered. The floor was crunchy underfoot, with what looked like claw marks on the large stone walls. The square room was bare except for a large heavy-lidded casket with "treshure" written unevenly on it in gold paint.

Val squeezed herself through the door frame spying the Herald edging towards the chest "if summat looks too good to be true, it probably is mi dear" Val cautioned, though her words were probably unnecessary given how many blatant traps the party had walked into already on this adventure.

The Herald turned and nodded at Val "yeah, I thought that, but then I thought Ansafety isn't currently here to look all smug if that turns out to be the case, so that lessens the blow for a kickoff. Besides I'm much smarter and more dexterous than Bumli." Val nodded, unable to fault the logic.

The Herald put his hand on the ice-cold clasp took a breath, turned it and heaved the lid open. Inside was a note written in the same crude writing as the lettering on the casket, it read "sir prize sucka!". On picking it up, the Herald had disturbed some kind of counterweight and the chamber door slammed shut and a whiny noise filled the room as gears and pulleys moved in the walls around the cave. The Herald looked around in panic which was heightened as he noticed the spikes protruding from the ceiling as it began to slowly lower down.

The Herald bolted past Val crossing the chamber in three large, hurried strides and began hammering on the now firmly shut door "Edin, Ansafety, Bumli... Trig, help!" he wailed.

Val closed behind him and put her arm gently on his shoulder as the Herald began to sob at their plight "there, there, what's up love?" she asked calmly.

The Herald spun round eyes wide in fright "the spike ceiling about to stab and crush us painfully to death?!" he asked in dismay.

Val began to feel one of the spikes pushing on her bronze winged helm "hmm this?" she stated in an even voice, touching one of the descending spikes. "OK Sorted." She crossed to the far side of the chamber where the gear noise was coming from and put her fist through the wall, yanking the lever behind which stopped the descent of the ceiling, Val nodded pleased with her work. She loped back across the room gently picking up the Herald to move him out of the way of the door before effortlessly pushing the firmly locked door open.

Ashen faced the Herald spilled out of the room and stumbled past the rest of the party who were waiting outside, and went off looking for a quiet corner to cry in.

"What happened?" Trig asked, a note of concern in his voice.

Val replied, "I think the poor thing got over stimulated."

Act 4 Scene 6: Waking The Undead

The king lay in the bed in his cage regretting showing willing and going to the party last night, he really shouldn't have drunk so much wine with his gruesome enemies, but what was he meant to do? He was used to being there at parties entertaining guests, pressing the flesh, drinking, eating extravagant food some kind of reflex had kicked in and against all odds he'd found himself going with it. A couple of the zombies had been surprising raconteurs.

He rolled over, the scratchy duvet slipping further off exposing his bare torso to the cold. He felt his wife's slim arm next to him he felt his way up it until he cupped her hard, cold bony head in his hands. With his eyes closed he moved close to her ear and began to whisper "I'll say one thing for our captors" he started "they know how to throw a decent party" he began to open his eyes and saw that his wife had lost a lot of weight. And flesh. Slowly through his clouded mind it dawned on the king he was in bed with a skeleton. He let out a scream, which the skeleton joined in on, and both leapt out of bed.

"Have fun last night?" the queen's voice cut in from the other side of the cage. The king made his way over to join his wife on the crate on which she sat, whilst the skeleton sheepishly let itself out.

"I didn't... it wasn't... I thought it was you... I mean..." the king spluttered and gave up. The queen was secretly taking pleasure in his clear discomfort. She had forgone the party on the small principle it was with people who intended to kill them to raise an undead army with their corpses. She'd watch the king and the skeleton stagger in singing songs about they would be rocking you, or something, before they both collapsed unconscious on the mattress only waking now.

"In three days", time, we're going to be sacrificed so that some two-bit necromancer can raise The King of The Undead to lay waste to the land and still you found the time to party with our captors?" the queen spoke slowly and sternly, really not able to understand her husband sometimes.

The king shifted uneasily on the crate, risky given the high potential for a splinter in the bottom. "They won't succeed, I thought if I could ingratiate myself with them I could find out more about their plans and work out an escape route." The queen arched an eyebrow, and the king decided it best if he shut the flip up.

Outside the cave the figure in the mask was coming down sweeping and sighing at the mess he encountered. His shuffle and sweeping noise broke the silence though not the tension. The queen fixed her eyes on him "I didn't see you at the party last night strange one?"

The Apprentice didn't break from his sweeping "Not my kind of thing, didn't seem right. Besides I had some very important texts on the between world to read and finish as quickly as possible" he muttered.

The queen stood and moved closer to the bars to see if she could further regard this strange figure who had attached himself to the necromancer for no obvious reasons. "This Ringost is a dangerous idiot, and he treats you terribly. His plans are clearly lunacy, and I can't believe anyone would be stupid enough to follow that." The Apprentice shoved heavily with his broom at some detritus, he didn't want to begin to try and guess what it was, on the floor.

The queen decided to change tact slightly "sure he may succeed in sacrificing us, but don't think The King of The Undead offers any solutions to what you are after. And don't let yourself be defined by Ringost and his actions. I'm sure you're capable of so much better if you want to."

The Apprentice propped the broom against the wall and turned to look at the queen. "Is this the part where your try and persuade me to free you?" he sighed wearily "because even if I did this gave is a hive of scum and villainy you wouldn't' get ten yards away."

The queen let out a loud "pft!" and went to sit back on the crate seat next to the king. "Not at all. You're the architect of your own destiny, but you've got yourself really into something here, I hope you know what you're looking to get out of this." The king put his arm around his wife, and she squeezed his hand, having decided to forgive previous skeletal faux pas.

The Apprentice muttered something inaudible. He then moved closer to the cage "let me see if I can get you some breakfast" he stated. "It's a strange time we all find ourselves in, best to tackle it on a full stomach, I think."

The Apprentice made his way off dreading to think what state he'd find the kitchen in given the rest of the cave was such a mess. He'd never seen anywhere so untidy, and it was a bloody cave.

Act 4 Scene 7: Re-charging The Batterings

Another turn another interminable long corridor. This one different from the previous ones by virtue of a bookshelf someone had put to the side to make it look more studious and some sign with a bland platitude like 'homes can be made from any material but the best homes are made from the heart' that some people in the realm thought made them seem more philosophical and interesting, when it didn't. Plus, it ignored the fact human organs were a terrible material to build properties out of and even if you managed it successfully, you'd look like a serial killer.

The party had been searching the cave for what must have been close to twenty-four hours now and if anything were more lost than when they started, and they'd started as lost as that key you'd put in a real safe place to keep it from getting lost and if you could only remember where that was then it was a very clever idea.

Out of sheer boredom the Herald went to the bookshelf and picked up the largest tome, a bottle green volume with faded gold trim. Trig moved close in behind something about what the Herald had in his hand triggered a memory in the fog of his brain. "Careful with that one my friend, that's the Fabled Book of Spells. It has some powerful wizardry in there if you care to learn it."

"Funny the things people leave lying around" mused the Herald. He opened up the book and flicked through its faded pages to look at the spell names 'Distraction Cat', 'Pogo Pants', 'Dances with Hedgehogs', 'Cor Blimey Strike a Lightning', 'Flaming Pheasant From Above', 'Contradict a Goose' 'Shield of Bread'. The Herald shook his head snapped the book shut and put it back on the shelf, he had no time for such useless sounding spells, but he made a mental note to look into getting some pogo pants at some point.

Val, who had been pacing the corridor at this point, seemed to get some inspiration from somewhere deep within "I'm completely bloody sick of this. I'm very, very sober and very, very bored!" She yelled.

Ansafety's wide eyes glinted from the light of the Herald's sword. "You have a better idea than ploughing on through the corridors?"

Val cocked her head to one side as she gave it some consideration "ploughing through the corridors eh?" she then concluded this idea with a "Raaarrrgghhhh!" as she charged at the thick stone wall at the end of the corridor, smashing easily through it as if it were papyrus.

"I'm not paying for any of this damage out of expenses" the Herald clucked disapprovingly.

Not losing any momentum Val carried on spiraling through the walls in her path the next room took her through a small green walled room where a goblin was sat on a bucket going through his ablutions "hey!" he called, trying to look fierce so as to be seen to be doing his job as he was doing his job, as Val steamed through ignoring his attempts as she ploughed on.

Val was now sprinting down a new corridor her wall bashing had given her a short cut to, in her path stood two enormous wooden armoured trolls who on seeing Val coming raised their enormous clubs ready to engage. Val didn't slow one bit just barreling them to one side causing one of the trolls to burst into tears. The rest of her gang were at full pace behind doing all they could to keep pace "sorry" the Herald managed to the trolls as he passed, not quite sure why he was apologising.

Val carried on this charge for a good ten minutes, storming through walls, monsters, doors, buffet tables, pillars, wall mounted grizzly bears, expensive looking vases left on narrow plinths, bellowing loudly as she went. Reaching a marble floored corridor, a familiar looking ogre was stood to one side watching the dervish coming towards him "oh you took the long route in the end did you, well each to their own, still you've managed to come this far and your only yards away from…" Plotpointe began as Val passed him giving him a swift kick in a delicate area out of reflex. The ogre crumpled into a heap managing to wheeze out "… oof! Well, that's gratitude for you…"

The rest of the party followed just behind on seeing Plotpointe on the floor Ansafety stopped and knelt next to the giant. "Sorry she is just in the zone, nothing personal" she reached into a pocket in her cowl and produced a salve wrapped in a leafy pouch "here, rub this on the affected area" she said as she stood getting ready to rejoin the sprint and catch her companions "its pile cream but it should do the trick. I think. Maybe. Can't make it worse."

After what seemed like endless running and the lactic acid biting hard in his legs, the Herald managed to call out to the vast figure of Val as she was about to charge another wall "Val, Val wait!". Val slowed her charge and turned to smile at the Herald, who was now bent double trying to regain his breath. "This plan is no better than the last one. We're covering essentially the same ground albeit quicker and more violently."

Val looked the Herald up and down "it's OK Herr love, I appreciate you're new to this, but it works out in the end, a solution always presents itself. Besides Quicker an' more violently is the title of me biography."

The Herald still gasping for air began again "But... cough... what... what... give me a minute..." knackered the Herald leant on the wall to support his weight and screamed as the wall, which was actually a secret door, opened sending the Herald crashing through landing painfully on the hard stone floor on the other side.

"See! You're getting it!" Val said happy at the Heralds lucky discovery. She stepped over the prone fop and into the new room. It was a large room, lit by a single brazier on the far wall. The brazier gave off a strange, eerie green light and shadows of twisted shapes danced on the walls.

The chambers walls on which the shadows spun were lined with strange dagger, swords, axes, and sharp stabby things. At the far end of the chamber next to the brazier was a suit of gold armour which held a rune and gem encrusted blade which caught the green light reflecting across the room its brilliance.

Val gave the newly upright Herald a nudge in the ribs, further knocking the wind out of him. "You see? Sword of ow-chee!" she laughed as the rest of the party entered the chamber "exactly according to the detailed plan!"

Act 4 Scene 8: In Better Spirits

Ringost had managed to shake off his 'dark fug' that had been plaguing him from the exact moment the drunken party had finished. He'd sworn that some powerful demon had cast a powerful ennui spell on him at the party, either that or he'd had that dodgy pint (that one pint out of the ten you have that causes you to feel rough the next day). Either way he was feeling nearly human again and back to doing what he did best; namely being grumpy ordering the Apprentice about.

With two days to the ceremony, the time had come to prepare to break for the cover of Ringost's cave and move operations out in the open to the ritual site in the North of the realm. The Apprentice had a number of scrolls Ringost had tucked under his arms, a curved dark bladed dagger in one hand, a set of scales in the other hand and a large backpack laden with necromantic brick a brack, which he suspected Ringost was going to try to sell to tourists as they made their journey.

"You know what, I think I need one more cup of tea to get me back to full fettle" declared Ringost. The Apprentice made an audible groan and began to relive himself of all his burdens, he was just in the process of sliding off the backpack when Ringost spoke again "On second thoughts, we've only a couple of days before the ritual needs to be completed, lets strike while the iron is hot eh?" The Apprentice made an even more audible groan as he began to repack the items up again, extremely annoyed at this tedious waste of time.

Ringost stared at the calendar he'd had the Apprentice nail to the cave wall, a far from easy task to carry out. Many a nail was lost to the bent bin that day. He smiled at the date with a ring around it "we're close, so close, people will come to know and respect the dark forces in the world, but more than that, they will respect me, no longer will I be invisible and seen of no importance. They will know, nay fear my name" Ringost shouted the last words.

The Apprentice wobbled a little bit with the items impacting his balance "this is about making things more even and fair like we agreed Ringost? This isn't about you or me is it?"

Ringost had a look of confusion for a moment and then regained his composure "yes of course it's about making things fair again. Though I think there will be some subsidiary personal benefits. It will be worth it my young apprentice." He said unconvincingly to his companion.

The Apprentice didn't have the energy to pursue this line of questioning, currently his legs buckling was his prime concern. Though the initial idea he had struck up with Ringost and the direction it seemed to now be taking vexed him greatly.

He wandered off unsteadily to load the gear. "If this is all about you being jilted by some girl who wasn't into your poetry as a teenager, I'm going to be very annoyed" he muttered to himself as he left.

Act 4 Scene 9: A Little Sword And Sorcery

"Well, 'ere we go!" Val said to herself as she strode confidently across the chamber floor.

Ansafety let out a long sigh that had the Herald wondering if there was some kind of steam trap that had been set off. "You don't have to say it Ansafety" the Herald cut in "we're all thinking it." Hoping that getting it out in the open would somehow placate the Elf's sense of disappointment.

Ansafety puffed out her cheeks "Fine!" She said the word several octaves above her normal voice pitch causing some mice to stick their heads out of the floor to see what new giant rodent companion had entered the room. She drew her bow once more shaking her head as she did so.

"Seems to be the way these things go" Trig stated searching in his cloak for the right offensive magic but finding himself distracted by the discovery of a pork pie in one of the folds, which he preceded to eat.

On reaching the suit of armour Val let out a slightly disappointed sound on finding that the mythical Blade of Ow-Chee was about the size of a letter opener and the knight's gauntlet holding it was actually really small to give the blade a larger appearance "bloomin' false perspective" she muttered. Despite its small size, the blade was covered in numerous runes which must have taken a steady hand to craft. Most of the runes were of stickmen (or stickwomen it was hard to tell given the size of the edge of the blade) flexing their muscles and laughing whilst stabbing large creatures with a small blade, subtlety in ruins had clearly not been the specialism of the creator.

Val placed her open palms either side of the blade "all duly noted, but we're going with plan A" she said out of the side of her mouth finally addressing the obvious trap they were walking in to. She rapidly brought her hands together and clasped the blade "Aha! Another win for plan A!" she declared triumphantly.

Her call of triumph was met by a crack reverberating around the room as the ceiling collapsed down the middle sending huge pieces of rock and debris hurtling towards the party, scattering the Herald and Edin down one side and the rest of the warriors down the other. The rubble settled many feet above even Val's head "Crikey that was close!" Bumli stated, failing to notice the enormous rock that had landed on his boot. Ansafety went to check on the condition of Trig.

"I believe that was just the start love" Val replied with for the first time some wariness creeping into her voice, as a platoon of trolls in thick rusted armour, wielding oversized rock clubs, which would have been better described as just some big rocks, emerged from a newly created hole in the wall.

Trig once more delved into his robes to see what magic he had for the situation or failing that if there was another pork pie he'd forgotten about "I don't remember that ogre warning us about this" he stated.

"An' that was why my pre-emptive kick in the nuts was so warranted. I knew it" Val responded trying to reason her earlier act of mindless violence.

****

The Herald gingerly picked himself up off the dusty cold stone floor, he'd got familiar with for a second time in a short space of time. The new chamber the collapsed ceiling had forced him into was dank and dusty and his blade was only offering limited light. The rubble had messed up his centre parting which he was seriously not happy about. He then checked for broken bones or bleeding and was reasonable satisfied everything was in place.

The Herald looked around for Edin who appeared similarly unscathed but was starting at the pile of rubble with a strange wistful intent. The Herald looked at the pile of stone and concluded they wouldn't be able to get through that to get back to the other four any time soon.

A low snarling sound snapped the Heralds attention back to the room they were in. Seemingly there was a gap that had opened in the far wall and descending some steps that had become visible was some kind of sorcerer, in animal furs and an iron goat's head helm, who, in case his various magic spells didn't do the trick of causing his opponents a headache had brought along his pet dog, which seemed to be a cross breed between a huskie and an armoured ogre, a breeding program truly not to be dwelt upon. The sorcerer's fur robes billowed as they grasped their staff tightly and began to mutter an incantation.

The Herald slapped Edin on the back "Ha ha they don't know what they're messing with, I'll give you the pleasure of this one old chap, I'm sure he will be a doddle for you to duff up."

Edin stared at the ceiling and simply shrugged. The mage was starting to draw a power from invisible particles in the room causing the hairs on the Heralds arms to stand up. His doggy thing couldn't have been literally any more straining at the leash.

"Err, Edin?" a nervousness replaced the previous cockiness in the Heralds voice.

Edin finally turned to face the Herald, acting like he had all the time in the world. "That confounded name again, must it torment me forever thus?" He reached for a notepad he'd seemingly concealed from even himself, tucked under his belt. He once more stared mournfully at the rubble on the floor "such wanton destruction. Stone and bone and for what? That one might prove themselves master of others through might? We must throw off our shackles, reveal our true selves and say 'no more!' We are better than the violent urges we lower ourselves to. What world is it that is predicated on mindless violence and low humour?"

The Herald had panic in his eyes now, hurriedly fumbling inside his tunic as the chamber was filling with a strange energy as the tendrils of magic drew further into the sorcerer's now glowing staff. "Edin!" he shook the barbarian by his massive shoulders "well done spotting and commentating on all that, but you failed to notice the large sorcerer and his even larger terror beast who are but a few feet away and about to tear us apart. Fighty time. Please!?"

Edin leant against the rubble and stroked his chin "and we fight again today, for what? To fight again tomorrow? The day after? A constant cycle of fighting? Where has it ever got this world? One long dance of fists until the end of time?"

"Edin!" The Herald cut in loudly "For Fu…. Aarrggghhh!"

The sorcerer's blast took the Herald clean off his feet and backwards into the wall. The Herald turned his gaze to Edin, a rasping chuckle emitting from under the helm. He began to once more draw power into himself as he descended the steps further, less cautiously now, seeing his prey were putting up no defence. Edin took the whole thing in with a look of cold indifference.

"Such dark spells as these spell darkness for those that succumb to using them. You have looked into the abyss many times, my friend, and just maybe the abyss has glanced back at you and found you wanting" Edin lectured the warlock to total indifference on the magic user's part, although it was hard to tell given the helm covering his face. He stepped closer still to the barbarian, so as to be able to give this hulking figure an up close and personal blast of foul magic.

The sorcerer closed the gap to a matter of feet, his beast glowering angrily at his heels ready to tear flesh should his master provide the opportunity. At this point there was a whooshing sound followed by a dull metallic clang as the heavy unlit ceiling torch chandelier landed heavily on the sorcerer and pet clearing them both out.

"Almost like we planned it wordy!" A voice called from the corner as the Herald stood sword in hand by the rope that had up until recently held the lighting up. Edin looked at the Herald and made to speak "To save you words and both of us time, the talisman of obsidian" the Herald lifted the charm around his neck "pretty useful against a magic user" The Herald smirked "that and some top-quality playing possum on my part. I knew that amateur dramatic troupe I joined would come in handy one day, and not just for the mastery of dressing like a dame."

Edin merely shrugged and went to speak again but once more the Herald cut in "No need to thank me and definitely no need to go on some junior scholar musings about the nature of what just happened. No what our energies go on, is finding a way out of here and back to the others."

The Herald began feeling along the walls for some kind of lever or hidden door. He leapt out of his skin when the rubble had a huge part of it disappear in a shrapnel of small stones. The Herald gripped his blade tightly warily, ready for another confrontation. A huge figure stepped through the newly created hole and looked at the out cold sorcerer and animal "oo you did well there love! That's a pretty averagely sized pet ol' goat head has" they spoke. Val looked at Edin and the Herald "you two beauties alive? Good, then stop mucking' about. Come on!"

She turned and went back through the gap in the wall, allowing none of her companion's time for recovery. When Val was on a quest she really was on a mission.

She stepped over the unconscious trolls which took quite the long stride "I've found a way to the outside up ahead, there is a simple door. If we'd come in that way it would have saved us a load of time and muckin' about y" know."

The Herald went to speak but swallowed down his frustrations. He caught up with Val "there is one thing, I think Edin took a heavy knock to his head, he didn't want to fight, which is remarkable in itself but then he went very, and I mean *very* wordy. He was like a different person."

"Oh, so you've finally met Tarquin?" Val asked her chuckle bouncing off the walls as she stomped down the corridor.

Act 4 Scene 10: The Breath Of The Wild

The companions pushed hard at the heavy door and the air and light flooded the stuffy corridor. They spilled out into the now humid day catching their breath. Val slammed the door hard behind her, catching the Gorgon who had finally caught up with them hard in the face. The Gorgon really had brought nothing to this adventure.

Trig gingerly made his way over to a rock for a seat and slowly caught his breath looking a little pallid and confused. Ansafety made her way over to him and took a seat next to him her hand resting on his. Edin padded around the group talking to himself, something about the temporarily deceptive illusive beauty of a summer's day or some such nonsense.

"Well, that was a blast wasn't it?" said Val beaming, seeming to have had a genuinely good time in the dungeon. "OK everyone back to the horses an' let's see what beasties to batter this adventure throws at us next!"

"Hang on" Ansafety cut across anger laced in her voice "Trig needs to catch his breath. I need to catch my breath. We all need to catch our breath." Ansafety caught Edin walking up to some rocks composing a song about dragonflies out loudly "Nearly all of us need to catch our breath."

"Nonsense!" Val shot back through a smile that looked a little forced "we're all ready to go, we've an important date with destiny! Or aint you been listenin' to Herr all this time?" she spun her newfound blade around her fingers, it not being large enough to spin around her hands "We got what we came for, did a reet professional job an' now we push on. Like we've always done."

"Like we've always done... huh...?" Bumli muttered under his breath flexing his arms to get some life back in them.

"No time like the present to go and give a good chinnin' to that Necromancer fella." For once the Herald wasn't worried about the time they had left to save the world, he was absolutely knackered and worse still just found out he'd chipped a nail in the ceiling collapse.

Trig looked at Val "about err... oh yes... about that blade, that is a powerful magic artifact and as such, with great power comes..." Val wasn't paying attention and leapt at a rock in the cave slope cleaving it easily in two with the magic weapon, Val made an impressed sound at the sharpness of her new toy.

"Yeah, got it magic power blade. Tell you what its mega sharp, should do a Necromancer up a right treat!" she said giddily. Val began pacing towards the horses.

Wearily Bumli got in stride with Val "my Dwarven skills really helped us get that blade, no?" he puffed his chest with a sense of pride.

Val laughed loudly "you mean before or after we rescued you from the pit?" she smiled not unkindly at the dwarf "it was my brilliant leadership and fighting skills that got is this prize. I always sort it for us in the end eh?" Val lengthened her stride as Bumli stopped in his tracks, his chest deflating like a burst ferret's bladder.

Edin shrugged at all that was going on and went to help Ansafety with getting Trig up and to the horses. The Herald moved his attentions from his nail and took a large gulp of what was left of his water and followed in. He was feeling something he hadn't felt about this quest before and couldn't place it, something felt different, an unresolved tension amongst friends.

Act 4 Scene 11: Sled Led Fled To Raise And Wed The Undead

Ringost sat next to the Apprentice in his ramshackle wooden sled, he was unable to sit still, giddy as he was at the journey they were about to make to the sacrificial site. Ringost cracked his whip, and the zombie donkeys began to pull the sled. "You know we had a perfectly decent coach and some alive horses we could have used? Would have been a lot comfier. Quicker too" stated the Apprentice matter of factly.

Ringost dismissed him with a wave "yeah but it doesn't have the same poetry" he concluded showing off the oversized gap in his knowledge about poetry just as a zombie donkey released some zombie manure for the sled to bump over. Ringost also seemed unbothered with matters of getting to places at a speed above a slow crawl.

A couple of powerful shire horses dragged the king and queen in their mobile cage alongside the sled, Ringost gave them a sarcastic wave. The renowned warriors of the Thunder Hooves tribe had to frustratingly keep slowing the pace of their mighty steeds as Ringost had made quite clear he was to be at the front of this travelling party.

Behind them the orcs, sorcerers, trolls, goblins, boglins, sell swords, wraiths, skeletons, evil elves, twisted barbarians, skeletons and thingies rode their steeds; a variety of horses, zorses, undead horses, seahorses, hogs, bats, big cats, penny farthings, giant worms and gophers. The Take The World On Foot tribe of warriors panted hard as they tried to keep pace as best they could, regretting their motto and oeuvre.

Further back still the aggressive Comeandaveago clan warriors from the Mancunian region were having a row between themselves over who got to ride the biggest horse, despite the fact all their horses were essentially the same size.

Ringost was awash with excitement at the journey taking place and seemed drunk on the deeds that he had lined up to take place. Ringost looked over his shoulder into the back of the cart and gestured at all the various orbs, scrolls, idols, standards with strange and often slightly crude drawings etched onto them "these my young Apprentice are our sacred objects. Items only the truly powerful and enlightened understand, that can create so much change, so much control" he seemed to shudder with delight, the Apprentice regarded the items he was pretty sure one was a pez dispenser with a skull painted on it.

"And these are our people" Ringost opened his arms wide at the travelling party that surrounded them. The Apprentice was starting to wonder if Ringost was actually maybe still drunk from the night before. "These good orcs, they're our people. These skeletons, you know they are our people. These people…" at this point, the Pants Halfway Down mercenaries ran past with their backsides out as they chased a hedgehog "…I'm not sure these are our people. Did we really hire that lot?" Ringost shrunk into his seat, the wind somewhat taken out of his sails.

"We hired them as they were cheap" the Apprentice clarified "we're going to war teamed up with the people who put in the lowest estimate" he stated as the party carried its slow ass journey on to the sacred scarred and scary sacrificial site.

Act 5 Scene 1: The Desolate Forest Whittaker

The party had ridden in an enveloping silence across the fields from the cave. An atmosphere the Herald couldn't put his finger on, but some kind of fission, a blister which if popped contained a harmful puss.

The team began to ascend a long drawn-out hill, a dark foreboding tree line beginning to take up the view in the distance. "Is that what I think it is?" Ansafety muttered to Bumli at the back of the pack.

Bumli spat "aye. The Desolate Forest." He wiped the back of his arm on his brow "we won't be going through that though. Surely?" his question hung in the air unanswered.

The posse rode on harder in silence the dark twisted trees now taking up most of their view in front. They could see the details now, the smooth dark bark of the trees, vines choking around the trunks, jagged branches like dislocated limbs daring anyone to try and force their way through. The dense foliage seemed to dampen all the sound so that no noise escaped from the darkness of the tree line a dangerous silence awaiting whoever entered.

A switch seemed to flick on in Trig's head and he spoke what all were thinking "Val" he cleared his throat "you don't mean to take the route through there? We're going around right?"

Val did not break her stare from straight ahead "windchimes, an' some ghost-based carvings some yokels have carved into the trees. It's no more haunted than the gord at my side, though I'll grant you that's had some evil spirits in it in me time" she had little humour in her voice for the first time the Herald could remember "we've a necromancer to beat, a world to save, it's the quickest most practical way and that's all there is to it."

Bumli grumbled "you never said we'd be coming this way."

Val turned and looked at him "yes I did love, very specifically at the start of the adventure, I had the map out an' pointed to it an' everything. We've always been coming this way, its unavoidable."

Bumli looked into the middle distance "I don't remember that bit, I must have been doing some Dwarven meditation at the time" he muttered. After a pause, Bumli swallowed down hard "Still, this way? After last time? Have you forgotten or do you choose to ignore it?"

Val's seemingly limitless patience snapped "Forget?! The thing that knocks on me minds door every morning for the whole of me waking day?! No, I've never forgotten. Not for a moment. The only surprise is the moments where I'm distracted for a little while an' don't have that thought coming to invade me 'ead space."

Ansafety was alongside Val now and Trig began to speak in measured tones "we are sure of your pain Val; we all carry it. But…"

"… No Trig" Val cut him off sternly but with no aggression towards him "this is the route I must take, I'm not sure it's the path for ya. For any of ya. I can get this done an' still have time to give that undead geezer a kick in the ghoulies. Kill two ghost type things with one sword" She kicked her horse up towards the reach of the trees "Sometimes you choose a route an' other times a route chooses you…" Val's voice tailed off.

Ansafety pulled her horse up keen not to enter the tree line "what do we do?" she said to the rest of the party with doubt in her voice. Edin, Bumli and the Herald pulled up alongside her, Val further riding into the distance, not giving a single look back.

Bumli scratched his beard "I think she believes she can slay demons, maybe we could have helped her, but I don't think she wants us to help her, it's her private battle. She's even tougher than she is stubborn, I think we have to let her do it. I think."

Edin squinted at Val's figure as it disappeared into the darkness of the forest "it is the within that pulls at Val, only she can decide how that defines who she is and what she does." No one in the party had the energy to groan at the cliched quality of Edin's words this time.

The Herald pondered for a while before speaking up "I still have a quest, with the world resting on it, and Val and that blade are the best chance that quest has." He let out a long breath as he thought "I'll go after her, we made a pact at the start, and we stay together. Thanks for your help friends, I'll do all I can to look after her" the party decided not to point out the folly of the Herald thinking he could offer any protection for Val. They solemnly nodded and quietly wished their foppish companion all the luck he could find, they knowing what awaited.

With that the Herald spurred his horse on knowing he faced a greater set of unknown unknowns than he had known in this known life of his.

Act 5 Scene 2: Popping Out For A Spell

The Denizens of evil, or good as they saw themselves as no one really wants to admit they're the bad guys, despite all the snake motifs they wore and poisoned blades they carried, pulled up to the ritual site. A dust plain with no visible plants or animals populating it. The area had an unnatural quiet and stillness to it, though it helpfully had a brown sign to help tourists find it, which spared the riding party Ringost's terrible map reading skills.

The plain was dominated by a circle of dark, uneven, unnatural stones some metres high that called out to the skies, fingers grasping up from the ground to pull down any who came too close. Truly this was a place where foul magic occurred and where hippy orcs came to get drunk in the summer.

Ringost immediately made himself busy causing a flurry of activity with his instructions for the unpacking and placement of items that had been brought with them. "Not there, no there, there!" He barked pointing in a vague spot unhelpfully as some raiders carried a heavy plinth and orb device.

The Apprentice got the feeling Ringost wasn't especially sure what he was doing but was using the time-honoured management trick of where he had a gap in his knowledge making up for it with bossiness at underlings. He was getting particularly aggressive with a goblin, which being smaller that Ringost gave him a sense of superiority, over the setting up of an object that the Apprentice was pretty sure was a kettle for the brews when they got a break, if they got a break, he realised now he should have asked about the breaks.

The Apprentice placed a number of scrolls on the makeshift dais that had been built nearest the largest of the stones in the circle, a large, jagged tooth of granite. The Apprentice couldn't help thinking the dais was a little wonky and was sure he saw the mercenaries walk off with some parts of it when they couldn't figure out where they went in the construction, the instruction papyrus that came with it being as much use as a spell of swift farting in a firestorm.

The Apprentice shuffled over to where Ringost was gesticulating wildly at some goblins and cleared his throat twice "So… err… we're really going to do this are we?" he asked, eyes focused intently on a spot on the ground.

"We are!" Ringost declared breezily not reading the tone of the Apprentice at all, intoxicated as he was on the macabre operations that were taking shape. He was paying particular attention to one of his acolytes to make sure he hung the barometer evenly off one of the stones.

The Apprentice shifted the weight in his stance "you know, it seems like a lot of potential destruction and loss of life. We don't want to spill any blood do we. I mean if nothing else, think of the administration that will cause when we're in power" he addressed Ringost.

Ringost wrenched his view from the large object being carried into the centre of the circle "what?!" he snapped and then paused to consider the question some more. "Look, the current rulers, who see what they have as the natural order of things and are not open to challenge, have been allowed to carry on without any question or resistance for too long. Orcs and trolls have been persecuted and forced underground as 'unnaturals', ogres made to carry out heavy manual labour without being asked what they want to do with their lives, wizards outside their cosy circle chased away as they fear their capabilities rather than seek to understand them. Their rich friends given more and more perks to get wealthier whilst the poorest suffer more and more at the bottom. The gap between those at the top and those at the bottom is wider than a constipated dragon's release turd" he patted the Apprentice on the shoulder "is it right that we allow that to carry on just because 'that's how it has always been'? We're in a unique position of being able to make a real difference. We're not setting out to hurt anyone, whether we do, or not depends on how they react to our course of action. They just have to meet our demands…"

"… and by meet our demands, you mean bow to you?" the Apprentice cut in.

Anger flashed across Ringost's face but then passed like a gentle wave as he recovered himself "It's a little more than that wouldn't you say?" he asked rhetorically "though yes, I must see their loyalty. They've nothing to fear if they show me that and follow my rule, which will be considerably better for all of them."

With that, he went to inspect a magical standard that sagged on its staff as no wind passed through the plains, thinking he was going to have to employ a couple of Orcs to continually blow on it to give it a little life and drama. The Apprentice remained rooted to the spot, churning his thoughts through his head.

Act 5 Scene 3: Searching The Forest For A Cure

Val and the Herald had been riding in the eerily quiet dank of the forest for some time and it was starting to eat at them both, though neither said anything about it. It was slow progress as each step was potentially hazardous for their horses as the floor seemed perpetually uneven, moving even, with unknown dangers under the leaves that covered it.

A sullen silence hung over Val and the Herald felt it best not to interrupt her and to disappear into himself for a while, a place he was very comfortable visiting given his levels of narcissism.

After what seemed like an eternity of pushing through branches that tried to grip and pin them, the Herald decided to pluck up the courage and break the silence. Slowly he moved through the bracken, but at a pace quick enough to get him level with Val.

"Windchimes an' puppets" Val spoke before the Herald had even had time to think of how he was going to break the standoff.

"Huh?" was all the Herald could muster by way of response.

"This place" Val nodded her head at the dark surroundings "they call it The Desolate Forest, its nothing of the sort, it's just kids putting windchimes an' strange puppets in the trees to spook any would be travelers through it. You'd have to be pretty cowardly to be scared by any of it" The Herald hoped Val hadn't seen that frightened flinch he'd done at a particularly scary looking puppet of a llama in a tree earlier.

The Herald took in the gnarled trees, the jagged limbs of the branches and shuddered. He decided to just go for it "What was that with the others before we came in?" he asked, slightly apprehensive to what the response he may receive would be.

Val didn't deflect her gaze from straight ahead "that?" she gave the Herald a quick glance "that was old uneven ground being walked over. Still, you've stuck with me this far, you've every right to know."

She shifted uncomfortably in her saddle, she seemed older and less full of vitality than the Herald had seen from this big ball of life "Our party used to be one larger, 'Will the Unwise', an ironic name, he was as smart as a whip that un, brain nearly as big as his heart, he was a proper leader, not like me. Anyways, there were rumours of this haunted forest, populated by some dread demon, locals put a good coin on whoever could purge it. Too much of a challenge for me to resist, Will advised against it knowing a little bit of the real danger of a demon, but my gang, my rules, so I laughed off his fears, I laugh most things off, regardless of how funny I find them." Val caught a leaf as it fluttered past from a tree above and inspected the veins in her fingers as she turned it over.

The Herald didn't interrupt the silence that was filling the gap. In time Val had seemed to gather her thoughts again "So we all came to this supposed Desolate Forest or The Wooo Woods as we called it" She smiled thinly at the memory "we were laughing all the way through making jokes about the windchimes being rejected from Ansafety's next song an' all that. Truth be told we weren't expecting to find no demon an' even if we did, I'd yet to come across something I couldn't chin. We carried on a couple of miles into the heart of the forest, not too far from the spot you an' me are in now" Val seemed to grimace at a point only she could see.

"Anyways we set up camp an' were around the fire, drinking, being bawdy, the usual affair, when a cold chill envelopes us all, a weird stifling air, though nothing that scares us too much, we've all been on too many adventures an' seen too many things to be easily spooked. We readied our arms to face whatever came, there was this great crackling sound, but we couldn't put a direction on it or see it, but something started to attack us, seemingly from all sides at once, a strange shape, forever just at the corner of our vision. We protected ourselves as best we could, but it was beyond our comprehension, we threw everything at it, swords, axes, arrows, holy water, foul language, cups of tea but it just seemed to pass through the air as if it didn't really have any physical form. The crew were gettin' nervous, an' this just seem to embolden the thing."

Val took a couple of breaths "Even I realised it was time to admit defeat, we didn't have the right tools to defeat this thing, I shouted at me lads and lasses to fall back while I tried to hold the thing off, if I could get any kind of bearing on it. Will didn't think this the best move an' went in front of me to try and protect me from it an' well... he didn't make it out, but we did. We paid a price that day, how we paid a price" again Val fell silent and patted her horses head affectionately.

"We never really talked about what happened, we should have but... you know..." Val trailed off.

The Herald attempted to gather his rushing thoughts "and now?" was all that came to him.

Val's booming voice was but a whisper "well now I have this I guess" she looked at her new blade. "That an' a determination to right some wrongs that I should have done long ago. Let's hope that's enough. I wouldn't feel right if I didn't try though."

The Herald pondered the story he'd just been told "you know, if we fail against this demon then we fail the world, the necromancer and the King of The Undead wins."

Val smiled at the Herald "well we best not fail then eh love, I've a reputation to uphold" she said as brightly as she was able. The Herald was glad he was situated in a woods with a lot of natural spaces to go the toilet as he was suddenly feeling very queasy about his prospects.

Act 5 Scene 4: Midday In An Imperfect World

Ringost's moods were shifting unpredictably from elated to dark and pretty much experimenting with spending a minute or two with all the points in between. It was obvious the ceremony and the thought of power excited him but there was something else in there causing him to be sullen and withdrawn at times. It was like living with a teenager who had a date that his parents kept trying to advise him what to wear for it. As the time of the ceremony got ever closer, the more his moods seemed to swing ever further.

The Apprentice had been doing his best to mainly stay out of his way, halfheartedly pitching in with the various ceremonial duties he didn't really understand and wasn't entirely convinced were achieving anything. Mostly though the Apprentice just watched, trying to understand what was going to happen and when and what he would need to do. He watched and he waited.

The hired swords seemed in decent enough spirits and given the presence of the undead, indeed they were literally and figuratively. They seemed to have no problems with what they were undertaking looking forward to a new world, in which they had a greater stake in, or at the least a more chaotic world from the one they understood now. Either way they were chasing something different, regardless of if it was actually better or not, it would be different from what they knew. The Apprentice suspected with some though it was just they were looking forward to some violence, though he wondered if they had thought fully through the implications of The King of The Undead and the true meaning of violence that came with his return.

In the middle of the stone circle, the giant mirror took up prominence. The Apprentice could see Ringost regularly looking at it longingly, or was it with fear, or both? This was the spot where The King of The Undead would make his entrance and begin his reign, the Apprentice knew how he felt about it, he was as apprehensive about what he would see in the mirror as that time he work up as a teenager and could feel a spot so prominent it was positively throbbing. Though he also thought he'd had too many thoughts about teenage years very recently and these thoughts were not offering him the distraction he craved, if anything could. The Apprentice watched and waited staring at the mirror.

The king and queen remained quiet in their cage; a passive dismay etched across their faces. The Apprentice toyed with going to talk with them, or even maybe just setting them free and ending this thing one way or another, at least he'd made a decision if he did that. He wasn't sure what either would really achieve, it's not like if he set them free they had much chance of getting very far given they were in the middle of a desolate nowhere surrounded by the undead and bloodthirsty mercenaries. Somehow he suspected outdoor survival skills wasn't the royal pairs forte, they probably had servants to do that for them.

And yet despite everything he felt some loyalty to Ringost and his plans and the potential opportunities they opened up. However much he turned everything over in his mind, it seemed any kind of coherent answer remained forever just out of his grasp, like the goblet of water you put on your bedside table after a heavy night's drinking.

Things had become incredibly serious of late. The hour was getting ever closer, he just hoped he had some certainty when it arrived. In the meantime, he just watched, and he waited.

Act 5 Scene 5: A Demon With A Blade

Val and the Herald dismounted their steeds in where Val reckoned the heart of the forest was, or at least it was a spot of significance for her. Very little light permeated from the branches above meaning a constant gloom hung over them. Val had become quieter and quieter, withdrawing into herself, her natural effervesce and humour vanquished for some time, the demon already taking a heavy toll. The Herald felt it was like questing with a different character in a different tale.

The Herald had much he wanted to say, wanted to ask, but knew he would gain no answers at this time. He was as aware as ever of the encroaching time limit for the necromancer and the imperative to stop that, and yet somehow it seemed an irrelevance when he saw how Val was. Still if it came to it he would have to leave Val to beat her demons on her own whilst he would try and stop the necromancer, his undead army and the King of the Undead on his own. Some chance he had of that, still he'd get mentioned in songs, very short songs with a very brutal sudden ending, but songs, nonetheless.

Val was pacing a short space of flat damp ground muttering to herself and practicing sword sweeps with her new enchanted blade. Suddenly she paused. The Herald froze too, he could feel something himself, the air was different, cold and yet bone dry, it became harder to catch his breath, to think clearly, there was a tension clawing at the pair, gnawing at him, wanting him to surrender up what made the Herald himself, the Herald felt disorientated like he was watching himself out of body from an unnatural angle.

Val remained utterly still but the tensing of her muscles betrayed her. There was an unnatural popping noise and quicker than the Herald could follow, Val had the blade of Ow-Chee drawn and in a defensive stance. "Now would be a good time to prepare yourself Herr love" she said quietly through her teeth. The Herald raised his sword but even the magical glow of the blade failed to penetrate the gloom.

The Herald saw some shape moved from the corner of his eye, it closed on Val in a heartbeat, who got her blade up just in time sending purple sparks flying from the impact to be immediately extinguished on the moist forest floor. The sulfurous tang filled the Herald's nostrils making him feel slightly nauseous.

The Herald spun to trace the dark shape but as quickly as he moved, he couldn't ever fully see it, it always remained on his periphery somehow. Luckily Val seemed to understand its movements better, and the presence was more than happy to go for Val rather than the confused Herald. Again, she clashed with the shape sending more sparks into the sky, a moment of strobing light. Again, the shape vanished. It wasn't the attacks that were causing the Herald the most dread it was the creeping silence in between them.

Once more the loud pop and the shape was back hurtling at Val, who seemed to manage to counter this time raining a number of blows which filled the forest with an unnatural purple light. The blows were delivered with such speed and ferocity that the strain could be seen in Val's face she continued to bring the blade many times at the demon, strikes that would have felled nearly any creature in the land. Another huge stroke that must surely have finished the fight and yet everything still felt wrong to the Herald, there was still a wrongness burrowing under his skin.

Val sagged and panted for breath; the effort having taken a toll on even her. Physical might proving no advantage in the fight with this creature.

Before the Herald could ask Val if she was OK, there was another pop, despite her fatigue Val rallied at speed and sent a blow of huge power at the shape coming for her. The shape vanished and yet still the electricity in the air remained.

Val slumped realising she couldn't beat the nightmare, she let go, let go of everything, the hurt, anger, guilt, grief and fear. She accepted who she was, all the good she had done and the brightness that she brought into this world and that was enough, it always had been, the demon may take her, but it wouldn't, couldn't take that. The air popped again, the Herald sprinted to get close to Val but the shape in the corner of his vision was quicker, the demon was on Val now and she was defenceless, the Heralds heart dropped and yet the demon vanished again on reaching Val, who remained motionless.

The fear eating ever into the Herald told him the creature was still present and was looking to finish this, if it had given up on Val for now, then it would come for him. He raised his sword and spun left and right to see if he could see anything, he held the talisman of obsidian tightly, knowing deep down its powers were useless against this foe's evil ways.

The Herald jumped in shock at a sudden noise from his left "Herald love" Val spoke quietly "Let it go."

The Heralds eyes still flicked left to right, adrenaline pumping as once more the tension in the air built "of what?" he managed to blurt out.

"Everything. Your fear, anger, insecurities, all the bad stuff love" the air was crackling and the hairs on the Herald's neck stood up rigid, he kept his sword high its light offering him a narrow view of the forest.

"Who says I have any of that?" the Herald snapped back at Val tension coursing through his body.

"Are you kiddin' me Herr love? You've got a massive spud snack on your shoulder" Val came back with conviction in her voice then in a softer, soothing voice "Herald, drop it. Remember all the good that you are and that you do. That's enough love an' it always has been." Finally, Val said "empty your mind."

The Herald still remained in a battle stance "having zero thoughts in one's head comes a little easier to you than me Valkyrie" he replied to Val with an attempt at dark humour. And yet Val's words cut to the Herald, what good was it doing trying to fight this thing, why go out on a negative mindset when he could remember happier times and have them coursing around his mind as he passed, if we was going to go out he was going out thinking of the best times.

Trembling he lowered his sword, leaving himself totally open. Once more the loud pop, closer than ever to the Herald and moving at him at hellish speed, he could feel foul air on his face, sweat poured off the Herald and yet he kept his thoughts away from darkness, into some memory of a more content, peaceful time somewhere else. The shape was inches away now a horrible hissing sound firing at him and yet it washed over him and when he opened his eyes, he could see nothing but an empty dark forest, which seemed now to hold much less fear.

He finally exhaled and was aware of an arm around him pulling him close, for the first time in as long as he remembered the Herald relaxed and accepted the comfort of an embrace. He turned to Val "what happened? We were done for surely?"

Val smiled at him, she seemed to grow in size back to the towering hulk he first met "demons are drawn to the negative, real or felt. You can't simply slay some demons with force, but you learn there are more powerful things that they can't beat. Those are the feelings to hold onto, the rest you have to let go or the demon always gets you."

The Herald allowed himself a smirk "careful there Valkyrie you might start to sound like Edin."

Val allowed herself a small laugh as they started walking towards their horses "you see" Val stated, "I think this has proven what I told you all along, never to overthink a plan!"

The Herald was too weary to state he hoped that wasn't her plan for defeating the King of The Undead as the two saddled up ready to finish this adventure they had started together.

Act 5 Scene 6: Clearing

Val and the Herald had been riding hard through the forest for some time, leaves kicking up wherever the hooves landed, the horses fed off the urgency of their riders. The pair had lost in their own thoughts for much of the journey but with each pace further the mood between the pair lifted further, Val's seeming to rise much quicker with her natural exuberance regained.

The Herald ducked under a low branch and brought his steed level with Val, he now felt ready to engage in conversant again. "we're going do this aren't we?" he part declared breezily feeling lighter than he had for such time after he had encountered a demon.

Val chuckled "shouldn't go tempting fate love" she mock admonished "I met Fate once actually" the Herald's eyebrows once more got acquainted with his hair line at this revelation "they told me they hate people doing that, still nice geezer and a mean pooh sticks player" the Herald looked at Val for a while, but could not work out if that was true or not, but he'd learned long since to doubt her at his peril. "But yeah I'm gonna teach that necromancer that its good manners not to go raisin' Kings of The Undead. Plus give him a little extra bopping for interrupting my nice day out in the pub."

The Herald put the depressing, one donkey village pub that he had met Val into the back of his mind, she must have meant some other drinking establishment, literally every other drinking establishment other than that one, personally he preferred the idea of fighting the fearsome undead ruler of the beyond to having a drink in that place again. "There is something that I've been meaning to ask?"

Val brushed her hair out of her face with her gauntleted hand "what's that love?"

"Edin… Tarquin… whoever, a barbarian built for dishing out large sword and fist-based justice, when we got split up in the dungeon, at the point where I needed him at his most violent, he went all weird and very wordy on me, he'd no interest in fighting, but I was worried he may start wielding poetry at the enemy" the Herald blurted out, unsure if he'd remembered it right now he tried to vocalise it.

Val laughed heartily her voice bouncing around the forest "and if he had written some poetry it would have been more lethal that his blade for your enemy I can assure you of that much!" Val managed to get her laugh under control, the Herald kept alongside being patient with waiting to hear the story.

"OK, you deserve to know the fable love" Val suppressed another chuckle behind her gauntleted hand "so Edin Skullsplitter was… is the immensely powerful barbarian of legend. The strongest fighter in the land, yours truly excluded obviously. One day he decided to take on the feared quest to kill Hopkins the powerful blue lightning dragon of the South. Seems he misunderestimated the power of this dragon, or more pertinently how much booze he'd drunk before going to fight it."

Val steered her horse up a slope where the trees appeared to thin, and more natural light filled the riders welcoming faces. "Anyways, he came a little unstuck to say the least and was mortally wounded in this encounter, the dragon wasn't looking so pretty afterwards either for that matter."

"So, he escaped its lair with what little life force he had remainin', got on his horse an' got it to ride like the wind to the great mystic, the only one with the potential powers to spare his life. He got there just in time, she took pity on 'im, given he bought plenty of her home brew an' biscuits down the years, an' she performed the 'I'm gonna git your soul sucka' spell on him. This spell essentially steals the lifeforce from the nearest human an' transfers it onto the wounded. This nearest human just happened to be Tarquin Sate, a philosophy, poetry an' general student of the tedious. Problem was he wasn't so up for giving up his life that easily thank you very much. So, the spell was semi successful Edin didn't die but nor did he get the life entirely to 'imself. Ever since then Edin an' Tarquin have been having something of a timeshare fight over the body. You get me Herr love?"

The Herald seemed to simultaneously shake and nod his head "err... not really, that doesn't seem to make any logical or even theoretical sense to me" he laughed lightly at the thought.

"That's magic love!" Val cackled "never seems to make much sense if you think about it too much, but it can be bloody convenient if you're in a spot an' you can't think how to get out of it though!" She chuckled some more "the great an' not so good writers and story tellers throughout the land have always used magic to get themselves out of some plot inconsistency they've created for themselves. Feels like a cheat to me, but then, I'm no writer."

Val paused to think over the conversation and became a little wistful for a moment "when we've sorted this necromancer an' any of his dead boring accomplices out, I need to make it up to Edin, an' all the others. Me stubbornness can override me manners and considerations sometimes. It's a failing I need to work on."

The Herald wondered if he should point out it was more a case of if and not when they defeated the necromancer but thought better of bringing the mood down. "They're friends Val, friends get it and forgive the things we get wrong."

Val nodded and encouraged her horse up the increasing gradient of the hill, the full light of daylight now winning its battle against the forest "sign o' the chimes!" Val called back to The Herald.

"The what?... Oof!" The Herald rubbed his head after it clattered through some low hanging wind chimes in a tree, a tinny, irritating melody played behind him and in his head.

Val made no attempt to suppress her laugh "told you, bloody kids and wind chimes!"

****

Sometime later whilst still riding, the Herald dexterously took in the alignment of the sun in the sky and made some notes in his journal. He drew his gold compass and looked at how the shadow of the sun cut across it, he made a few more notes in his journal, as he used these notes to try and calculate how long they had before the ceremony started. Finally, he pulled his calendar out of a pocket in his cape and checked the dates, he tried to control his horror as he saw today was the day of the ceremony. He kicked his horse on further.

After hours of hard riding across overgrown fields the Herald became aware of a persistent noise he couldn't place but that grew louder, it slowly dawning on him that it was the sounds of wings. Large powerful wings of some vast creature. Frightened he looked around seeing in the distance behind them some form of horse with the plumage of a large bird closing on them "Val I think we're in trouble here!" he bellowed to his companion.

Val spun to look where the Herald was pointing, no doubt there was a rider in amber hued armour riding a winged stallion who was about to pull up alongside the two riders. The rider lifted their visor revealing two violent coloured eyes underneath "What ho Val how goes it?" the rider called out to the Valkyrie.

"Oh, hullo Lady Derbyshire how ya doin'? Sally the fourth is in fine flying form today isn't she?" Val called back happily.

The Lady Derbyshire kept her steed level, her wing tip a matter of inches from the riders playing merry hell with the Heralds fringe. "What japes are you up to today my friends?"

Val laughed "ah you know, gotta kill a necromancer before he raises some old pale, stale male in chainmail who will destroy the land, not the first time that's happened eh? They make some habit of it no love?"

"Ooh sounds a blast!" the winged rider called back "need any help?"

The Herald was about to shout back "Absolutely we need all the help we can get, we're badly out of our depth, outnumbered and if this necromancer succeeds the world becomes a dark place for all for eternity. Oh, and just to mention something I was keeping quiet so as not to panic anyone, but the ceremony starts today and that winged stallion you're riding looks really fast."

But before he could get that out Val said "nah!", to be fair the Herald probably have gone with something shorter. "We got this, plus I'm sure you're really busy love."

"Well yes, I'm nipping to the shops as I'm out of artichokes so you're not wrong on that front Val. Shame I'd have been up for those larks otherwise. Ah well, the next time." Lady Derbyshire dug into Sally and the beast beat its wings hard and began to climb higher into the sky "Good luck my fine friends, artichoke sandwiches at mine later if you fancy!" she called, her voice getting quieter as the distance between them grew and with that she disappeared into the distance.

Val spun in her saddle to see the Herald giving her daggers, currently with his eyes but he had weighed up the pointy thing on his belt option too. "Y'alright there love?" Val asked cheerily.

The Herald was incredulous, but he'd got used to being in this state and was getting better at articulating why he was feeling this way now "firstly, why did you turn down the help? We're massively outnumbered and some winged support would have been of real use."

Val was about to answer the Herald's rhetorical question when he continued "secondly, flying steeds are a thing and we're not using them? We could have completed this quest days ago on one of those things!" he stated barely keeping his ire in check.

Val shook her head bemused "Ah yeah, they're quick but you don't get the sights, smells and feel of the land that riding gives you, so I don't bother with them as a rule. Plus, those things guzzle fuel, they eat a lot of hay so they're expensive to run and you can spend an eternity waiting for your turn to get on the runway in the village and hit the sky. Besides, flying rides feels like cheating, it makes things far too easy."

The Herald went to pick all the holes, contradictions and the bits that were plain nonsense in Val's answer but decided against it and just made a mental note to add it to the list of quest gripes he'd been keeping in his diary.

If he survived, he'd write them all up and give Val a presentation on them, maybe see if he could get a wizard to rustle up a laser pointer spell to add emphasis.

Act 5 Scene 7: It's Been A Hard Day's Come Together For Tomorrow Never Knows?

Bumli crouched over the pile of twigs and leaves he'd assembled, grumbling to himself as he fingered his tinderbox. He was having mixed results in getting this fire going, mixed somewhere between bad and awful. Trig snapped out of staring into space and watched his companions' troubles, he drew some powder from his robes and began an incantation as a small orange orb grew in his hand. Bumli saw Trig starting his wizardry and quickly intervened instructing the wizard that he was ok. Unfortunately, Bumli leaned too close and singed his beard on the nascent fireball in the enchanter's hand.

"Not a bad spot" declared Ansafety, who was unusually attempting small talk, leaning back on her pack and taking in the view of the distant hills that stretched beyond the horizon. She produced something long and wrapped in leaf from her tunic and nibbled absent mindedly.

"Verily!" confirmed Edin as he scribbled furiously in his journal "natures beauty challenges our senses with its wonder, can we ever truly capture its ephemeral essence with mere words?"

"You certainly blinking can't!" Bumli muttered loudly eliciting chuckles from everyone in the group who wasn't called Edin. He tried to settle himself in front of what he convinced himself was a roaring fire but was more a single twig that had caught up offering as much heat as the legendary Holy Underpants of Thendor. He detached a flask from his pack that contained some of Blessed Bean's incredibly strong ale, he took a huge slug which sent his eyes on a journey wandering in different directions, before passing on the flask.

"These rolling fields" Ansafety spoke into the sky "remind me of when we fought those Bear People in the fields of Sally" she reminisced, a trace of a smile on her face.

"Bear People pft!" spat Bumli with mirth "the usual village missing their idiots. Idiots in some manky fur. One of them was wearing a rug I swear!" this observation always raised a laugh from the group, and it got a light version of its usual response this time.

"Truly a bunch of minor ursa major" Edin rumbled his bass chuckle "Ansafety got two with one arrow if my memory is not a false prophet?"

Ansafety gave a mock bow with her bow. "All in a day's work. What was that spell you used Trig?"

Trig again snapped back his distracted gaze from the distance "hmmm... spell... oh yes, I think it was the great flamey pole cat familiar I summoned on them, seemed to chase them away. I think it got stuck up one of the bear people's trouser leg." The group laughed as their focus was drawn onto the now more like an actual fire fire which was starting to crackle.

As the sun began to set behind the distant hills, Bumli decided what this group needed to get a bit of fire in their bellies, perhaps close to literally, was some of Jen and Berry's Insanely Lethal Firewater (the poison sign on the bottle really should have been a giveaway to any purchaser that this was not a drink to be trifled with, nor make a trifle with). He pulled the small flask from his tunic and took a swig, he held onto the ground to make sure he remained sitting upright as the powerful liquid sent a conflagration through his body. It wasn't an unpleasant experience. He took a quick extra measure for good measure and passed the flask onto Edin.

"So…" Bumli cleared his burning throat several times "we've made our point now, we should probably go and help Val and that foppish twerp she's got herself lumbered with. She'll be needing us?"

Silence hung over his proposal broken only by the slow snap of the fire sending embers chasing into the sky. Edin changed position to sit a little more upright. "Using the balance of probabilities, I err towards the reformation of our erstwhile companionship, though fear that may be doomed to recycle the same outcomes of what our fellowship ever did leaving us in some kind of loop of repeated behaviour, so that consideration weighs heavily on my decision making adding melancholy notes of doubt." Bumli went to argue with Edin, then agree, then paused as he realised he had no idea what Edin had just said, though he suspected Edin probably didn't either.

The fire danced in Ansafety's large eyes flickering in the uncertain wind. She took a swig from Bumli's flask knowing the damage it would do to her perfectly in sync elven body. Her voice was a husky whisper "you heard Val. She isn't one for subtext or mixed messages, she doesn't want us. So what? We chase her around like we always do following her whims and choices pretending it's all OK. Like we've done for years, how has that worked out? I think that path is done and there is no sense in retracing our steps along it." She traced a spark from the fire with her fine fingers "If we hadn't ended this quest" she glanced at Trig "this quest could have ended us."

"We've taken part in much more dangerous adventures" Bumli countered "and our own skins haven't usually been much of a worry, not when there are people to save and rewards to be taken." Bumli looked like he was going to continue but dropped to silence.

"I've never been worried about my life!" Ansafety said fiercely. She took a breath and continued in a calmer tone "but it's getting harder and riskier for us all. Val has been in these situations, and *she* has always got out in one piece. I'm sure she will be OK, I'm sure…" Ansafety rubbed her temples "Besides, she doesn't want us there we all heard her. Its best this way."

Trig who had remained quiet throughout poured some blue-coloured dust into his hand and blew on it. A colourful azul pattern of a neon donkey floated into the sky before disappearing. "Val is rash and says things she may not mean and means things she does not say, though maybe this time it really is a quest only she can take. Who knows where her and our adventures finish up. Though right now, I am a tired old man who needs his sleep. Things often look different after a good sleep I find."

"Good luck getting a good sleep in that twig frame Bumli is calling a shelter!" Ansafety managed to force some levity causing the group to chuckle.

After a moment, silence once more befell the group as they all considered what they now were and what would and could be, doubt seemed to be the answer to every question they asked.

Act 5 Scene 5: Time To Undie

The Orcs were on their tea break, amusing themselves with an impromptu but elaborate shadow puppet show onto one of the large sacrificial stones. One particularly big and tough looking Orc proving adept at doing silly high pitch squeaky puppet type voices.

The Apprentice pulled himself away from the (more entertaining than it had any right to be) show and took the decision to go and see the king and queen. He'd grown tired of Ringost's mood swings and inconsistency, which worsened as the day shortened and the ritual neared. He thought maybe seeing the royal couple would, he wasn't sure what it would do when he thought about it, but he felt compelled to do it anyway.

The Apprentice made his way through the bustle of the preparations throughout the stone circle and stood a few feet from the cage of the imprisoned couple. On getting this close he realised he didn't actually know what to say, luckily the queen started the conversation for him.

"This how you saw it playing out when you got involved in this plot?" she stated flatly eying Ringost grinding a variety of items with a pestle and mortar in an agitated fashion. Ringost then began wrestling with a centipede to try and find its thirty fourth toe to cut off, for the very specific spell he was working on.

"I didn't get into necromancy thinking it would all be pulling ghouls out of the hat and sawing sirens in half" the slight hint of ire in his voice giving way to resignation. "I knew the dark powers inherent in the magic, but thought maybe something extreme, or the threat of something extreme might change things a little, rebalance some of the world. Too many people sat feasting in ignorance whilst others go hungry, but this…" his voice trailed off as he took in the site, where mercenaries shared crude jokes in the face of the building evil and dark invisible forces crackled.

The queen's voice dropped an octave and sounded like a soothing balm to the Apprentice "You've not made all your choices yet, nothing is done, whether you change path is for you to decide, what can you live with? What do you want to live with?"

The Apprentice continued to stare into the distance, churning those words around in his head. His hands went to his mask, and he took a step towards the cage before catching himself and stopping. "You know what really gets me about necromancy?" he asked the royal couple, who were sideswiped by the strange question "it's the grossness of all the spells. It's all 'eye of this', 'giblets of that', 'slimy bits of the other'. Does no spell just require a little coriander a bit of water to thin the potion? It's like they're almost willfully trying to be disgusting to prove some kind of point."

The king and queen exchanged bemused glances as the Apprentice carried on "they must know it looks disgusting and like the kind of thing a villain would do." He turned to walk away and called back over his shoulder "I'm in control as I ever was. I fully know what I'm doing" A statement that may have carried more power if he hadn't clearly stubbed his toe on a rock as he made it.

Act 6 Scene 1: I Spy Something Beginning With 'D' for Danger, Decking, Daggers, Dancing, D'Enemy, Death, Dunces and Delicacies

The Herald edged cautiously along the cliff edge keeping himself low. He sucked on the oyster flavoured lollipop (a treat in high company, but certainly an acquired taste, generally acquired by having no taste) he'd saved himself for the moment he was feeling most stressed, and after a number of scrapes which had come close, he'd decided now was his most worrisome. He could see in the distance a strange orange beacon glowing into the encroaching dusk.

The Herald lowered himself down to lie flat on his stomach. He produced his spy glass and focused on the direction of the eerie light.

The Herald sucked harder on the lolly and his legs began to involuntarily jangle. About a league away, he guessed, he wasn't actually sure how far a league was, but this felt like it could be that distance, there was a stone circle with a lot of figures engaged in frantic activity. The fires and braziers they'd lit accounted for some of the light, but it was the strange, disconcerting glow in the centre of the circle that vexed the Herald the most.

He looked at the clear night sky above him, he reckoned they had about an hour before the ceremony would begin. "Val? Val?" he hissed between his teeth behind him.

"What's that love?" Val boomed as she stood directly behind the Herald, the shock of which sent him spitting his lollipop out, about a quarter of a league he guessed.

Once the Herald had reset his heart to a more reasonable one hundred and twenty beats per minute and put it back in the right part of his body he hissed at Val some more "will you get the cripes down before someone spots you?! And try to keep your voice lower than an ogre that just stubbed its toe on a Manticore!"

Val wasn't sure why the Herald was so highly strung, but she just shrugged and sat beside him. Stealth wasn't really Val's thing; she was about as stealthy as a particularly large oak Treeman in clogs (and have you ever tried to fit all the roots of a Treeman into a clog?! It takes quite the shoehorn) on a cobbled lane attempting to catch an ant by surprise and whack it one it on the chops with its branch.

The Herald began to trace his spyglass around the light, to see what the immediate dangers he could see on the site. The views made for grim tidings, he puffed out his cheeks and began to whisper to Val "OK, this isn't going to be easy. He has a literal army with him and that's just the figures I can see and some of them are big, bigger than trolls by the looks of it. It's going to be extremely tough. But I think we can do this, if we get to the East of the preparations without being spotted then that route in looks less guarded, we take out the sell swords there quietly, we might be able to get at the necromancer, put him down and the main threat is over. Who knows with him out of the equation the army may give up, if not we'll have saved the world at the cost of our…"

The Herald cut himself off startled as he was by the sound of horse's hooves pounding, he quickly got himself up into a fighting crouch before it dawned on him the hooves were coming from behind his position as Val passed him winding her way down the undulating slope next to the cliff face. She had her sword in her hand and shook the jar she carried on her horse, which woke the sprite in it up who began to do a passable attempt at singing Ride of the Valkyries, a song by Ricardo Wagnerleaf the elf musician.

The Herald found himself jumping on the spot in frustration. Realising he had to help out his lacking in subtlety friend, he raced to Flighty Joanna. Through his superior riding skills, he soon found himself down the slope and level with Val, she smiled warmly as he pulled up alongside.

"Val!" the Herald spat "what the blinking heck are you doing?!" Somehow the Herald avoided using appropriately ruder words. "This is suicide, our only chance was stealth!"

Val continued to beam at the Herald "nah love, that army, they're just an inconvenience, we'll get through 'em easy!" she began to laugh. Despite himself the Herald began to chuckle, then chortle then finally a full belly laugh erupted from within. "Now you get it Herr love, the ultimate destination for us all is always certain death, so remember to enjoy the journey!"

Now on the flat their speed picked up and they closed the gap from the cliff to the stone circle by half, they kicked their horses on some more. The army the Herald had spotted had raised the alarm and began arranging themselves in a stance to meet the charging riders.

Along with this threat, the members of Ringost's army that had been hiding to the side of the canyon began to pour out of the rocks to complete the trap. Large Orcs with their clubs and axes and smaller humans in ornate armour with their short ornate swords and also joining them, a collection of have a goes with whatever weaponry they could cobble together, one appeared to be wielding one of his shoes as aggressively as he could, the intimidation somewhat lessened by him shuffling along painfully as his bare foot kept stepping on small stones.

The Herald's face set in alarm but Val just turned to him and gave him an encouraging grin as the two released their battle cries as they charged towards whatever fate awaited them.

Act 6 Scene 2: Do Not Disturb My Friend, He's Dead Tired

Ringost pulled a red powder from a pouch felt it between his fingers then put it back in the pouch, before pulling it out again and throwing a little over his shoulder, he didn't want any bad luck right now. The Apprentice was at a preparation table just a short space away trying to find ever inventive ways to look busy to the necromancer. Standard employer/employee behaviour really. Unfortunately for the Apprentice this was his first job, and he hadn't had the practice from a low paid job of maximising pretending to do work whilst actually doing a little less than the bare minimum you could get away with.

An elegant square shouldered warrior bustled her way through the preparations, her polished steel armour reflecting the dim light giving her the appearance of having an eerie aura. "My Lord, we have the enemy engaging us from the West" The Lady Heaveho said matter of factly, her use of the words 'My Lord' dripping with barely contained contempt. Standard employer/employee behaviour really.

Ringost broke into a wolfish grin "finally. I was beginning to get offended no one was trying to stop me." He took out an eye of newt from his robe and popped it into his mouth, beginning to suck "and the troops we placed for this eventuality have engaged?"

The mercenary nodded, her face set somewhere between annoyance and amusement. "Of course, we've engaged, we're professionals in these matters!" The Lady Heaveho was irked at Ringost's micromanagement, standard employer/employee behaviour really. She regained her composure and continued "so far the battalion are about holding them both back."

Ringost spluttered and spat out the eye he was chewing on hitting a passing Orc, who made a mental note to saying nothing to Ringost directly but to report the incident to the OR (Orc Resources) Department. Standard employer/employee behaviour really

"Both?!" Ringost asked incredulous.

The Lady Heaveho was really struggling to hide her grim mirth by this point. The Apprentice had given up the impression of work (though it was hard to tell the difference) as he listened in intently to the conversation. "Yes, My Lord, one is some unknown streak of goblin urine warrior in fancy clothing with a five gold pieces haircut, the other is Val Kerr." The warrior took pleasure in watching Ringost's face drop as she slowly drew out the last name.

Ringost's not especially deep voice rose an octave, making him sound like the Old-World insect singer Bee Gee "Reinforce the line with troops from the South and East, get those damned am dram Orcs there and Ant as well, throw some sharp goblins at their head if you must. She. Does. Not. Get. Through."

The Apprentice sidled over to Ringost "something to worry about sire?" He asked cautiously.

Ringost flattened his rumpled tunic and then flattened his even more rumpled hair, regaining his composure. "No… no. Not at all. The troops will crush them with malevolent ease and even if by some miracle… well that won't happen. Plus, I have more than a few contingencies up my spacious wizard's sleeve." Ringost told the Apprentice not sure if his words were true or not but wanting to give him the words he thought he wanted to hear to keep him compliant. Standard employer/employee behaviour really.

Ringost turned and fixed his gaze on the mirror in the stone circle that was beginning to draw in the orange light it had previously been spewing out, he allowed himself a satisfied half smile "Besides, it's all academic really, they're too late."

Act 6 Scene 3: A Giant Punch Up

Val swung blades, fists, feet, knees, elbows, teeth, nose, buttocks and any other part of her body she could use in an offensive manner (and Val knew a lot about offensive manners) to push her foes back. Wherever her smite landed, her enemies either fell smited, or thought better of getting a smiting and performed the fighting maneuver known as 'getting the hell out of the way of the smite.'

Even the Herald was performing admirably, seeming to draw strength from Val's presence. He nimbly dealt out blows to the opponents below his horse using his elite riding skills to ensure he kept the horse moving and the enemy engaged on his terms.

"I think we may be getting the upper hand here Val!" he bellowed above the noise of the battle "not much longer and we will... pants..."

"I'm not surprised you're panting love, its thirsty work this brawling lark eh? I could murder a goblet of ale after I've murdered this ailing goblin." She laughed as she bopped a fighter on top of his helm sending it retracting into his body like some kind of upright steel turtle.

The Herald wheeled his horse closer to Val, slashing at figures as he did so "no, I mean pants, as in we're in trouble here" he shouted, darkly pointing to the horizon as numerous, men, women, scary creatures, and other thingumajigs came into view over the ridge including some towering figure who was easily three times the size of Val.

Val paused dropping the goblin she was holding by the lapels (clearly a goblin from the 'Always Well Turned Out' battle clan). "Hmm… that… yeah a minor inconvenience I grant you, shouldn't cause too many problems."

The Herald rolled his eyes and shrugged, he had long since learned that Val treated any kind of obstacle as something to be bashed around the head until it ceased getting in the way, even if it was a weather hazard blocking the route, the Herald could not shake the memory of the punch up Val had attempted to have with some snow, with mixed results, though Val was determined to call it a draw. The Herald took a quick swig of his fire water and prepared for the next wave.

The troops they were currently battling began to disengage, retreating up the slope so as to look brave with the reinforcements arriving, pulling a mixture of aggressive and taunting faces, except for one goblin that hadn't quite mastered it and merely looked quite wistfully cheery.

The two armies, if Val and the Herald counted as an army, eyed each other up over the ground that separated them. A moments silence eerily drifted over the battleground between them as the two parties tried to psyche each other out. After an extremely short period, Val's boredom threshold gave way "bugger it!" she started her battle cry, shook her theme music up to start it over again and kicked Power into action. The Herald sighed and encouraged his horse at the foes his quietened battle cry betraying his nerves.

The opposing army took their cue, and an enormous roar filled the valley as they rushed down the slope to engage and tear these interlopers apart.

****

The Herald could feel his stamina (not exactly a selling point to start with) wane, his arms were growing ever heavy and most of his effort was now going into avoiding the blows that came his way. Joanna was doing sterling work, kicking out at would be assailants. Val seemed, if anything, to be gaining more power no matter what came at her; soldier, Orc, Troll, Tree Beasty, lost tourist asking for directions it soon regretted its life choices and thought it should have spent more time with the career's advisor at school.

At this point, the giant, who had been taking great interest in the battle without getting involved decided to play his hand. In a couple of loping strides, he was up to the Herald, tree trunk club raised above his head. He emitted a foul bellow that caused the ground to tremble before bringing his club down hard. The Herald managed to steer his steed out of the path of this strike, but the shockwave of the impact dismounted him and sent him sprawling. Val disappeared in the dust the attack kicked up.

"Val?!" The Herald yelled into the debris where she had previously been riding. "Val?!" again he called with some dismay in his voice.

The Herald was literally yanked out of his search by rough hands on his shoulders, as the enemy soldiers pressed home their advantage on the distraught and now totally vulnerable warrior.

Act 6 Scene 4: Hanging On The God And Bone

The orange glow in the centre of the stone circle grew initially imperceptibly duller, it was much like the energy saving candles some people used in their homes. It seemed to draw what light remained of the day into it, leaving the area bathed in an impenetrable blanket of black. The moths had long since flown off deciding this mirror had promised more than it was now currently delivering.

The little light began to pulse at the rate of a resting heartbeat. Skeletons lit makeshift torches around the stones to provide light away from the faint glow.

Ringost's brow dripped with sweat as he concentrated on the potions and powders he mixed in front of him. The Apprentice passed Ringost a goblet of what he hoped was slightly stagnant water as the necromancer took a brief pause from his incantations.

Ringost drained the goblet, though much of it had dribbled down his chin, and faced the Apprentice, a dark fire playing in his eyes "get the king and queen prepared at the sacrificial stone, it is nearly time" he said darkly, his voice on the brink of cracking. The Apprentice swallowed hard and managed to nod.

The Apprentice weaved his way through the cadavers and mercenaries who were keeping alert for trouble and insuring messages were passed between all sides of the sacrifice area. Some seeing their supervisor Ringost was otherwise engaged had taken to just vaguely looking busy whilst surreptitiously doing the Daily Chain Mail crossword they had hidden in their codpiece.

Reaching the cage housing the royal couple, the Apprentice produced the heavy rusted key from his belt and turned it slowly in the lock. He began leading them to the centre of the stone circle, the king and queen taking in the amount of soldiers around them and realising escape at this point was an impossibility.

The closer they got to the pulsing of the mirror, the more uneasy the Apprentice felt. His skin prickled and a nausea tried to overcome him, forcing his to swallow down bile, it reminded him of the last time he had a night out in Ye Olde Wetherspoons. He pointed the monarchs to a large granite rock with a pair of manacles hammered into it. He locked their legs into the cold metal and pulled the key out.

The queen opened her mouth to speak but the Apprentice spoke first. "Some extremely dark things are going to happen here, things that will defy explanation. Right now, you have no chance of escaping, and the world will fall. Ringost is using a lot of power and at some point, everyone's attention is going to be on that glowing mirror and what is happening in it. And then, then, well it's all up in the air really, I guess."

And before they could process and reply to the Apprentices words he hurriedly turned, went to put the manacle key in his belt but somehow seemed to miss and dropped it close to where the royals were chained before he purposefully strode off, thoughts weighing heavy on his mind.

Act 6 Scene 5: What Would You Do If I Sprang Out Of Tune?

The strong arms kept the Herald pinned on his knees. He was surrounded by a bloodthirsty gang of bandits, mercenaries, Orcs, Goblins, furbies and scary things that had yet to be codified. They all seemed happy to have captured one half of the duo who had just administered quite the smackdown on their number.

The Herald stared at the hard stone ground taking in the pattern of the rocks, incapable of rational or helpful thought. He'd failed. Failed Val. Failed his gang, no his friends. Failed the Kingdom. And failed himself. Again. He felt numb through those he'd let down, his only redemption seeming to be that he wasn't going to have that long left to dwell on it too much.

A large pair of fur lined rusted armoured boots came into his vision. Slowly raising his head, the Herald found himself staring at an enormous Orc, his elaborate albeit crude and spiky armour covered his intimidating physique. A large flat blade hung to one side of his waist, a large leather-bound book of prose to the other.

The Orc cleared his throat "you have a noble countenance" he paced from side to side "no that's not it" he muttered and then seemed to quietly practice a vocal scaling before settling on the deep bass to speak with "that's it" he smiled to himself. He returned in front of the Herald "you fought well" he growled "but now your quest ends, it's nothing personal and apologies for the savageness of this, but we get paid in good gold for any intruders heads we return to that little idiot who thinks he is running things over there. And gold can fund a lot of plays and useful Orc endeavours."

The Orc drew the large blade and tested its weight "I really don't like the barbaric nature of it but you humans and your nature…" he rested the sword on the Herald's shoulder, the cold of the steel pressing his neck with its icy touch "it's a hoary old cliché, and I'm loath to use it, but any last words worthy adversary?"

A few notes of regret played across The Herald's mind, the people he'd let down at first, the time he'd wasted, the family he'd wished he'd communicated better with, but then better things, the thrill of the adventure he'd been on, the laughing he had with his newfound friends. Just friends. His mind cleared and he looked the Orc in the eye "do what you have to, I've known what it is to be alive now, death is just the natural full stop to all that" he declared sounding much braver than his stomach told him he was feeling.

The Herald felt the coldness leave his neck as the sword was drawn back but the killing blow didn't arrive. "Not so fast eh green love?" a familiar voice came from the rubble as a covered in dust beige Val forced herself from the rocks "you think this is the first time I've been stoned?" she asked rhetorically.

The Orc paused a fraction with his blade and with Val that was fatal, she'd closed the gap to him in the blink of an REM eye and knocked him to the floor. The rest of the troops that had been stunned by this appearance gathered their senses and sprang back into attack mode.

The Herald used the confusion to roll free of the arms and pick up a sword to give Val all the help he could offer, which truth be told wasn't a huge amount of help to her. He spun through a number of attacks and got level to her "I thought you were…"

Val cut him off with a hearty laugh "you think some oversized eejit with a stick is going to put me down? The day that happens is the end of the world love!"

The Herald was going to point out that it was nearly the end of the world but thought better of it as A. it would be churlish B. it would also be pedantic and no one like a pedant and C. he was too busy avoiding having pointy things stuck in his body at the time being for churlish pedantry.

The Herald fought with renewed vigor seeing that he had a friend back with him. Val just fought as she usually did with happy and violent abandon. They were cutting swathes through their would-be assailants. The large Orc, Allt was bellowing at his troops and some trolls to take up a defensive position just back from the fighting. A dark robed figure hung back well out of the way making gestures of casting spells but not actually doing anything of note, still he really put a lot of effort into his show and that would probably have bumped his combat grade up to a D minus at least.

The Herald parried a blade designed to cut him in half and countered with a punch to the stomach of his attacker who lost his balance due to his trousers being halfway down. "Val that massive Orc giving the orders, the one that was about to take my handsome head and ruin my haircut, I reckon if we take him down the others may break."

Val nodded "sounds a plan love, lets teach him the error of his ways with a thick pointy ear". The Herald got behind Val as she began her charge that sent foes scattering like rag dolls as she powered through them. No matter the opponent when Val reached them they were soon divorced from terra-firma. The Herald knew if he stayed behind Val he'd be OK.

Val's seemingly unstoppable force met the immovable object of Ant who had stepped into Val's path and sent her flying back, just missing the Herald as she went, with a well-aimed kick to her chest.

Val's distance from the Herald now left him exposed. Very exposed. Using his blade and quick feet he dispatched the first attackers who came at him, but once more was overwhelmed by numbers who dragged him back in front of Allt.

"I'll get it done this time fair Valkyrie" he called mockingly across to Val who was rising to her feet somehow not taken out by the kick of the giant. Despite that, it was no use she was too far away to close the gap, she wouldn't be able to save the Herald this time. The Orc swung his blade with monstrous power at the Herald's neck.

A loud "clank" echoed around the battlefield as the Orcs blade was catapulted from his hand mid swing by a preternaturally well aimed arrow.

A blue glowing apparition of an enormous turkey appeared in the midst of the Orcs sending them scattering as the turkey breathed fire bolts from its beak. Truly a strange summoning, it wouldn't be an easy one to explain at the tavern afterwards, it was kind of a 'you had to be there' sort of creature.

A new sound filled the air as what sounded kittens having their souls tormented but turned out to be bagpipes floating across the skirmish. A squat powerful figure not wielding any trousers but wielding an axe as well as the bagpipes as a weapon, and a giant of a man made of pure muscle met the scattering troops sending them reeling.

A further storm of arrows rained down pinning the warriors who held the Herald who used his satchel to smack the Orc holding him away "not just for putting things in Em Queue" he muttered satisfied with himself and then wasted no time getting to his feet, retrieving his sword and helping to press home this new advantage.

The Herald fought his way to the twin fighting piston of Bumli and Edin. "I've never been so pleased to see a trouserless dwarf and a Barbarian that carries a book of poetry as a weapon. Good to have you back Edin!" he called cheerily. The hulking barbarian merely grunted in return as he sent two unfortunate soldiers catapulting into the rocks several feet away, with a lazy flick of his wrist.

Where the warriors' blades didn't clear a gap, the storm of arrows from Ansafety or weird oversized plodding exploding creatures of Trig took up the slack. The enemy began to get confused by all the random angles their supposed quarry were coming at them with.

Despite being vastly outnumbered, but not out violenced, the heroes began to thin out their opponents fighting wedge. Allt, the largest of the Orc who had tried to take the Heralds head twice, waded his way purposefully through the retreating forces cutting a direct line to his, shouldn't still have a head on his shoulders prey, stepping in front of the Herald Allt declared "sorry old chap, its manifest destiny that you go down and your wealthy four tet brings us some high-quality theatre productions."

The Herald looked at Allt and smirked, he raised his sword to his head by way of salute and took up a fighting south paw stance "OK green meanie, let's see how good you are on your lonesome tonight."

The Orc waited no longer, his patience long since gone with a howl he lunged forward with a swing of bone slicing power, the Herald's superior reflexes meant he easily ducked and came back with a nimble lunge that the Orc was only just quick enough to sidestep.

This move enraged Allt further who came at the Herald with a combination of swings from varying angles and heights, the Herald using all his skill and nous to dodge and weave all the attacks, every sword stroke from his opponent falling short. With a frustrated roar the Orc raised his sword above his head in two hands and brought it down hard at the Herald, the Herald stepped back but the Orc had cunningly moved him, so his back was against the cliff rock face, seriously curtailing his room to maneuver. The Orc swung again at chest height, the Herald having no option but to parry, the strength of the incoming attack sent pain shooting up his arm and the Herald staggered back into the rock face.

"I don't think You've too many of those left in you, do you?" Allt sneered with a gloating tone, he decided now was the time to finish it as he raised his sword for a final swing.

"Between a literal rock and a hard place methinks!" the Herald managed by repost as he raised his stinging sword arm. Allt swung with all his might, the Herald used the last of his energy to actually go towards the blade and duck at the last possible moment, feeling the wind of the swing on his back. The Orcs hit smashed into the rock face, the impact dislodging debris sending it falling down onto the Orc knocking him out cold.

"Rock on!" the Herald declared in celebration, inordinately pleased with himself. "Hey guys!" he called to his companions who were elsewhere in the battlefield "I just made a pun after taking out my opponent, why don't more people in life do that?" Despite being in the middle of a fight the heroes still found time to look disgusted at the poor state of the Heralds punning.

The giant had been watching the tide turn on his comrades from a tree he'd made into a makeshift stool. He decided now was the time to get involved again, these midgets couldn't be trusted to win a battle. He uncurled himself from his perch and in a couple of enormous strides he was coming up on the biggest source of the loss, Val. "Will you kindly stay down this time please? I don't want to have to inflict any more pain that I have to. Well maybe a little more pain." He snarled and raised his club.

Val went to adopt her most defensive stance which could best be described as 'violently windmilling' and chuckled "I'm sorry love, but do you think you 'it me for any other reason that I let you?" she eyed the giant up and down, mostly up "never been 'it by a giant before, curious to feel what it was like was all."

The giant bellowed his rage flecks of spit showering the land like putrid rain, he swung hard, his club missing Val by some distance, his next few swings proving similarly unsuccessful. The giant paused and sighed "so it has to be like that again, does it?" he raised the club above his head ready to splat Val under it once more or knock her down with the shockwaves at the least. He brought the vast club down, Val watched it carefully all the way and at the last minute jumped onto the club and seeming to defy gravity ran up the branch to the top and kicked Ant in the head, knocking what little sense he had out of him. Val dismounted the giant with a surprisingly graceful leap and roll, a couple of goblins forgot themselves and applauded the athleticism, one holding up a '9' scorecard that he carried on him for reasons difficult to fathom.

"I guess you weren't too big for my boots!" she shouted triumphantly "hey whadya know, the Herald was right about that punning!" again her team looked non plussed at best at this idea.

With the giant and Allt down the remnants of armies seemed down on the idea of further punishment from these aggressive combatants and took up a formation of legging it in the other direction.

With a satisfied nod Val put her sword in its scabbard "the joys of taking names, and some of those were really 'ard to spell" she said to herself. She turned and found herself in a semi-circle of Trig, Ansafety, Bumli and Edin. The Herald decided it best he hung back and see how this one played out.

The two parties awkwardly weighed each other up like some drunken halflings at the last dance of their school ball. Eventually Val broke the silence "come 'ere" she opened her arms wide after a short beat Trig made his way to Val followed by Edin. Bumli and Ansafety exchanged glances and followed joining in a large embrace. The Herald followed and through his arms round his companions from behind, being pleasantly surprised when he felt a squeeze back.

"I've missed you guys" Val said quietly to the group before quickly following up with "I'm sorry, I was an idiot and selfish, thought the best way to resolve my problems was on me own, I was so wrong" she smiled wistfully "but by not trying to beat me demons or beat meself I've beat me demons and freed meself."

"Ha getting soft there Valkyrie" Bumli came back surreptitiously dabbing his moist eyes with his beard from within the huddle.

The group separated and Val took in Ansafety and her singed barely there trousers "still insisting on using that oversized battle standard eh Ansafety?"

The elf looked nonplussed but that might just have been standard nonplussery from her. "As I said, it's a sacred battle standard" The Herald followed her gaze and saw atop her thirty-foot pole was a lightning damaged tapestry with the image of some elven nobility being served grapes with a look of disdain on their face as if the server had just violently broken wind. The Herald assumed the disdainful look must be an elven thing.

The Herald disengaged, "what now? We don't have much time at all."

"But we still have enough time" Val countered "told you I'd got the timing all planned bob on" she declared convincing no one "let's finish what we started together" the group nodded their agreement at this plan before joining Val in an elaborate high five routine which the Herald attempted to participate in but having never seen this act before either just looked like he was mainly attempting to sway away flies.

Act 7 Scene 1 And You Will Know Us By The Wail Of The Dead

The mirror in the middle of the stone circle seemed to draw ever more light into it, despite the pitch black of the night, it was somehow sending out more darkness sending visibility at the site to near nothingness, despite the placement of the torches. The previous pulsing glow had become more of a defiant unnerving ember. Shapes moved across the mirror in a macabre dance, never staying still long enough to reveal their true form. Even the skeletons looked a little uneasy with it all and they were skeletons and not easy at expressing unease on their skull faces.

The Apprentice had reached peak queasiness, his stomach was knotted (and not one of those simple knots they teach you early on at scouts) and his breathing came in uneven lungful's. The moon was minutes away from the point in the sky where its light would hit the mirror. Ringost had ordered the tallest skeleton, Florence, to attach his special stone to the top of the mirror and this was beginning to glint in the moonlight.

The Apprentice reasoned that maybe there was time yet, he crossed to the dais where Ringost stood in some kind of trance, repeating some unfathomable mantra, he guessed it was the words of the ancient Shaman

Scatmanjohn and drinking from a goblet which even from this distance the Apprentice could detect a copper tang.

As he edged closer to Ringost the Apprentice grew more and more unsteady. He got within feet of Ringost, all feeling around him had an innate wrongness he couldn't understand. He looped his hands in his belt by his dagger before finally plucking up the courage. He spoke "master?" Ringost didn't reply merely staring ahead repeating some obscure chant into the night.

The apprentice put his hand on Ringost's shoulder "master?" he asked more firmly this time, something seemed to snap in Ringost, and he broke from his chanting a clarity passed across his eyes.

"What is it my young apprentice?" he asked, an uncertainty in his voice.

The Apprentice took a breath and decided to go for it "we have to stop, these are dark forces beyond our control, we should not, cannot inflict these onto the world. We've proved our point; the land now knows what we are capable of. This world will now engage with us on more even terms I'm sure. We've already won without having to go any further. We currently look very much like the bad guys but with a bit of spin maybe we can get a few people on side? There have been less plausible redemption arcs in the history of this world, in a few years you might get on Strictly Come May Pole Dancing and the public will take you to their heart when you show your poor dancing."

Ringost slowly nodded a relief etched across his face "I… I… you're right, we can now try and make a world for all, we have the weight of our potential to get engagement from those that rule. To be a little honest I was getting a little creeped out by some of the grossness in the spells and…" Ringost was cut off as a commotion broke out. The nearest skeletons charging towards the king and queen who had reached the dropped key and broken free of their chains and were making a royal rumble.

"What is this?!" Ringost's eyes darkened over again "no my friend, it will not be over until we teach this world what real power is!" he stated as dramatically as he could and then began taking up his chanting again as the shapes in the mirror began to writhe ever more frantically.

Act 7 Scene 2: Charge Included

The Six huddled by a rock staying out of view as much as possible, reluctantly in Val's case. Trig was doing his best to see if he could do his bit to help by searching for his mind for any rock impersonation spells, but alas could only think of a pebble spell which added nothing to their camouflage other than a cherry on a cake type effect.

The Herald trained his spy glass on the scene that was unfurling at the stone circle a hundred yards or so away. "Well do I not like that. What is going on in the middle of that stone circle, I do not like one bit." The Herald involuntarily shuddered and raised the glass back to his eye "there is something happening near that strange dull light source, if source is the right word, I can't tell what is going on but if I didn't know better I'd say it looked like a fight?"

"Lemme see!" Val answered eagerly, always up for watching a dust up and yanking the spy glass from The Herald and in the process nearly dragging him off his feet, attached as the spy glass was to a chain around his neck "Luckily this is my area of expertise love, that's definitely a fight!" Val turned to the Herald and released the spy glass to give him a little more oxygen. "Well Herr, you're one of us now and probably the brains of the outfit" Ansafety scowled, Trig was staring absently into the distance and Bumli looked wrongly slighted "What are our tactics?" she gave him an encouraging smile.

The Herald pondered a moment "hmm, well the East still looks our best bet, if we can get close maybe we can make the most of that commotion to sneak up and then we could try and take out the last remaining guards before quietly closing in... charge, we charge full frontal, throwing windmills and taking names and let them worry about us. The patented Sir Kevin of Keegan and Val Kerr approach!"

The gang looked at each other, wide grins plastered across their faces.

"I mean, we'll probably all die. But it'll look pretty spectacular. We might even get a decent song made out of it for us." The Herald concluded with uncertainty in his voice.

Act 7 Scene 3: When Many Tribes Go To War All You Can Do Is Play For A No Score Draw

The many various mercenaries and skeletons were wrestling with the king and queen to subdue them. Despite their vastly superior numbers, they were under strict instructions that no royal blood was to be spilled at this point, the king and queen had no such worries hacking with the swords they had picked up at anyone that got too close, it was a bit unfair really. Slowly through this shuffling dance of swords they were edging towards the edge of the stone circle and potential freedom, they just had to last out a little longer and the moon would pass.

A muscular mercenary in burnt orange lizard scale armour turned to Ringost his arms stretched open "without force, those two chinless wonders are getting the better of us little dictator, the communication line where we were fighting off the invaders has gone quiet, not a good sign. I'm done with all this nonsense" he sheathed his sword and said something out of earshot to his troops who also began lowering weapons and turning their backs.

The Apprentice took in this development with curiosity, turning to Ringost to see if he would realise the folly of now continuing, he was losing the will of his soldiers and with that a lot of his muscle. Ringost's eyes seemed to glow red under his hood, he spat out an incantation and swept his arms around him. Slowly all the fallen skeletons and undead creatures began to rise, snapping limbs back into place, or tucking them in their belt for convenience if they were chopped off. They moved in on the king and queen and mercenaries surrounding them.

"You need more faith in my powers sell sword" Ringost growled nodding at the lead skeleton. The Skeleton approached the mercenary leader and with a sly grin across its face slipped a blade through the side of his armour, dropping him to the ground. A crackle and snapping sound appeared from the mirror and out stepped a skeleton in burnt orange lizard scale armour, it bowed its head at Ringost. The Apprentice looked on aghast and guessed this ghastly new Geist spell Ringost had used was as the mirror was now working to full power.

Across the battlefield more skeletons turned their weapons on the stunned mercenaries, each time a skeleton replacing them stepping from the mirror. "The dead, so much braver and so much more compliant" Ringost declared with a sneer of satisfaction, his voice betraying a dark crack.

"Yeah and they can match you for personality" The Apprentice said out of Ringost's earshot.

The skeletons were less worried about the impact of a royal sword and overwhelmed the royal couple "hold our royal guests please my loyal subjects, I would like to see this one out myself." Ringost ordered like the megalomaniac he was becoming.

The vast ranks of the undead man/bone handled the king and queen to the sacrificial alter that lay at the front of the mirror. The Apprentice was making numerous calculations in his head and none of the sums coming back were in any way palatable, his hand once more rested on his dagger hilt as he weighed up his options.

Ringost drew the curved blade from his belt and made his way to intercept. The moonlight was beginning to hit the stone that rested at the top of the mirror, Ringost could have cut the king and queen down there and then and raised the King of The Undead, but like all tyrants and little men he couldn't resist a final gloat. "Your *loyal* subjects failed you" he took great delight twisting the second word "and now me and The King of The Undead shall rule these lands with our… my loyal troops. A new more interesting reign begins."

The king was too resigned to his fate to speak but white hot anger flowed through the queen's veins, she had many things she wanted to say; about how The King of The Undead would clearly betray Ringost, how a land of the undead was no land at all, how she pitied Ringost's pathetic existence, how death of the innocent was not the way to address the inequalities he felt, eventually she settled with "Ringost you pillock" which about seemed to cover everything.

Ringost let out a maniacal cackle that the Apprentice had caught him practicing in the mirror a couple of days back, he had to admit it came across more effective outdoor in the moment as it echoed off the great stones. He raised his blade to strike down.

"Not a good idea Necro love" a commanding voice boomed across the circle as Val stepped from behind a pillar, five other figures emerging from other stones their heroic charge proving something of a nonevent given that everyone was too busy with the royal pair to have seen it. Val and her team had weapons drawn and a determined glint in their eye, Val spoke again "I've a few bones to pick with you."

Act 7 Scene 3: If The King Comes At You, You Better Not Miss

The six heroes (as it feels safe to now call them) began closing the cracked land towards Ringost, the Apprentice the king and queen. Ringost kept his view alternating between the royal couple and these interlopers closing in on him. His skeleton troops formed around him. The Apprentice was trying to stay as detached as possible wondering how this one was going to play out.

Val drew the blade of Ow-Chee the low light of the mirror still managing to reflect its powerful albeit extremely short blade. "I would hope you know what this is love?" she queried "in case you're even dumber than ya look, and that would make ya bloomin' dumb, this is the end to your madness. So, you can surrender now an' that should lessen 'ow much ow I dish out."

Ringost hesitated for a moment and then something flickered across his eyes, and he began his default laughing mode again. He nodded at the massed undead ranks around him "elite troops but rendered in unlife, they don't feel pity, or pain, or remorse, or fear and they absolutely will not stop until you're dead."

"Sounds like the tax office to me." Bumli muttered to Edin causing his barbarian friend to boom out a laugh that echoed across the dark battlefield.

Ringost ignored this slight as best he could, he was going to look like the competent leader in front of his troops. "You think they worry about that shrunken blade you hold in your hand?"

"I bet it's not the only shrunken thing around here!" Ansafety went with a surprisingly crude repost causing the others to snigger once they'd got over the surprise of that type of joke coming from her.

Ringost shook his head slowly "joke all you want but the laughing ends now. Some would argue the laughter stopped the moment you took the unwise decision to start this little adventure." He stated, perhaps pertinently. He reached into his robes "we outnumber you about ten to one, maybe eleven, I haven't done a proper count, plus I've also taken a few extra precautions, anyway," he produced a small draught of liquid in a bottle and drained it in one. All the veins on his body began to glow with a sickly dark green colour and his eyes took on a ridiculously intense stare.

Val's patience for dialogue was long used up, though in truth she'd only gone in for it in the first instance as she wanted to look professional in front of the royal couple. "What say we show this dead head how we do things upstate old new world style!" she stated spinning her blade.

"Thought You'd never ask" Bumli rumbled swinging his axe of repeated vengeance a sudden roar came from the six as they charged the few feet between Ringost and his cadaver army.

The clash of steel on steel bounced around the canyon, the undead seemed to draw power from the mirror close to them making them a far tougher proposition than they initially seemed, though this was a minor inconvenience to Val and her gang as they chopped their way through their opponents, though the undead had the power to regenerate, which felt a little like cheating to the Herald, and this was slowing their progress somewhat.

Val had the advantage of the blade of Ow-Chee and being Val, she was proving particularly effective making the undead dead dead, rather than semi dead dead. Ansafety was nimbly weaving out of blade strikes and pin cushioning her opponents with arrows. Trig kept close to her sending the undead scattering with his sonic hedgehog blasts and explosive powders. Bumli chopped through assailants with ease every time his axe landed it went into jackhammer mode repeatedly smashing into the victim, splintering bones. Edin had grown tired of using his sword to grind the bones of his foes and had instead taken to hitting the skeletons with another skeleton he had picked up, occasionally he seemed to pause as if he had some ideas for musings in his book.

Despite the lethal effects of all the fighting techniques come mindless violence, it was taking them time to get to the king and queen.

Ringost was finding the whole dance highly amusing, but it was taking up his time, time he needed to complete his spell raising the undead and he needed his concentration elsewhere, but if he risked turning from the battle for even a moment to complete the ritual one of those intruders could potentially get him off guard.

It was time for him to end this himself, he had the powerful, combustible spell of the Stare Oid running through his body and an anger to cut down these would be heroes who dared mess with his plans and dreams. "Apprentice, you Jeremy and Nancy" he nodded to his large skeletons bedecked on black armour with a flame motif "watch our royal guests, their time is incredibly imminent!" The Herald nodded unconvincingly, ignoring the tautology.

Ringost took a few steps towards the fray, the giant barbarian spotted him and made a fast and loud bee line towards him his sword again in his hand he swung at Ringost who simply took a step aside at the speed of a heartbeat and gave a swipe with his arm that sent Edin hard into one of the sacrificial stones. Ringost was struggling to suppress the joy at the power currently coursing through him.

The ever-watchful elf had seen what happened and unleashed a deluge of arrows at Ringost, who with his newfound speed simply stepped aside, the arrows pinging off the stone behind. The last arrow he caught and snapped in half in an act of supreme showing off.

The elderly berobed warrior flung shapes of squirrels that exploded on impact with anything. Unfortunately for Trig that anything was anything but the necromancer who always seemed one step ahead of his aim. Ringost made an elaborate gesture and a shockwave travelled out from where he stood sending his attackers off their feet.

The dwarf and the foppish one were still standing and dodged through the skeletons that came at them to get to Ringost. The human reached first his light up blade clearly visible in the darkened battlefield, but his precise rapid blows didn't even get close to landing. The Dwarf joined in with his hefty axe, but neither could get near to landing anything telling before Ringost overpowered them and flung them back painfully.

Ringost felt a massive force thud into his back sending him staggering forward, he gathered what was left of his senses, which wasn't a lot truth be told and realised one of his own skeletons had been flung at him. He looked around and saw the massive, imposing figure of the Valkyrie but four sword lengths away looking extremely angry.

"Hurt me friends would ya? Time you were taught the errors of your ways you little wet fart!" Val closed the distance to Ringost in a heartbeat, she swung the knife of Ow-Chee, but with the potion inside him Ringost was too fast even for Val. She came again ever persistent until Ringost lifted her and threw her hard into a stone pillar.

Ringost smiled and dusted his hands off unaware of the cliché he was enacting. He began to turn figuratively to the task of the sacrifice and literally to where the king and queen were when he noticed out of the corner of his eye the shape of a large angry armoured lady getting up.

Ringost shook his head, no living thing should have been able to shrug off the attack he just inflicted, surely. He had no time for any other thoughts as the Valkyrie had closed the gap swinging rapid blows again, he was just managing to avoid them, he ducked under the next attack and grabbed Val by the throat and again flung her into a stone with all the power he could muster, a sickening thud greeting his ears from the impact.

Happy with his work Ringost began making his way to his undead minions. His black heart nearly leapt out of his mouth at the voice that came from behind "oi! Short arse!" Val was rising despite her clear pain "I can do this all day and all night, most weekends and a few bank holidays too, if I have to!" she growled. Her colleagues were gingerly getting up and forming beside her, seeming to be stronger within each other's company. With Ringost's attention on fighting he had neglected re-raising the undead and he was looking a little light on soldiers.

They began closing on Ringost utterly focused on bringing him down, Ringost wasn't sure how much longer the potion would last and began backing up "Apprentice hold them!" he yelled, the Apprentice looked at Ringost agog and stayed routed to the spot. "Fine then you weak fool. My loyal followers take them down" the handful of skeletons that remained moved to engage Val and party, a silent murderous mass who were dashed on the rocks of our heroes who were in no mood to be stopped by a bag of bones and continued to make ground on Ringost.

With panic in his eyes Ringost fled to where the king and queen were with his two remaining skeletons. He snatched his sacrificial blade off Jeremy and grabbed the struggling queen by her wrist.

"You tried, and frankly it was a much better effort than I expected from such a collection of oddballs, but you were always destined to fail!" he called across the battlefield as the sound of fighting died down, the heroes could see what was about to happen, but all were too far away to do anything. "You may have had superior arms, but time was always the enemy and now it has run out for you and this land". The gang looked on helplessly as Ringost raised his twisted blade to strike the queen.

Act 7 Scene 4: I Get By With A Little Help With My Friends When Fighting Yelping Fiends

Ringost brought the blade down hard and direct towards the queen's chest. At the last minute a painful stinging sensation on his hand sent him staggering back. He tried to gain his senses, quite an attempted gain, to find his assailant and his gaze finally focused on a small yellow and black shape which was swarming around his head making a dread buzzing in his ears.

Shocked Ringost could only stumble back arms flailing around like a giant water wheel trying to rid himself of this tiny infernal intruder. The night sky seemed to grow lighter as an image of a stag projected into the sky, a heavily antlered figure swung in from a rope (what it was attached to was anyone's guess) kicking Ringost hard in the chest, sending him further back from the queen and into one of the sacrificial stones, only the last remnants of the potion prevented the attack from complete incapacitating the necromancer.

Ringost's rage was bubbling over, but with the Stare Oid potion now worn off off he didn't have the physical prowess he had before and was extremely vulnerable. He regained his balance and tried to gain an understanding of what was going on.

He was shocked further when an invisible force yanked the blade from his hand "Yoink!" came a disembodied voice from next to him as his sword began to float off from behind the rock next to half a human. Ringost's anger was vying with perplexion for his overriding emotion. "She-Ra-Ra-Ra catch!" the invisible hand released the blade, and it flew through the air to be caught athletically high up by a cartwheeling pom pom wielding lady in a glittery leaf costume.

With incredible agility and a few catchy rhymes thrown in for free she darted away from Ringost leaving him gob smacked, tired, angry, smarting from a wasp sting and in need of a quiet space to have a cry or a poo or a cry and a poo, whatever best combination of crying and pooing he could fit in really.

Ringost finally stood up straight and did the best he could to regain his composure, he smartened his robes and straightened his hood so he could see properly. "What in the name of the great ungrateful dead sewer grate is a going on here?" He screamed at the party.

"I'm Stagman" came the reply from the powerfully built man in the unconvincing stag costume. He threw a smoke bomb and appeared next to Val; the magic somewhat lost by the fact everyone had seen him run to get there.

Ringost took a cautious step forward weary of the wasp still circling closely by, of all the foes he currently faced this one scared him the most. Despite his daily dealing with the dark heart of magic and the evil dead he surrounded himself with he was still a human and thus massively scared of wasps, he hadn't been able to lose that part of his being when selling his soul to the dark gods. "Can someone with a brain cell. Or a vocabulary greater than two words answer my previous flipping question?" he demanded looking unoptimistic of that answer coming from Val, Bumli, Edin or that weird antler bloke.

Val still fancied her chances of giving him what he thought he wanted "simple love, they're called friends, you may not be familiar with 'em but they're amazing an' they'll always trump any evil!"

The Herald stifled his laughter "you did well new team members!" he called warmly to She-Ra-Ra-Ra, Beastmaster, Stagman and the half invisible man as they formed up around the six original heroes. Edin tipped his sword to his new companions, Trig bowed generously, Ansafety gave a mock half curtsey and a wink and Bumli gave his friendliest monosyllabic anger grunt. It was quite the display.

A stress headache cursed through Ringost's head, but he wasn't beat yet. "Spare me the friendship cliché nonsense. It is of zero match to dark magic, and I have a trick or two more up my sleeve yet!" he looked to the Apprentice who was staying close to a stone pillar trying to be out of the way of the fighting as much as possible, his eyes behind his mask betraying his fears. "Use my teachings finish it my young apprentice!" Ringost ordered him.

The Apprentice shook his head "it's done Ringost, I'm done. We maybe could have proved a point if we'd done this the right way, but raising the King of The Undead, that's not the way forward, it never was. It isn't you; it isn't me, it isn't us." He attempted to reason.

Ringost just about subdued his anger eating at his insides "luckily that's two tricks" he said before beginning a rapid incantation and the dagger wrenched from the hand of the one called She Ra-Ra-Ra and through the Control Object spell Ringost had performed he was able to launch this blade at the queen.

The King saw the steel making its way for his wife's chest and at once he overcame his paralysis of fear and threw himself in front of his partner. The blade lodged in his chest, a spark flying from its tip drifting up into the night then floating towards the mirror, as the blood seeped down the edges of the weapon. The queen bent by her husband her body shaking. The Apprentice also hurried over to the royal couple.

Ringost hesitated dumbstruck, uncertain at what he has just done, before something overcame him, the other side that had been his unwelcome companion these last weeks, and he began laughing wickedly "brave at last king, but your gesture changes nothing, royal blood was all that was needed, and royal blood is what I have."

The spark finally fluttered into the mirrors surface and extinguished on impact. A quiet momentarily descended the battleground as those present paused trying to work out what had happened and what to do next. A rumble started in the ground, a barely perceptible purr to start with, growing into a shake, finally an invisible wave of total darkness powered from the mirror knocking all around it off their feet with raw malevolent power.

Finally, the pulse in the mirror began again, sending light out in a steady rhythm, the light changed to a bright purple sinister light as a red boot with grotesque faces carved into its metal stepped from the mirror.

Act 7 Scene 5: Flail At The King Baby

Something in the air tore and a weird cold clinging dampness enveloped the sacrifice area. A blanket of quietness engulfing the surroundings as if the world was covered in thick snow.

The only sound to penetrate was the steady step of a pair of heavy boots coming from the mirror. A tall lithe figure in red armour shaped in the manner of tortured faces around the contours, with a cloak of impenetrable black stopped and absorbed the area. He took a huge breath seeming to absorb the taste of conflict that had just been and the prospect of bloodshed to come. It was hard to read his exact expression given the constant sneer on his hollowed-out features.

He took another step trying to ignore the fact he'd just stepped in some horse dung "I hate this pathetic realm" he muttered darkly to himself.

He looked down with amused contempt where the queen kneeled by her fallen husband. A masked figure stood behind her his hand resting on her back, the shaking in his shoulders betraying the feelings behind the mask. Eventually he addressed her "A waste of tears, former queen. His death has enabled an upgrade on ruling around here."

Surprisingly, the Herald seemed to be the first to break from the spell the appearance of The King of The Undead had caused. With what was an impressive guttural roar for him he charged the undead king swinging his blade with blind fury rather than the usual practiced elegant sweeps. A previously unseen emotional rage burned at the Herald and his cries were louder and earthier than they had ever been before. For a second the features of the red armoured figure seemed surprised, but they soon slipped back into detached amusement as he easily ducked and parried the rapid flurried blows of the Herald.

The Herald had to be at the peak of his prowess as the undead king countered at preternatural speed, he swung hard at the king and although he parried, the tip of the Herald's blade caught the king on the cheek drawing a dark black blood. The King merely laughed and dabbed a gauntleted finger in the blood before tasting the liquid. The wound began to slowly close in front of the Herald's eyes. The King obliged with the cackle he felt the situation and tradition merited.

The Herald went on the attack again but if anything, the undead king was getting faster and stronger a red blur of explosive power. He moved out of reach of all attacks before sending the Herald staggering feet away with a massive backhand. "You're lucky, pathetic one I want you alive to bear witness to the start of my reign…"

"… of terror?" countered the Herald as he regained his composure.

"Not to me!" laughed the king "I'm having a great time!"

Val had finally gained what passed for her senses "Enough is enough, I've had it with you murder thinkers on this murder thinking battlefield!" She showed the king the blade of ow-chee she held in her hand "I think even you know what this is love? An' what its gonna do to your soulless existence?"

The King of The Undead wryly considered the blade "Ah that old piece of cutlery? You think that actually works?" he asked neutrally, giving off the air of not being concerned at all.

"An Orc in a pub assured me it does. Or was it a tree sprite in an inn? Could have been a grotling in a kebab house now I think of it. Either way, don't matter, seemed to work well on the sack of bones that passed for soldiers around here, I'm gonna prove it works on big sacks o' summat else. I'm gonna do you up a treat mate!" Val pulled herself into her best 'well angry crane' stance before charging at the king.

In support of her charge a hail of arrows flew into the king before finally he disappeared in a green acrid smoke of an explosion as Ansafety, and Trig lent their weight to the battle with whatever projectiles they could master. As the smoke cleared, the king remained where he stood. He exhaled and the arrows dropped off his body like cheap fridge magnets, the scars the explosion and arrows caused quickly healing over, bones snapped back into place with a resounding crack.

Val barreled into the king, but he was impossibly quick and very much a match for Val in the strength department and she could not get a single blow to land. He kept his eye on the smaller of Val's two blades ensuring he was out of its reach at all times. He knocked Val back many times though she was too strong, too determined plus too daft to know she was beat.

Having come to, Edin grabbed the king from behind as Bumli came charging from the flank. The King merely performed a rapid bow sending the giant barbarian over his shoulder and into the incoming dwarf collapsing them in a heap of limbs. The Herald tried a sneak stab from the blindside hoping the king's attention was back on Val, but the king seemed to see all and powered him back into Trig with a thud. Ansafety lowered her bow to help her stricken comrades.

With an economy of effort Stagman, She-Ra-Ra, Beastmaster and the half invisible man were all felled as they charged in to confront this malevolent force.

Val continued to fight on, but she could just not master this foe and land any kind of telling blow. She went high with the blade of Ow-Chee and this time her opponent managed to flick it from her hand with a clever parry before planting an enormous kick that would have snapped an Orc in two but just sent Val staggering back with a loud "Oof ya bugger!"

The King of The Undead spread his arms as if acknowledging an invisible crowd. He hadn't been slowed, let alone stopped by the mightiest and most available heroes of the realm. He took in his stricken opponents "that, that was all you had?" as he spun his blade deciding he'd had enough play and he no longer needed witness to his powers. Time to finish this tedious dance.

Act 7 Scene 6: Mirror Pilgrimage

The King of The Undead paused to acknowledge the undead army surrounding him who had all dropped to a knee, being a megalomaniac, he found it hard to ignore and deference or simple bottom kissing went a long way with him.

Ringost swallowed his nerves and stepped to the front of the skeletal gathering. The King seemed to smile at him, though as always it was hard to be certain of his expression and thoughts with his features. "You did exceptionally well Ringost Arr, now match my army and show your fealty and kneel to me."

"Your army…?" The King of The Undead's face twitched "… yes of course master, your army." Ringost slowly dropped to his knee.

The sickening smile once more lit up the undead kings' features. "Good… good now rise, I may yet make use of a necromancer of your limited powers" he rolled the words 'rise' for dramatic effect, being the lord of the undead forces didn't also stop him being something of a showoff who loved to act up for a crowd.

Ringost rose painfully to his feet, kneeling wasn't something he was good at or expecting to do, Necromancer's not usually having much time to practice yoga. "Master, you said I would rule most of the lands, that was the deal was it not?" he asked with as much certainty as a cat looking at the door to go out on a wet night.

The King of The Undead stared at him for an uncomfortably long time before snorting "We did. Deals change though, just be grateful if it doesn't change any more. From even here I can see this land has gone soft, the best heroes they can pitch against me are these jesters" he pointed at Val and her scattered team. Seeing the colour drain from Ringost's face he continued "Provide me with good service and I'll ensure you get the rewards you deserve."

"I'm actually more of a fool" muttered the Herald as he slowly made his way to his feet helping his companions in regaining what passed for senses between them and checking the severity of any injuries and for any fatal tears in his expensive clothes.

A slight figure had crossed over to the party clutching the blade of Ow-Chee with serious intent. "Fools, have you not being paying any kind of attention?"

"I've got news for you pal" Bumli grunted "In case you weren't paying attention, we just got our asses kicked" He pointed at his steed Nice who had taken a knock from the shock wave but otherwise seemed happy enough eating the sparse patches of grass.

The Apprentice groaned his annoyance "You've got to focus, if you fail The King of The Undead enslaves the land and all must bow to him and do his bidding. You don't get multiple chances on this one."

"I fail to see how that system is especially different from the current system of monarchy we have" Bumli muttered.

"Bumli!" Ansafety dug him in the ribs "the king just died, show some respect."

"Yeah, Dwarven Lords forbid we should have a range of views on hereditary rule at this time…" he said before deciding to say no more for now.

"Are you all done?" the Apprentice asked irritably, his voice cracking, he shook his head and finally lifted his hood back and slowly undid the clasp on his mask before removing it. In the blue moonlight a familiar set of features were set in a near mirror of the Apprentices haughty features.

The Herald gulped hard and stepped in front of his friends who had their weapons raised "Brother?" he regarded the man in front of him. "What is this madness you've got yourself involved in?" Wearily the brothers circled each other before embracing awkwardly.

The Herald stared at the ground "there isn't the time to properly explain, at first I thought I was there to act as the insider, keep the kingdom informed of Ringost's nefarious plans, be ready to stop him, though maybe I lost myself, got drawn into the idea of a more even realm, I didn't think it would ever come to this." he paused "and now our father…" His voice croaked on the last words as he and the Herald stared at the prone form of the king some yards away, as the queen still watched over his body.

The Herald wasn't sure how to act, wry amused detachment rather than sincerity his forte. Before he had chance to say or think anything else, the Apprentice composed himself "Right now we have to be focused on one thing, that's the pure evil in the red armour. Look you're not going to beat the King of The Undead in this realm, he's too powerful, too alert and even if you got him, he just retreats to the nether realm to lick his wounds and wait for the next idiots to try and bring him back." Val was about to contradict him and tell him if she hit him, he'd stay down but the Apprentice continued "However, if we can get him back in that mirror we can beat him. I think…"

The group looked at the Apprentice with doubt and suppressed anger. The Herald gave a half smile and stepped next to his brother putting his arm around him. "My friends this is my younger, but less smart and clearly less handsome brother Brookerston the fourth. Or Brooker to those that had the misfortune of growing up with him." The Heralds forced smile betrayed the lack of mirth in his words.

"It's a terrible name, but it still beats the Apprentice", Brooker muttered to himself.

The group continued to stare at Brooker and the Herald. "Hang on!" Bumli said "So that pile of dung the Herald is… that means… we've had a prince amongst our group all this time?" Ansafety smacked her palm loudly against her head in frustration at the slow wit and loud expositional dialogue of the dwarf.

Val stepped forward, "Alright Brooker love, everyone gets a second chance with me. We're listening" she could see her party shifting a little uneasy "I can speak from recent and past experience that we all make mistakes in our lives, it's what we do when we're given that second chance eh?" she could see her words had got through by the way the attention of her group fixed on the former Apprentice "OK Brooker, better make what we have to do pretty ruddy good eh?"

Brooker cleared his throat "Well what we've got to do won't be easy, and we're only going to get the one shot at this, but I need you to drive him back into the mirror. Once he is there, I'll take care of the rest" He indicated to the blade of Ow-Chee "I'm going to need this sword? Dagger? Knitting needle?" Val looked gutted to be giving away something sharp and pointy but nodded her ascent. "Our chances aren't great here, but good luck to us all hey?"

"Real motivational speaking guru aint he?" Bumli muttered to Edin.

As the party began to ready their weapons again and said their war chants or rudest words they could think of. Brooker caught the Herald's arm "Tarquentin, good luck, I know we never really said what we felt and I don't think there is enough time ever, let alone now but... you know... all the best", he squeezed his brothers arm speaking the words "for mum and dad, for the realm. And for us, eh?" as he separated and made his way to the sacrificial zone and the mirror that dominated it.

The Herald stood stunned wishing he'd known what to say, but maybe for once it wasn't words that were needed, what had passed between the brothers maybe had said all there was to say. Bumli sidled up alongside him "Tarquentin?! That's actually a real name?" he roared with laughter despite the imminent danger "figures."

Despite himself the Herald broke into an uncontrollable laugh and shook his head "I'm getting ridiculed for my name by someone called Bumli. Bumli Air Quaker?!" Bumli chuckled and slapped him hard on the back, Edin gave him a goofy thumbs up before drawing his enormous sword. "What a time to be alive… for however much longer I'm going to be alive" the Herald stated darkly.

Trig caught up with the Herald and handed him a potion "what is it?"

"Err… let me remember now its… err… Potion of Jazz Eel… yes that's it dear sir. Makes you very hard to hit and work out your timings" Trig semi explained. The Herald grimaced and took a slug, it tasted of milk, liquorish, and pond water topped cheese and onion crisps, but even worse than that. It still was considerably more drinkable than anything Bumli had shared.

Val fixed her gaze on the king who was still drunk on the fumes of spilled blood, battle and the minions bowing to him. "let's do this eh?"

Val didn't wait for a response knowing her team were totally ready "Oi King Tit!" she yelled across the battlefield, instantly gaining the attention of The King of

The Undead who sneered "We've got unfinished business" she drew her mighty broadsword and gave it a theatrical spin whilst advancing into a fight that might be her last, though Val knew no fear.

The King merely laughed by response and motioned for his skeletons to stand down, he was quite capable of dealing with this response he was sure, especially with that small, enchanted blade seemingly lost to the battle. "What again, as someone from another time and another realm may, or may not say 'The definition of madness is doing the same thing over and over and expecting different results'. I'm going to enjoy inflicting the same results on you and your sorry rabble." He drew his cruelly serrated longsword "I think you've born enough witness to my return, this time you all die in agony" he began to close the ground to the group in long light strides.

Beastmaster looked slightly panicked "Err, do we have a plan here?"

The Herald laughed "Of course we do, same plan we've always had - get stuck in, use every part of your body as a potential weapon and if all else fails, chuck a few windmills! Nothing is off limits" Val beamed in pride at him and his newfound appreciation for the tactical nuance of a battle.

"I'm Stagman" Stagman agreed reaching into his Stag Bag for some Stagarangs to chuck at his foe.

The King had closed the Gap to about five metres between the two parties. A roar broke from the group as they began their almost certainly doomed assault.

Act 7 Scene 7: Brothers (and Sisters) In Arms (And Legs And Knees And Elbows And Headbutts...)

Val was naturally first to reach the foul king, planting an enormous sword blow that the king just about managed to turn onto his misshapen shoulder pauldron, he grunted and pushed Val back closing the distance to get a sword stroke in but finding himself unable to move is arm as Bumli and Edin held it, their combined strength just about matching his.

With great effort the king just about managed to shake them off, scattering them back and was about to engage with Val when a large explosion from Trig threw him off balance before a giant glowing orange animatrus goat charged him and butted him two metres back towards the mirror.

The king went to regain his balance but found himself unable to move as Ansafety had fired arrows of high piercing that pinned his cloak to the ground. The king yelled his frustration, he was fond of the stylish elan the cloak gave him as he unclasped it and let it flutter to the ground. This was already more resistance than he had anticipated after his initial onslaught. He was looking for which foe to engage and kill when a figure swinging on a rope (again begging the question of attached to what in the clearing, it made no sense) kicked him back saying but two words as he did so.

Whilst off balance an agile rhyming figure cartwheeled in and gave him an elegant kick further backwards "take that foul king, I hope you feel the sting, of my mighty kick, let's face it you're just a pin di…" She-Ra-Ra-Ra took evasive action to avoid the counterattack. He was within three metres (about ten feet for those creature stuck in, but insisting on, old measures) of the mirror. He was struggling to concentrate on the battle as a small insect was swarming around his head and kept coming back no matter how much he swatted at it. Even The King of The Undead in his dire immortality was perturbed by a wasp, he wasn't stupid.

Letting out a scream of pure hatred, the king beckoned for his skeletons and Ringost to enter the fray. The Skeletons rushed from their position Ringost was more tentative and held back.

Val was once more back on her feet "Tankwestminster or whatever your name is, with me. The rest of you keep them bag of bones away!" with that Val and the Herald sprinted to engage the frustrated and confused king.

Val went to shoulder barge the king who managed to block having the strength to somehow resist her force. The Herald came sliding in "Ba ba ba ba de da da dada bop!" he scatted as the potion coursed through his veins and he swung his sword with great speed and unusual shapes and although not landing any telling blows, he was keeping the king distracted and annoyed at the jazz nonsense he was producing.

Val joined in throwing large blows with her sword which forced the king into a defensive stance as she pushed him further back. The Herald went in low to try and take the king's legs, but he was regaining his focus and saw the attack coming aiming an enormous kick at the Herald, only through the speed of the Jazz Eel potion did the Herald avoid the full blow of the kick as he was knocked off balance and stumbled down "Bop de boo de bummer!" the Herald sang out as he fell. The king allowed himself a satisfied smile.

Val came rushing back in with large swings. The king was managing to deflect these with ease, not realising Val's intention wasn't to make contact she was pushing him further and further back with each swing. He was less than two metres from the mirror now.

Val went for another powerful swipe, but the king regained his composure and turned it aside. He countered quickly and sent his sword arrowing for Val's body, Val managed to turn the blade a little but not so much that it didn't pierce her front armour sending her to the floor and rolling away with a pained "ooh you rough sod!" Dropping Val amused the king greatly and he raised his sword above his head in two hands ready to deliver the telling blow.

The king began his run forward to deliver the final swing not noticing the Herald on his peripheral vision who stepped in front with the grace of a minor seventh chord and put all his might into a quick kick in the kings undead never region. The kick had some power and combined with the undead ruler's momentum it packed real heft.

The King howled in a high-pitched pain as he reeled backwards within a metre of the mirror, his face contorted in agony, a look replaced by shock as a blade pierced him from the side as the queen pushed the sword with all her might into the gap at the side of the king's armour, who staggered back with the sword still in him. "Nice one de do dum. Thanks mum!" the Herald yelled in an improvising manner.

"Sweet move love, you're finally getting it" winced Val as she rose unsteadily to her feet. "Ooh that sod broke me jugs!" Val cursed and looked where the blade had pierced her armour but not the pottery she carried around her neck, which had almost certainly just spared her life.

"Route one" The Herald acknowledged, less nonsensically as the potion began to wear off. He went to help Val up, but she waved him away "I've had worse love, and there is a bigger priority right now". She regained her feet ran and drop kicked the king who was still groping to remove the sword from himself sending him to the mirror, as it looked like he was about to pass through he managed to grab the side with both arms and prevent himself passing to the other side.

The King laughed seeing the best plans his opponents had made fail, they thought their combined might would get him through the mirror and they had come up miserably short. However, in his gloating he hadn't counted on a disgruntled employee as Ringost came slamming into him from the side, The King managed to draw his dagger and run Ringost through as he impacted, but not before the pair tumbled back through the mirror.

The King looked bemused as he found himself on the other side looking out "This? This was your plan? Get me back in the mirror? It's too late the spell has been completed, I can now step out of the never realm whenever I like, this changes absolutely nothing. Pathetic!" he rumbled.

Brooker had simultaneously stepped from aside one of the stone pillars "Good work brother" he nodded at the Herald "you may make something of yourself yet" he laughed and then plunged his dagger into his own chest.

"No!" the Herald wailed forlornly as Brooker's form slumped, the queen stepped alongside to console her son despite the pain she was also feeling. Both were surprised to hear Brooker's voice again from inside the mirror.

"Perhaps it was unwise to teach me about the never realm?" he asked as he appeared in the mirror next to The King of The Undead. The King was unable to lose colour from his face but even his contorted features revealed this was something he wasn't expecting. Before he could react, Brooker had plunged the blade of Ow-Chee deep into him.

The king's features seemed to wither in on himself his voice a hollow high pitch rattle, the skeletons the others were fighting merely disappeared to dust. In his dying throes the king managed to reach in a pouch on his belt and pull a dark stone like object which he cast from the mirror "one final gift!" he managed to mangle out before crumbling into fine dust which dispersed into the realm within the mirror.

The stone rolled to a stop just away from Val, the Herald and the queen. After a moment it began to shake and then double in size, then double again. Limbs began to branch out and snap into shape before skeletal wings grew and bore it aloft a creature of easily ten metres long. The creature opened its huge mouth, showing its rows of serrated dagger like teeth and roared, a sound so dread that the Herald made a mental note to change his underwear should he survive this encounter.

He turned to Val who winced again, whether from the pain or this development he wasn't sure. She raised her sword once more "great, undead dragon. There's something you don't see every day."

Act 7 Scene 8: Being Chased By The Dragon

The dragon stretched out its limbs and its cold lifeless eyes took in what was around it. A stone circle with many bodies lay around it and a few humans staring at it in awe or fear or both, not that it mattered to the dragon it would destroy all equally. It roared again as it decided which prey to torment first.

Bumli raised his axe "this is beyond ridiculous now. We spend ages getting rid of them orcs and mercenaries, then we use all that time defeating the necromancer, then the pale bloke in the shonky armour we chucked in the mirror and now a bleedin' scrawny dragon. Some people don't know when to call it quits." Edin raised his eyebrows in agreement next to him.

The Herald swallowed down his loss knowing he had to deal with this oversized problem first. He gave Val a slap on the back and forced a smile "Dragon eh? Undead one at that. Bet you've fought loads of those!" the tremor in his voice betrayed his bravado.

Val's face stayed unusually passive "yeah love, had a tussle with a few dragons, generally to a stalemate and we've gone our separate ways after. But an undead dragon without the blade of Ow-Chee, well that's a new one on me, gonna be summat of an interesting challenge." She moved her sword between her hands testing its weight as the dragon's putrid breath covered her in an unpleasant breeze, something she was generally used to from camping with Bumli.

"If this is it, I got to tell ya Herr love, it's been a blast" she raised her sword as the dragon began to beat its wings, its unreadable stare fixed firmly on Val's group. The rest of the party wearily formed up alongside Val ready for the unknown.

"Here kitty, kitty!" Trigs voice from behind completely threw the party and yet this seemed to take the dragon's murderous attention.

Spinning, the party saw a bright orange fluffy dragon shape, inside of which controlling it like an illuminated puppet master was Trig. "Knew I had some Pretend Dragon spell somewhere in my repertoire" he spoke to the group. He turned his gaze back at the undead dragon "fetch!" Trig ran past the party, the undead dragon and towards the mirror.

"Trig no!" wailed Ansafety but to no avail. The undead dragon's attention was totally occupied with the glow moving towards the mirror it turned and with a few beats of its wings it was beginning to catch up with Trig who was pumping his crazy legs as quickly as he could.

He finally reached the mirror a strange shudder overtaking his body as he crossed the reflective threshold. The undead dragon was swiftly behind keen to attack its glowing doppelganger, as it reached the dark reflection it retracted some limbs so as to shrink into itself to be the size to be able to cross the glass like threshold into the mirror realm which was simultaneously the size of the pain of glass and a never-ending world.

Both the forms were now close together in the new realm "Smash the glass friends" Trig said in a surprisingly calm voice. Ansafety shook her head, her eyes welling up. Trig spoke again "There is no time for doubt. My time was done long ago, I was going to end up in a way I didn't want to reach, it's better to end like this. I've had more fun than I'm ever going to be able to express. Now do what you know you must do."

Ansafety raised her bow, her normally controlled movements jerky, her hands shaking, she drew the string, even in her grief her aim was true the arrow hitting the mirrors surface sending the glass shattering into a glittering explosion the orange glow bouncing off the shrapnel before fading as the parts of the mirror fluttered onto the wasted battlefield.

Ansafety let out a tortured scream, Bumli made his way over to her and awkwardly hugged her.

The battlefield finally knew silence.

♥

Act 8 Scene 1: You've Got To Fight All The Wights To Party

The Queen had opened the castle to all the land and all creatures that dwelled within it. A party to celebrate the heroes who had vanquished the attempt of the forces of evil to subjugate the land and to celebrate the lives lost and to appreciate the joys of just being alive. For others it was just an excuse for a right royal knees up.

The Wokes (they looked like small cute furry bears, but they'd eat your feet if given half a chance) had been invited for their ability to play the skulls and helms of the defeated foe like a xylophone, truly it was a niche act. Some bravely tried to get tunes out of the skeletons that had turned to dust, without much joy. Though it sounded better than the middle-aged band Ye Lighthouse Familee.

The Wokes had been joined onstage by Ansafety's band who were proving many hands make light work of creating truly awful music with some jazz and bone inflected soul music (which somehow managed to be much, much worse than that sounded).

Up in a wing of the castle, away from the party, the Herald lay on his bed staring at the ceiling. He'd been avoiding the celebrating, he wasn't in the mood, he wasn't sure if he had the mood in him anymore. A dull emptiness he couldn't grasp gnawed away at him. He couldn't find it in himself to pretend to be happy and celebrate after all he had lost.

A knock came at his door and the queen entered with Val squeezing her frame through the high arched door frame behind her. "Tarq, come join the celebrations, they're very much in your honour" the queen encouraged at him, and Val nodded her agreement.

The Herald continued to stare at the ceiling "How can I? I lost my youngest brother, my father and my friend and I'm meant to show up like I'm ready to party?" He played with his thumbnail distractedly.

The queen sat by the Herald and lay a hand on his chest "and I my youngest and husband. There will be no soothing that loss I feel in every waking minute. And yet am I to abandon everyone I know? Abandon myself? Perpetually mourn until my time comes? Or do I acknowledge all that, carry that loss the best I can and be the person I need, and am needed to be?"

Val took this opportunity to speak "it don't go Herr love, but it don't have to be your constant definition either. You've too much to offer the realm to disappear permanently into grief." Val started to sit on the bed, felt it sag and heard the creaks of the frame and quickly sat up before her extra weight broke it.

The Herald smirked at Val's sit-down, stand-up dance. "I've pretended to not be a prince for so long. Maybe for tonight I can pretend to be a celebrating prince?"

The queen took his hand "who knows? As a wise person will say, you spend some time pretending to have fun, you might have some actual fun by accident. And you need feel no guilt for living your life." She passed the Herald his party shirt (the one with the oversized ruffled sleeves made of gold leaf, finest silk and a material the royal alchemist had created called polyester). "Now come with me, I've something to show you" the queen added mysteriously.

The three wound themselves along the labyrinthine corridors of the castle, taking a spiral stair hidden behind a drape into the royal sub cellar. They found a hidden chamber by pulling the sword of the knight's suit of armour in the hallway. They entered the revealed chamber, and the queen lit the brazier on the wall. The Herald's eyebrows shot up so high they were now probably on one of the floors above. In the centre of a chamber was a mirror twice the size of a human, four times the size of a halfling and six times the size of the leading actor of the land, Com Troose.

The Herald stared at the mirror cautiously. Slowly a light shape began to form, the Herald's hand instinctively went to his sword until the image gained focus and he found himself looking at familiar features a near mirror image in the mirror. "Brooker? How? You're not dead?"

Brooker looked to be playing his thoughts around in his head and how best to explain "not alive, though not dead either, it's a bit like the effect of watching amateur dramatics. It's a dull soulless place, a bit like you're average Weatherforks chain inn. The King of The

Undead, taught me how to get to the nether world, and that was his downfall, alas he didn't teach me how to get out. That's why I couldn't help you with that scrawny dragon. I remained stook here, helpless."

The Herald's thoughts raced around his head like an angry wasp drunk on cider looking for someone to pester. "Wait though, if the King of the Undead could come back from the other side then with you, maybe you can too, we could…"

"… perform necromancy?" Brooker cut him off. "I think that's what landed us in this trouble in the first place isn't it?" He looked at the Herald and the queen and smiled "No I'm afraid its best the dead remain dead, that's the natural order. I think it's time for me to pass on into the other world, or whatever awaits, if anything does, when I leave this realm. I just wanted to say goodbye to my family who mean so much to me. There are so many words I want to say, and yet I'm not sure where to start."

The Herald managed to hold his tears "you don't need to say them brother, I know. Always have." The queen moved next to the herald and put her arm around him.

"Goodbye my weird and wonderful family, the realm is safe with the two of you at the helm. Well mum maybe, not sure you can be trusted brother!" The Herald managed to smirk at the joke despite his feelings of loss that stirred to the surface again.

The Herald stepped to the glass and placed his hand on the cold surface where his mirror image brother had his hand and whispered a few words into the surface. He stepped back to take in one last full look at his brother.

"'Ere Brooker love" Val spoke "Have you seen Trig there, he went in there to save us from the dragon, he's bound to be up to no good that way. Can you pass on my regards to the silly old duffer?"

Brooker shifted slightly on the spot "Well you see the never world, and that undead dragon I'm not sure he really..." he looked at Val and smiled seeing the eagerness on her face "... yeah sure I'll keep an eye out for him and pass on my regards if I see him." Val beamed at these words.

"Farwell and enjoy your adventures!" Brooker managed to say with forced cheer as his image began to disappear as it had formed. Once his imaged had fully faded, the queen nodded to Val who drew her sword and after a slight hesitation brought it smashing through the mirror sending shards scattering across the floor with a melodic tingle. "That's gonna be a bugger for someone to clean up" Val muttered to herself knowing full well the royal pair in front of her weren't going to get their hands dirty doing it.

****

The Herald took a moment to compose himself in the royal dunny before emerging to where the party was in full swing. There was drinking, eating, dancing, revelry, consuming, imbibing, bopping and charades going on across the huge chamber which had a few streamers put up to make it looks especially celebratory.

Em Que was enjoying showing off her new invention, a small cup like device where if you pulled the string at one end it set off an explosion of small shreds of papyrus dangerously in someone's face, she had told anyone using it to not point it in people's faces but it had fallen on deaf ears. The half invisible man was proving to be a half master of minesweeping unwatched drinks, which was unnecessary as all the drinks were free anyway.

Beastmaster and Beastmrs were using that control of wasps to keep the part of the buffet they liked protected by the patrolling insects. Stagman was to the side of the dancefloor pulling enigmatic poses and steadfastly refusing to bust moves, until a good-looking courtier asked him to dance at which point he relented and showed them his best stag dance (surprisingly impressive), the courtier asked his name to which he growled "I'm Stagm… Graham, I'm also known as Graham" as the two danced away to the unusual music.

She-ra-ra-ra was leading some highly coordinated dancing though anyone trying to keep up with her ended up on the floor in a panting heap of tangled limbs.

Bumli had returned to the chamber from the royal kennels a big smile across his face.

The Herald looked at his mum and marveled at the front she put on and the way she worked the room talking to all the guests, making everyone feel important.

The music stopped abruptly mid-song and the Herald spun to see a large group of Orcs and goblins had bustled into the chamber. He, like many others adopted a defensive stance and reached for the most dangerous looking piece of gold cutlery he could find on the table. The queen made her way to the stage "Ah noble orcs, you got my invite" she spoke clearly her words cutting across the room, she nodded at the kegs they carried "and you have brought some temple trashing trappiest stout, that is very kind. You are much welcome guests. Come join as and party as one land, one people." The queens' words had the desired effects, the tension disappeared, the music struck up again and the orcs began to mingle, a couple showing off a neat orcish wyvern waltz.

An orc sidled up to Allt and spoke quietly in his ear "bit primitive this party isn't it? I was hoping for some opera and a sit-down banquet."

Allt smiled a tusky smile at his companion "ha yes, but we will get some culture into these people one way or another. People are so much more susceptible to a good play when they've had a skinful I feel." With that the two orcs submerged themselves into the celebrations.

The Herald decided to join the party proper, he sidled up to Edin and gave him a playful nudge. "I'm glad we had you and not Tar quin for that last battle, otherwise we could have been really up against it!"

Edin smirked at the Herald "all your perceptions are miscoloured, my fine accomplice!" the Herald was stunned "me and the other gentleman have come to an accord, that we take a fairer share of our being and more interest in the others pursuits. I've come to enjoy the visceral pleasures of a noble punch up and Edin is learning the wonders of prose and poetry. His verses show promise though admittedly they do seem to be thematically about smashing a chap around the chops. He has also discovered that big heavy books are not only a fine read but also a useful tool for smacking an opponent where it hurts." He gave the Herald a slap on the back which left his brain rattling around his head, as Edin and Tarquin joined the dancefloor to show off some delicate baroque headbanging.

Bumli laughed as he watched Ansafety drain her goblet of Stonebeardy's Stern Stout and her plate of beetroot and black ox curry he'd bet she couldn't manage. He saw her break out into cold sweat and her eyes water as she managed the last bite "You'll rue that in the morning elf!" he chuckled not unkindly.

"Nonsense!" Ansafety let out an enormous belch "us elves have the constitution of a cast iron elephant... wooo!! I love this one" she yelped as the band struck up a tune she knew about mystic shepherds who journey to the unicorn at the centre of the world "come on dwarf, you and I are dancing!" she grabbed Bumli around the waste which was a bit of a stoop for her.

Bumli happily joined her on the now packed dancefloor "I'll have you know us dwarves are famed for our Minotaur trot tango!" as he began dancing as if he had been spun around several times and his limbs been placed on the wrong way around, either way the two started a giddily enjoyable dance.

The Herald made his way to the side of the dancefloor and stood there drinking wine from his chalice, playing down the sad nagging at his being. Val stepped over to him and gave him a hearty slap which sent his brain spinning the other way around and most of his wine down his fine shirt. "So, I guess you're going to rule the land in place of your dad eh herr love?"

The Herald smirked "Nah, it's not for me, I've still got much I want to do. And I'm too feckless, I just don't have enough fecks." He began topping up his wine from one of the jugs "Still I ascended to the throne long enough to make a few sensible legal changed. My sister is coming back from the fancy isles she has been at, and she will rule with my mum. Seems the best option to me, putting competent, honest, caring, compassionate people in charge. Who knows? It may catch on."

"Ah you can always rely on us sisters to lead love!" Val concurred "'Ere, I got you something" Val reached into her satchel and handed the herald some pottery that was vaguely in the shape of a goblet, or it could have been a piggy bank or perhaps an exploding dwarf star "made it meself, perfect for fine wine!"

The Herald eyed it up, spotting it wasn't even, made watertight, and contained several holes and would lead to wine all down his shirt. He smiled "it's perfect, I'll save it for special occasions... more special that this one." He casually put in on the table next to him as far away as his arm could reach.

Val beamed with pride "so what of the Herald now?"

The Herald swilled the wine around the top of his chalice "I dunno, I was wondering if there was some questing party he could join. He's pretty useful in a fight and has defeating the King of The Undead on his CV. Not to mention an undead dragon. I'd say pretty decent qualifications for any heroic outfit."

Val snorted "Some of that may have a small resemblance to the truth. Maybe me team does have a space but there are strict tests if someone wants to join us." She grabbed the Herald accidently squeezing the air from his lungs like some kind of accordion as he spilt more wine down his top. "Show me yer best dance moves and I'll consider your application."

The two made their way to their friends on the dancefloor "you know" the Herald began "as I'm not delivering messages anymore, I can't really be known as the Herald."

Val rubbed her chin "well to be honest with ya Herr love, what you were doing wasn't really what you would call bein' a herald, I'm not sure the name was apt to start with, I'd say you were more of a messenger boy."

The Herald had lost his momentum here he'd never thought about how accurate the name he'd given himself was or wasn't. He regained his (fancy) thread "anyway, I need a new name. I was thinking The Righteous Destroyer!"

His gang cracked up in laughter at him "Let's not get carried away eh herr love!" Val cackled. "Maybe the Semi Competent Thruster?!" the party laughed harder still. The heroes began dancing further in a happily uncoordinated way as Val said, "we may make a quester of yer yet!" to the artist formerly known as the Herald, her words blending into the music and laughter.

Allt spoke to the Orcs that had gathered around them "They are at their weakest, the time is now right for us to pounce, now is the time of the Orcs. Let's show them, let's blow their minds with the nine-hour comedy Farce of 'Oops vicar where are my pantaloons?'"

The party carried on unawares of this poor comedy farce threat that awaited and continued making enough noise to wake the undead.

Ye Ende (no refunds).

No Orcs were hurt in the making of this book, though one goblin did chip a nail.

About the Author

Olly is still a vaguely pointless human of the clan Dull Baldie from a drab suburb of Manchester. Maybe someone can edit his Wikipedia entry to make him something more exciting, a flying space monk armed with laser ears and Buckfast perhaps?

This is his second book after Intergalactic Trouble in Little South Manchester aka Man I wish I'd Given That Book a Shorter Punchier Title. He wrote this book after a couple of people said they enjoyed the first book (him mistaking politeness for sincerity), so in a way this book is society's fault. Don't rule him out writing a third book just to prove some kind of dangerous and tedious point.

May whoever reads this find a sentence in it they don't hate and possibly even laugh at the author's mistaken belief he can write, I think chapter 27 has a particularly amusing word in it. Like life, take enjoyment where you can find it and moan about the rest as you get stuck behind the metaphorical caravan (probably called something like 'The Maverick') of life being towed by a Nissan Duke.

Remember, we're all part of the same realm, we just wear different codpieces sometimes.